Escape to Yesteryear

J.S. Frankel

Published by eXtasy Books Inc, 2025.

Having special abilities and being looked upon as different is one thing. Being hunted down for having those abilities is another story altogether.

IN THE NOT-TOO-DISTANT future, there is no place for those who have special abilities. Hunted down due to their genetic abilities, those who are enhanced have only two choices: join the forces that would destroy them, or fight for their right to exist.

For Eli, who can transform his body to wood or metal, or Callie, who can emit bursts of intense light, they have to decide which course of action to take. The question is, how much are they willing to sacrifice?

ESCAPE TO YESTERYEAR

Escape To Yesteryear

———— ⚬ ————

By

———— ⚬ ————

J.S. Frankel

To my wife, Akiko, to our children, Kai and Ray, and to the many people who've supported me along the way. Eva Pasco, Gigi Sedlmayer, Joanne Van Leerdam, Sara Linnertz, Harlowe Rose, Richard Correa, Stephen Drake, Helen Dunn, Melissa Williams, V.J. Allison, Michelle Ann Holstein, Annette Mori, and so many more, I thank you all.

And to my sister, Nancy Dana Frankel, gone but not forgotten, this one's for you, sis!

Chapter One: The Hunted

EARTH, TWENTY-FIFTY-seven. New York City. June seventeenth, three PM. Times Square.

Times Square was crowded like a commuter train at rush hour, and as I walked along the crowded streets, the heat, smells, and sounds of the city assaulted my senses. I hadn't been back to Manhattan for over a year, and now, I was suffering a case of sensory overload.

Unlike a commuter train where a person got trapped and had nowhere to go, I could actually move, although not as freely as I liked. While sliding in and out of the ever-moving and ever-growing crowd, I did my ninja best to remain invisible and avoid hitting anyone.

As I did, an old saying popped up in my gray matter—*no news is good news*. Everyone knew what it meant, but these days, there was nothing *but* news, and all of it was bad. Domestically, things sucked, but they paled in comparison with what was going on outside our shores.

Russia had become the new-old boogeyman. They'd tried to take over Ukraine about thirty-five years ago—they'd failed—and after three more prime ministers, six brutal putdowns of insurrections, and two failed wars, one against Poland, and one against Hungary, they were back for more.

Poland had the backing of the US, as did Hungary, even though they had a far-right government. Both times, the Russians had paid dearly for attempting a hostile takeover.

Now, they were threatening to bomb the US for some trumped-up charge of espionage and the fact that the Russian ambassador to England had recently been assassinated. Our government claimed it had nothing to do with it, but try telling the Russians that.

The US, led by war-hawk ex-General Millard Anderson, someone who made Attila the Hun look like a churchgoer, hit back at the Russians with his own salvo in a recent press conference. *"Make no mistake. The US is more than capable of defending itself. Give us a reason, and we'll make sure your day is a bad one."*

One reporter piped up, *"Surely, Mr. President, you can't be serious."*

Always ready with a comeback, Anderson replied, *"Surely, I can. Let anyone try to stand against us. Russia, back off before we make you. China, stay the hell out of Taiwan's waters."*

Them was fightin' words, but Anderson had always been militant. He'd been a great general on the battlefield when he'd led American troops in Ukraine against the Russians, but that was long ago. He'd since traded in his rifle for a mic, but what he failed to realize was that the political battlefield was a different kind of animal.

Whatever...boasting aside, the Russians weren't going to back down, and their prime minister fired off his own verbal salvo, something about imperialist Yankee oppressors and whatnot.

What else was new? Not the new-old Cold War. I'd read about that in my history texts, and that had been a dangerous time over a century ago. Now, the Cold War was back, it was heating up, and cooler heads urged both sides to back down.

Me? I had other concerns. War was hell, but I was going through my own private hell. It wasn't easy being me. Eli Marks, eighteen now, I was one of the enhanced, a person able to shift my molecular structure to wood or metal.

There weren't that many of us, but in every country, in every part of the world, we existed. And because we did, society was afraid of us. Oh, the commentators spouted the usual aphorisms. *"We're all equal. We're one race—the human race."*

Call that bullshit to the nth degree. We weren't equal, and we never could be. The enhanced had attributes that set them apart from everyone else, such as super strength, speed, intelligence, or powers that could burn, freeze, disassemble matter, or rearrange it, and more.

And in individuals who were jerks to begin with, they sometimes went rogue. It happened. It could happen to anyone, enhanced or not, but with the enhanced, not many people could stop them.

So the governments around the world did what everyone expected them to do—they flipped out. After registering shock at our existence, they passed laws to limit us, forced us to register, and after that, they began rounding us up...

"Hey, watch it, buddy!"

I stopped and looked up. A large man stood in front of me, two feet away. He was gesticulating wildly. "I'm walking here. You wanna make something of it?"

"Sorry," I mumbled and moved around him, redoubling my efforts not to get into an altercation. It would've been easy to bring that slob down. A molecular shift here, a metal hand to the gut there...he would've been toast.

And I'd have invited big trouble, which was the last thing I needed. I'd moved here from Tacoma, Washington a year and a half ago. Manhattan was a great city to get lost in.

I'd lived elsewhere, but New York always drew me back. Perhaps it was the excitement that this city had, the aura of dynamism, and the practically limitless possibilities if a person applied themselves diligently enough.

But while I spotted the high-rise apartments and places to shop, I also saw areas filled with garbage and took in the sights of the derelicts and the drugged-out. They were the unwanted, even more than people like me were.

As well, there were well over forty places under reconstruction, all due to battles between the police and some of the enhanced who'd decided to make Manhattan their own private war zone. Property costs were already high, and the insurance rates had to be astronomical. Such was the price the government paid for fighting against the enhanced, who simply wanted to go their own way.

Unfortunately, going their own way often meant blowing stuff up in battles against the authorities, with the public caught in the middle. I then repeated my daily mantra of staying out of conflicts. It was the only way to live.

Living, though, meant eating and drinking. My throat was dry, and my stomach growled. I had a few dollars in my pocket, so I bought a drink from a sidewalk vendor and drained the bottle in three quick chugs. "You want another?" the vendor asked. "You're lookin' sorta on the skinny side, too. You eaten lately?"

To answer his question, no, but I couldn't afford to. At the height of five-nine and weighing around one-seventy, I'd always been lean, but if I missed a few meals, then I'd get the prisoner-of-war look, and I had to eat frequently to keep up my strength. "Uh, I'm a little light on the cash thing. Thanks, anyway."

The vendor, a fat middle-aged man with a handlebar mustache and limpid brown eyes, reached under the counter of his stand and brought out a sandwich. "Take this, kid. On the house. I don't need no one dropping dead from heat exhaustion or malnutrition, you get me?"

"Thanks."

There were still some decent people in the world, after all. He waved me off, and I retreated to the edge of a nearby alley to chow down. I appreciated the vendor's gesture, but I didn't want to rely on the kindness of strangers too often. I'd seen how people reacted to the enhanced, those who had superpowers, if that was how those who were enhanced wanted to be described.

Quick answer—they didn't. They preferred the term *people*, but try telling Joe and Jane Average citizen that. And since revealing myself wasn't on the menu, I had to make my cash last until I could get some more from the leader of my group, that is, if he was still alive.

ESCAPE TO YESTERYEAR

Wheels was his nickname, but his real name was Larry Fender. Short, fat, and totally brilliant, he reputedly had an IQ that was off the scale. An MIT undergrad in his early teens, he'd majored in physics and quantum theory. He and MIT had been in the process, he'd said, of building a wormhole tunnel. That was science fiction, as far as I was concerned.

"No, it's science fiction fact," he'd responded with a grin. *"MIT and I made it work. They used their funds to build an experimental tunnel. I provided the numbers."*

That was all he'd said on the matter, and he'd been widely respected by everyone back in the day. However, those days were long gone.

Still, I couldn't forget what he'd done for me. He'd hidden me after I'd run away from home with a girl named Callie. Like me, she was enhanced, and we'd gone from Tacoma to New York by bus. Once we got to the Big Apple, we hooked up with Wheels.

We found refuge in his lair—an abandoned subway tunnel—and that worked for a few months. It was quiet, safe, and shielded from all outside contact. In short, it was the perfect hideout...

Until the day that someone in our group betrayed us. I never knew exactly who it was. All I knew was that an alarm bell went off. We escaped just as the officers of the law crashed through the front door. Shots rang out, and a rumor went around that Wheels had been severely injured but survived. I wasn't sure. All I knew was that I'd gone from a safe spot into a land of uncertainty.

At first, Callie and I traveled together. We found refuge with families all over the country, one month here, three months there...finally, we ended up in Dallas, Texas. It was there that our peripatetic lifestyle caught up to her. She'd had enough, and she'd told me so one starry night in the Lone Star state.

"Staying with families is one thing," she'd said. *"But we need a permanent safe spot. Moving all the time...it just isn't good. I'm sorry, Eli."*

I care for you, but we can't be together. It'll be too easy for the government goons to catch us."

Much as I was into her, she happened to be right. Callie went her way, I went mine, I didn't stay in one city for too long, and I took any part-time job that I could in order to get enough cash to live on. I'd had a bank account that had been set up for me by Wheels, but there wasn't much money left, and I never knew if the authorities were onto me or not.

And so, my nomadic lifestyle continued, but like the proverbial homing pigeon, I'd returned to New York, hoping that I'd find others like myself...

"Hey, you, get over here."

A harsh, raspy voice interrupted my thoughts. The voice belonged to an officer of the AMA, the Anti-Mutant Association. Bright yellow uniforms marked them, and those uniforms were laced with khaki green. On a catwalk, they'd have made a horrifying fashion statement, but they were no jokes, never hiding behind civilian clothes.

They carried net guns, knockout gas canisters, and many other items that were designed to dampen or take away the powers of the enhanced. And for crowd control, they carried regular pistols.

In short, they meant business, but who were they after? I'd lost touch with everyone after Wheels' establishment went under, and I'd only known a few of the enhanced to begin with. Our leader's policy was that we shouldn't get too friendly with each other. That way, if we were captured by the government's thugs, we couldn't sell anyone out.

"You won't take me alive!"

That voice, high and whiny...it was Firebird, a guy in his mid-twenties, real name, Eric Darven. He and I used to work together when things were good not so long ago. Back then, Eric sported a muscular build but wore civilian clothes to hide his physique. With a head of flaming red hair, he stood out in a crowd. However, he rarely disclosed his abilities, and like my parents, he frequently counseled me not to show off what I could do.

Now, Firebird no longer had the impressive beach bod. He looked to be around thirty pounds lighter. He wore a soiled red bodysuit. Additionally, he sported a stubbly beard, and he staggered as if coming off a drunk or a chemical high.

Firebird had always been a little unstable mentally, mainly because he suffered from manic depression. He also had trouble when he tried to control his flame powers. A lot of the time, he couldn't. It took a toll on his psyche, and as our leader used to say, Firebird's mind was more than a bit scorched.

Still, he'd always had a good sense of humor, and he was always ready to take on a mission. Now, his only mission seemed to be getting through another day, and if the AMA had their way, he wouldn't be on the streets too much longer.

"Hey, you, Firebird, over here. Now," the AMA officer commanded. He had three other men with him, and they raised their weapons. Freeze-guns—they fired a spray that would freeze anything or anyone solid.

Eric stopped and turned to face them. His eyes were spinning, and a snarl wreathed his lips. Oh, man, he was toasted on something, and it wouldn't be long until a fight started. Mental problems or not, Eric was a good guy in my book, but he had a flaring temper, hence his superhero name.

Now, he raised his hands, and they began to glow. A crowd had gathered to find out what was going on, and while some of them looked on with fascination, most of the people stared in anger and fear. They'd never understand, but that was human nature. As for Eric, he didn't seem to care. "Back off, slime," he called out. "That means everyone. Back off or get roasted."

That was all the provocation the AMA guys needed. "Give up now, Darven," one of them said in a reasonable tone. "You didn't register, you're on the wanted list, and we don't want violence. C'mon, it doesn't have to end this way."

"Yes, it does," Eric replied, and flames in the shape of arrows shot out from his palms and fried two of the men in their tracks. They never had a chance to scream. The smell of burned flesh permeated the air, and more than a few of the people in the crowd threw up. The rest scattered like quail. "Come and get some!"

With that, the flames came out again, this time burning a section of a restaurant that had recently gone out of business. Fortunately, no one was there, not even a squatter.

Eric then glanced my way, and his eyebrows went up a fraction of an inch. He mouthed, "Eli, that you?"

I nodded, and a tiny wave of his hand meant that I should move back. I did so, but no one paid any attention to me. They were focused on Eric, who, in turn, stared down the AMA officers. In years past, they would've been frightened, but with their new generation of weapons, they had little to fear, except being in the wrong place at the wrong time.

The two remaining lawmen raised their guns and looked at each other before shifting their gazes to Eric with one AMA man saying, "Mister, this is your last chance."

More flames came from Eric, superheating the already hot atmosphere, and he screamed, "You won't take me. You can't take me!"

They could, and they did. One officer fired, and then the other. A fine spray of liquid nitrogen came out and encased Eric's right arm. It solidified, and then with a sharp crack, the entire arm came off, and he screamed while collapsing to the pavement. Blood leaked out from the ruined shoulder, staining the sidewalk red.

I had to help. Their guns couldn't hurt me, but they could slow me down. I started toward his position, but even through his pain, Eric shook his head slightly and mouthed in my direction, "No, man, don't do it. I'm done. Stay safe."

The AMA officers moved in, grabbed him around his shoulders, and hauled him away. His remaining hand was still twitching, but it wouldn't be for long. After he was gone, a few reporters raced over in their vans to film the aftermath and get the viewpoint of John and Jane Citizen.

Most of the people said they were scared. "I'm just your average office worker," a portly man in his fifties said to the camera. "I got no superpowers, I got no abilities, and I don't feel safe with them mutants around."

"I won't let my children watch any news about them," a young woman in her twenties chimed in. She held her daughter's hand. The girl couldn't have been more than six. "All of them, they're out to rule the world, and all we have is the AMA to help us."

A few of the other people voiced support and sympathy for the fallen ex-hero, with one elderly man saying that the government was being too hardline. "They destroyed that young man. Took off his arm. I saw it. They crippled him for life."

If Eric had a life. I doubted it would last that long under the AMA's loving care. The old man was the only one who'd voiced support for Eric, and he was soon shouted down. Someone threw a tomato at him. It hit his shoulder and exploded with a loud splat. Most of the onlookers laughed.

I'd had enough. I turned and walked away. Once out of range, I stopped near an alley, heaving deep breaths in and out. That had been a close call, and it was only due to Eric sacrificing himself that I hadn't been a suspect.

"Look at that," someone murmured.

I turned to my right and watched as six people assembled near an electronics store. The interviews with the citizenry were shown, and they also showed footage of Eric's arm freezing and then breaking off. Naturally, the closed captioning said that the scenes were intense and not suitable for children, but I doubted that any of the viewers cared. This was news, and gory news meant ratings.

Sick at heart over Eric's injury and probable demise, I shuddered and walked away, knowing that it could've been any of us, or all of us...or me.

Chapter Two: What Once Was, Part One

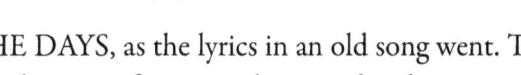

THOSE WERE THE DAYS, as the lyrics in an old song went. Those days hadn't been that long ago for me, only around eighteen months, but what a difference a year-plus made, and that probably came from another song.

My apartment lay near the Hudson River, my little fortress of aloneness. It was a grungy-looking, forty-year-old building, with a number of zombified drug addicts and homeless wanderers outside who made their daily rounds on their trips to nowhere. The gangs never went there, and neither did the police. It wasn't profitable for the former, and it wasn't worth it to the latter.

Call it my refuge, and at that moment, I needed a refuge. After the incident with Eric, my paranoia level zoomed into the stratosphere. I skulked along the city streets, took back alleys wherever possible, periodically glanced over my shoulder to make sure that no one was following me—no one was, as far as I knew—and finally reached my apartment just before five PM.

Once inside, I immediately locked up. My upgraded security system involved using three locks, a flip switch that was connected to an alarm system, just in case the AMA came around and I couldn't get into my enhanced mode quickly enough, and a warning light on my television. The alarms hadn't gone off so far, but having a healthy dose of paranoia had kept me safe, at least, so far.

I had no telephone, no smartphone, and no computer—it was my way of keeping off the grid as much as possible. Stay one step ahead of the authorities. That's what I told myself every single day. Make no friends, get close to no one. It guaranteed a lonely life, but it had kept me safe.

In fact, the only person I ever spoke to was my landlord. Ten minutes after I'd come back, someone knocked on my door. "Who is it?" I called out.

"Mr. Fargas, your landlord. How are you, Mr. Dollar?"

Wheels had given me that pseudonym, along with bankrolling my apartment and setting up a bank account for me, under the name of Joe Dollar. That's all anyone knew me as, if they ever bothered to ask my name...

"Mr. Dollar?"

I opened the door. Mr. Fargas, dressed in a faded sweat suit, short, unhealthily fat, with stubble that fought his razor and won, always yelled at his other tenants to pay up. With me, though, he was unfailingly polite. "I just came by to say thanks for the rent," he said somewhat apologetically. "Haven't seen you around much."

"I've been visiting relatives," I replied, hoping he'd take the hint and go away. Oh, wait, I hadn't given him a hint. "Now, I'm kind of tired. I guess, uh, you got everything?"

He nodded. "You paid me six months in advance. I wish all my tenants was like you."

Fargas left me, then, and I locked up again. It had been a rotten day, and I felt for Eric. He hadn't asked for what had happened to him, but the government had deemed him a danger, and he'd killed two of their agents. Grieving was something I was familiar with, and I'd deal with it on my own time.

My room itself was old, the furniture was old, but the couch, torn fabric and all, looked inviting, so I plopped down and closed my eyes. I didn't sleep, but the visions came, nonetheless...

Five years ago. Tacoma, Washington.

When I'd come out to my parents—and in this case, coming out meant showing off what a person could do, and it had nothing to do with orientation—naturally, they were amazed as well as frightened, and they counseled me that I'd never be accepted, no matter how good a person I was.

Abilities usually came around when a person hit puberty. It consisted of big changes that left the preteens or teens uncertain, scared, or angry. Usually, their reactions went through all three extremes, as hormones ruled, and it was tough for those kids to deal with those sudden changes.

In my case, my parents raised me as normal. Hell, I *was* normal. I had no idea of what my body could do, but when I hit thirteen, just after my Bar Mitzvah, I had a fight at school with a kid who was two years older, three inches taller, and around forty pounds of flab heavier. Fat kids could be strong kids, too, and this bullying pig's name was Bruce Rondo.

Rondo liked smacking other kids around, and he was an equal opportunity smacker, hitting girls as well as guys, younger kids, and sometimes kids his age. The teachers had repeatedly warned him, but Rondo, while possessing the scholastic skills of a gnat, more than made up for that lack by being as cunning as a rat. He always assaulted his victims before school, after school, or during breaks so that no one could catch him doing it.

The other kids were scared shitless of him. He came from a wealthy family, and his father had a lot of pull in Tacoma's food service industry due to owning six food-processing companies, and they lived in one of the nicer neighborhoods. So, we had a rich bully with no social conscience and no people skills.

Worse, no one seemed to want to be the first to put him in his place—until me. His one mistake was trying to kick my ass. He'd done it before, and naturally, being short and weak, and, yes, afraid, I didn't want it to happen again. I was in the men's room, doing my business at a urinal, when Rondo came in. "Hey, Marks," he called out.

Immediately, I turned my head to the side to respond, and I caught his smile, that nasty smile all bullies seemed to get when a fight was imminent. "Rondo, I'm not into fighting," I said after zipping myself up and going over to the sink to wash up.

"Too late. Lemme tell you, I don't like people. I don't like Jewish kids, don't like Italians, don't like black people...hell, I don't like anyone."

"At least you're equal opportunity," I said, trying to stave off the inevitable.

"Yeah, I am."

And with that, he strode over to launch a punch at my face. My only thought in that split-second was to steel myself for the impact. *Steel*...that concept flashed through my mind at lightning speed.

A nanosecond later, Rondo's punch connected with my cheek, a loud crack echoed around the room, and he recoiled, holding his now-broken hand. "What..." he managed to get out.

I hadn't thought of anything except steel...and then I looked at my hands. They'd gone metallic. Oh...call this a moment to freak out, and when I recovered, I turned to Rondo, who was clutching his smashed digits. "Try again, fatso."

He shook his head, the tears streaming from his eyes, and choked out his question. "What are you, man?"

"Strong."

Confidence, something I'd never had before, filled me, along with a sense of vengeance. Don't get mad—get even. And with that, I laid into him, not hitting his face, even though he deserved it, but instead, I went after his shoulders, smashing them until he fell to the cement floor, writhing in agony. The metal covering my hands suddenly reverted to flesh, and I staggered from a sudden bout of dizziness.

But the vertigo soon left, and instead of becoming Mr. Android, I settled for straddling his chest and smacking him around the face until it was red and raw and swelling rapidly. Result? He bled freely from his nose and mouth. I left him with a warning. "Rondo, this is the last time to pick on me or anyone. Got it?"

His eyes resembled slits, and he blinked at me. Narrow though his eyes were, the hatred still shone out. "Yeah...yeah."

I leaned closer to his now pumpkin-sized head. Four bloody teeth lay next to it. "Because if you do, if you tell anyone what happened, if you ever go near anyone again, I'll do ten times worse. And you won't be able to prove anything. You understand where this is going, right?" Fear replaced the hatred. "Sorry!"

Yes, he was a sorry mess of fat. Cue, exit the washroom. Later on, I heard that he'd been taken to the hospital with numerous injuries, including shattered clavicles, a smashed right hand, and the previously mentioned four knocked-out teeth. He refused to say who'd attacked him. All he said was that he'd fallen down the stairs, which didn't make a whole lot of sense, but it didn't matter. From that day on, he never bothered another student again.

Naturally, at first, I didn't tell my parents. I didn't tell anyone. But I explored my powers to see what I could do, and while it freaked me out at first, I soon realized that being different wasn't bad.

In fact, it was awesome. By concentrating hard, I could will my entire body—or any part of it, if necessary—to take on the consistency of metal or wood, the latter of which also came as a surprise when I leaned against a tree one day.

However, no other abilities surfaced. I couldn't stretch to impossible distances. I couldn't fly. In metal form, although my body weight increased to over four hundred pounds—we had two scales at home, and they broke when I stood on both of them, and the needle passed the two-hundred mark on each—I could also run three times as fast as a normal person.

In terms of strength, mine increased to five times what a professional strongman could do. I ran through walls at an abandoned apartment building, knocked down concrete telephone poles, and lifted steel girders with ease. One major problem, though—my abilities only lasted for five minutes.

As for becoming wood, initially, I thought it would only be useful if I wanted to float on water, but after testing my abilities—which meant banging my wooden fists against brick walls and such—I found that my bark was also ultra-tough, tough enough to smash through concrete, if necessary. Again, I could only hold that molecular transformation for five minutes.

But that paled in comparison to what was happening in the world. From the time my transformation occurred, more and more reports of enhanced people came from every country. Some of the enhanced could glide or fly, some ran incredibly fast, one of them could sprout up to eight extra limbs—everyone called him Octopus, for obvious reasons—and there were many others with even more bizarre powers. The big thing, though, was that we were different.

My parents found out that I was one of the different when I was fifteen. It was Sunday afternoon, my parents were downstairs, and I was in my room, practicing turning metal, then wood, and then back to flesh again. The more often I did it, the easier it became.

However, no matter how hard I concentrated, my powers never increased past the five-minute hold mark. Shifting into metal or wood was draining, and I often got dizzy, not to mention hungry.

Once I changed back to my default form, dibs on the refrigerator! Chalk it up to the molecular shift in my body. At any rate, I was in wood mode, and my mother came in with a load of laundry. "Eli, are you decent...oh."

Oh. That was all she got out before my clothes fell to the floor, and she slumped against the wall. I did my best to defuse the situation. "Hi, Mom."

"You're a...a tree?"

What to say? "Mahogany, probably, or maybe oak. I'm not really sure."

That didn't defuse anything, as she screamed and ran to get my father. Shortly after, my father called a meeting in the living room and shut the drapes. No prying eyes, he'd said.

It was then that we had the discussion. *The* discussion. I showed them what I could do, and they grew frightened. Not of me, but of what the government could do if they found out. "Dad, they're not going to take me away...are they?"

My father wasn't so sure. We were built alike, short and slender, with brown hair and mild brown eyes. We both had narrow faces, high, arched noses, and we even shared the same kind of loping walk. My mother had auburn hair, a pretty face, and a kind smile, although then, it was strained.

"Eli," she said, striving for calm, evidenced by her breathing in and out deeply, "We're your parents, but we've, er, we've been watching the news. I don't trust the government, and you can't go around looking like...that."

"You think the police won't like it?"

My father stared at me in disbelief at my naiveté. "Son, get real. No one will."

I didn't believe him, then, but I promised that I wouldn't go around showing off. School continued, people left me alone, I studied, and life continued.

However, so did my dreams of being someone different. In essence, I was. It wasn't a matter of what I could do. It was a matter of what I *could* do with the powers I had.

"If you have power, you have a lot of responsibility." I'd heard that saying before, or something similar to it. To me, at that young and impressionable age, it made perfect sense. Tacoma was a nice place to live, but it wasn't crime-free.

Not yet. And like the comic book heroes who'd found they could do the spectacular, the notion of being someone special and standing out while fighting the fight for truth, justice, and everything else that concept entailed, stood out. So, once I'd mastered my powers, at the age of sixteen, I told my parents that I was going to start training. "What for?" my father asked.

"To keep in shape."

My answer sounded innocent enough. My physique at that time consisted of a short-for-my-age lean body with no appreciable muscle mass. My father gave me a searching look and then waved his hand. "Just be careful."

So off I'd go after it got dark. Jogging took me to a different neighborhood two or three nights a week. During my rest times, I did a few sets of pushups, squats, lunges, chins where I could find something to hang from, and some other calisthenics that pumped me up.

However, the exercise was only a cover for what I really wanted to do—to stop crimes from happening. My first time, I went downtown to one of the seedier sections. It was summer, and I wore a pair of sweatpants along with a t-shirt.

I arrived in the neighborhood around ten PM. The streets were deserted. While nothing was happening on the main street, on a side street, two men were trying to break into a car with coat hangers. They were totally messing up, scratching the side of the car and swearing in frustration.

All right, make it happen. I morphed into metal, pulled a mask from my pocket, donned it, and strode over to them. Before I reached their position, I wondered what to say. All superheroes had catchphrases, but while I'd gone through a list during the past few days, nothing cool came to mind. Still... "Guys, it's late, and this isn't your car, so why not do something more worthwhile?"

They turned around and gaped. "What in the hell?" one of them said.

"Hell has nothing to do with it," I replied while trying to lower my voice and sound more adult. I also realized that I'd uttered a cliché and that I'd have to come up with better lines. "Come quietly, or you'll be in trouble."

Lord, that was another cliché. Both men glanced at each other, pulled out knives, and tried stabbing me. Their blades broke against my metal skin, and with a casual swipe at their jaws, I knocked them out cold.

"Tailor-made," I muttered, thinking that this situation was specially made for my skills. After thinking it over, it wasn't a great catchphrase, but it worked. Anyway, mission accomplished, and I practically skipped onto the main street, intending to go home...

"Jesus Christ."

The voice came from behind me. I turned halfway around, only to see a couple in their twenties staring at me. Time to leave, and I ran from the scene as fast as I could and got home in record time. By the time I burst through the door, I was back in my human form, sweaty, breathless, and trying very hard not to grin from the sheer excitement of it all.

My father had been perusing a magazine, but he stopped reading and turned to face me. "Have a nice time?"

"Oh, yeah."

OVER THE NEXT MONTH, I went out for my nightly runs three or four times a week, came home after beating up punks, and checked the news. Reports about a metal-man or a log-man were featured, and had a superhero arrived? Superhero, fine, but a log-man? That was...weird.

While checking out the various news sources on television or online, I'd raid the refrigerator. My mother commented that I was eating a ton, but added that I was a growing boy and needed more food.

On the other hand, my father remained quiet when I came home, but I had the feeling that he knew what was going on. Sure enough, he pulled me aside one night just as I was going for my run and motioned to the dining room. My mother was upstairs, taking a shower. Once the door to the dining room closed, he said, "Eli, you're not going out tonight."

"And why not?"

His lips thinned. He didn't appreciate my question, which he probably viewed as talking back to him. "Because this metal-man superhero stuff has got to stop. Your mother and I—we know. It's only a matter of time before someone catches on. Do you want the authorities to come here and arrest us?"

Wonderful...busted. "Dad, I'm just trying to do, you know, some good."

That sounded lame, but I'd said it, and now, I had to stand by it. He sighed and took a seat on a nearby chair. "Son, while I understand that this transformation is exciting, and while I understand that you want to help out, all this is going to do is bring unwanted attention to you, and to us. Is that what you want?"

It was time for me to protest, and protest I did. "Dad, no, I don't. But if the police can't do it—"

"Then someone else will. Eli, this isn't the right thing for you to do, even if you think it is. You know there's a possibility of being found out. Promise me you'll stop."

And if I didn't? After posing the question, his voice took on an authoritative air. "You would put me in a corner. You're my son. I would never turn you in. But to keep your mother safe, I'd ask you to leave our house."

He had me. The vision of him turning me over to the authorities flashed briefly across my mind, but then I dismissed it. My parents had always been good to me. I'd always felt that I could talk to them about anything—except this. Still, I knew that they truly didn't understand me.

ESCAPE TO YESTERYEAR

So I swallowed my pride and put my dreams of bringing law and order to Tacoma on hold, and I returned to my dull life of being Eli Marks, average student, social misfit, and wannabe superhero. It was time to put away those childish things.

That is, until I met Callie. After that, everything changed.

Chapter Three: What Once Was, Part Two

FLYING SOLO THROUGH high school had never been my dream. Every guy wanted to find a girl to spend time with, and vice-versa. For people into same-sex relationships, same deal. No one wanted to be the odd person out.

At the age of sixteen, I was still single, forever so, it seemed. And my mother just felt that she had to ask. We sat at the kitchen table at seven-thirty in the morning. My father was an accountant at a leading tax firm, so he always left early in the AM, returning around eight at night to have dinner with us. So my mother became my main confidante, and naturally, she felt that she could ask me anything...and she did. "Aren't there any girls in your class that you like?"

Oh, and to answer her question, something that was personal and which made me feel very uncomfortable, I wondered what to tell her. Should I lie and tell her that I was a stud with the ladies, or should I tell her the truth and say that I was a total washout?

Decisions, decisions...but in the end, as the old saying went, a boy's best friend was his mother. "I, uh, well, I haven't met anyone cool, yet. I'm still looking."

Call that a tactful answer, even though it was total BS. However, my mother nodded sagely, sipped her coffee, and said that I'd find someone. "There's always someone for everyone. You'll find that someone."

Maybe. As with all things in life, some people made their choice to lead a solitary lifestyle, while others had it thrust upon them. I fell into the latter category. It wasn't like I wanted to be the proverbial odd person out...it just sort of happened that way. Parties, dances, movie invites—they were reserved for those who inhabited the special world of the in-clique crowd.

And I wasn't part of that world.

What world, though, could I be part of? I'd heard about other enhanced people like me, but hearing about them and actually meeting them were two different stories. And if the reports were true about them hiding from the authorities, then I might as well have been living on another planet.

"You're sure you're not doing anything, er, extra-curricular?"

That came from my father a day after my mother had asked me the relationship question. I was three months shy of turning seventeen, and for the past couple of years, I'd heeded my father's words about not going all vigilante and taking out the bad guys in my spare time.

"No."

I'd come home from school at four that day, done my homework, my mother had made spaghetti and meat sauce—my favorite—and while I'd practiced shifting in my room, I'd refrained from going out and doing what I thought was the right thing to do.

Now, I lay on my bed, reading a novel about cat-people written by a popular author about forty years ago, and my father just had to knock on the door, walk in, and ask me that question. When I repeated my answer that I hadn't been doing the superhero thing, he'd asked, "You're sure?"

I put the book down and gave him the old look of extreme sincerity. "Yeah, Dad, I'm sure. Trust me."

"That's all I wanted to know."

He gave me a smile of father-son bro-ship and left me alone. While I was disappointed at his edict, as it turned out, two days later, his prediction of the government acting against the enhanced came true. The MRA—the Mutant Registration Act—passed in Congress. There was no public discussion. In fact, there was no discussion at all. Every country in the world passed similar acts.

All an enhanced person had to do was register. It sounded innocuous, but it wasn't, and my parents knew it. They said nothing to anyone, but they insisted more than ever that I hide my abilities. "People won't understand, Eli," they'd repeated over and over. "And people always fear and hate what they don't understand."

Cliché statement or not, it was true. Shortly after I'd turned seventeen, the roundup started. Those who'd come forward and registered had already given the authorities their addresses. It was a naïve notion on their part that they'd be left alone.

They weren't. When the government officials knocked on the doors, well, they didn't knock. They kicked the doors in. Naturally, fights broke out, and at first, the enhanced won, due to their powers.

After that, the government got smart. Via a presidential order, the top brass recruited scientists, engineers, and other people with skills to form the AMA. It had the government's highest clearance to do what it did. With the nation's top minds at their disposal, they developed weapons to neutralize the powers of the enhanced, or they got their own enhanced to do the dirty work for them.

And the end results were bloody affairs, with the enhanced—most of them teens—taken away. Of course, the government took their parents along for the ride, but it turned out to be a one-way ride, as no one ever heard from them again. The news speculated that they'd been imprisoned, but most of the ordinary citizens figured they'd been terminated.

Call it the slow creep of fascism, all done in the name of public safety. Upshot—I had to hide who and what I was. I stayed in regular human mode, walking away from most potential fights. It bothered me to walk away, but revealing myself to the world would've done more damage.

My parents said they understood, but they didn't. No one did, except Callie Sanda, a girl I met one day. It was mid-March, and being the dutiful student-slash-nerd that I was, I rarely went out after school was over for the day. No one ever invited me anywhere, so it was a case of me, myself, and I, and we were very good at doing the individual lone wolf act.

However, one Friday, I decided to go into a donut shop near my high school. I got a cup of tea, tossed in a little sugar, and I sat in a booth, quietly enjoying myself when a voice said, "Can I join you?"

I looked up. A girl about my age stood two feet away. On the short side of five-four with equally short, spiky blonde hair, an elfin face, and cool green eyes, she held a glass of cola in her hands and gestured to the empty seat beside me. "Uh, sure," I replied, summoning up my ballpower, which, to date, had been absent around women. "Have a seat."

She slipped in beside me, and I sipped my tea, wondering what to say. Girls usually didn't talk to me. At school, when I'd asked a few of them on a date, all I got was a laugh and a turndown, along with everyone pointing at the loser—me—and saying that I couldn't get a date to save my life. Welcome to Alone World, population one—yours truly.

Reality check—it hurt. Those girls were after the jocks and those who looked better. I didn't have those two qualities going for me. Maybe this time, it would be different. "My name's Eli," I said. "Eli Marks."

"Callie Sanda," she said softly. "Callie's short for Callisto. You should be careful."

Careful? "Why?"

"Check out the table. Your hand is wood."

I looked down, and...aw, hell. Sometimes, my body took on the consistency of metal or wood objects without me consciously knowing, and this was one of those times. I concentrated, and my hand went back to flesh. "Thanks, but aren't you freaked out?" I scanned her face for signs of revulsion and found none.

"No. It's all good."

"Yeah, you look good to me," a voice said.

Marvelous, a large, powerfully built guy in his early twenties, wearing a brown windbreaker that barely covered his frame, had come over to make his pitch. I couldn't catch a break. The first time a girl had spoken to me, and this guy had to come along and ruin things. As I cursed myself mentally for not being tougher, Callie let out a sigh and murmured that she'd handle this.

Right. With short dark hair, a tough pug face, and a crooked grin, he was trying for the bad-dude angle, and to be fair, he was succeeding. Callie, though, wasn't interested and said as much. Mr. Tough Guy, though, wouldn't be dissuaded, and he leaned over to rest his massive paws on the table. "C'mon, baby, trade up. This punk probably weighs one-fifty soaking wet. He doesn't even lift, and he ain't anything to drop your panties for."

"Neither are you," she replied with an edge to her voice. "For the record, you've got a dirty mouth, something I don't like."

A smirk lined his features. "Isn't that too bad. I speak how I speak."

Callie favored him with a nod. "I guess you do. All right. If you want to hear my honest answer, lean a little closer."

As he did so, she whispered in my ear, "Close your eyes. Tightly."

I did. A second later, a scream sounded, a bright light penetrated my eyelids, and I sat back, uttering a whoof of surprise. When I opened my eyes again, my vision was blurry. Someone took my hand. "It's me, Callie," a voice said. "C'mon, we need to talk."

Right...talk. We got up, and Callie told me to walk slowly. "I'll lead you out. Don't worry."

I made out a few objects on the floor. They were people. We bypassed Mr. Tough Guy and the other patrons who were holding their hands over their eyes and bellowing in rage and agony.

Outside, my vision cleared, and Callie pulled me into an empty alleyway. As for my new acquaintance, she exploded, kicking the empty crates in a fury and cursing Mr. Pickup Artist out. "That guy was a jerk," she said heatedly. "Somehow, I always manage to run into jerks like him. Story of my life." She smacked the wall with her palm for emphasis, and then recoiled from the pain.

"What did you do to him and then everyone else? Blind them?"

"Temporarily," she replied, shaking out her hand. "I had the feeling that you were, uh, someone like me, and I was right. My real name is Callie, like I said, but you can call me Sunburst, if you want."

To show off her skills, she turned away, and a bright light emanated from her. Even though she was facing the other way, it still made me squint. "Some power you got," I said with admiration.

When she swung around to face me, she arched her eyebrows. "You, too. I thought they were only rumors, but it's true. You're the log-man, aren't you?"

"Who told you?"

Callie said that she'd read about the incidents of a log-man or a metal-man online. Those reports always came from Tacoma, and they always happened in a certain area. "I figured from the descriptions that the punks gave, I was looking for a guy about your height. I just happened to come here, and I saw you go log-man, so...yeah."

I really hated that nickname. "I'm...I'm not the log-man." I sounded defensive, and then I toned it down. It wasn't her fault. "I can turn wood for about five minutes. I can turn to metal, too, but it's the same time limit."

To prove my point, I shifted into metal first, then wood, and then went back to my default state. Once done, she bowed as if to say, *I submit to your superior skill.*

After that, she sat on an abandoned crate, rubbing her chin and taking in a few deep breaths, letting them out slowly. "Do you get tired after changing your structure?"

"Yeah, but if I rest up, I'm good after a minute or so. It takes me time to get to the point of shifting again. I can't turn it on and off all the time."

Callie nodded. "Me, too."

I had to know something. "Do you have a catchphrase?"

She laughed. "No, but I thought about it, like, shed a little light on the subject, or let me brighten your day, but that would take too long. You?"

And I thought mine was cliché...but I didn't tell her that. "Oh, uh, I figure that if they were dumb enough to take me on, then they were tailor-made for me. So, I say tailor-made. What do you think?"

As soon as I asked her, a frown crossed her face. "That's almost as bad as mine."

Well, at least she was honest, and I laughed. "Yeah, my catchphrase sucks."

A smile replaced the frown. "Anyway, I'm glad I found you. I've been on the run since those maggots passed the MRA. Did you register?"

"No," I replied right away. "My parents know about me, but they haven't registered my name or anything. I, um, I figure I'll get by."

She sat up straight, all traces of exhaustion gone, and a look of fear flitted across her face. "You'd better figure different. I knew someone in my city like us. He disappeared a while back, but before he did, he gave me the name of a guy who can help us. I used to live in Oregon, in Beaverton, but I, uh, left home. I'm...my foster parents were dicks, so I left."

She'd used the past tense. "Were?"

"They're dead. I, uh, I don't want to talk about it." This time, an angry expression flashed across her face like a sun going nova, and then it faded.

"Sure thing," I said, not wanting to make her angry. "It's all good."

Callie nodded and offered a brief smile. "Thanks. That was seven weeks ago. So now I'm here. I'm staying with another host family. Home schooling. They're good with me being what I am."

I was curious. "You said someone could help us. Who?"

"A guy named Wheels. I don't know his real name. That's all the info I have, but I heard when he visits here, he hangs out at an arcade downtown. I got in touch with him, and he gave me a password. You interested, or should I go on my own?"

She didn't have to tell me twice. If there were other people like me—us—then I'd be foolish to pass up the chance of meeting them. "I'll go."

Two hours later.

The arcade was brightly lit, with people from six to over sixty playing the various games, napping on stools, or eating, and everyone seemed to be in a good mood. It was loud, with bright lights flashing, and for a moment, I was disoriented. Callie grabbed my hand and steered me over to a man who was playing a first-person shooter game. She tapped him on the shoulder and said, "Freedom."

He nodded, put down the gun, and then he gestured us to follow him over to a relatively quiet corner. "This is between us," he said as we walked. "Secrets stay secret."

Wheels was a bright, affable fellow in his late twenties, roughly five-six, round like a butterball, clean-shaven, with a head of close-cropped brown hair and average features, save for a large mole on his right cheek. His skin was quite weathered, though, and he blamed that on staying out in the sun too long when he was younger. He immediately said that he could help us. "Callie's special, in case you haven't figured it out."

"I've seen what she can do...sort of," I answered.

He chuckled. "Yeah, that's our Sunburst. Anyway, I don't get to Tacoma too often, but I'm here to help. I'm no friend of the AMA, so if you're thinking I'm a plant, think again. I could turn you in, but that's not my style."

That got me curious. "What do you want?"

"To help you out. They're after me, too."

33

As it turned out, Wheels had only his intelligence to rely on, not any physical gifts. His real name was Larry Fender, but he explained that his nickname was Wheels on account of his ability to run fast. "I know I don't look it, but I can do the hundred meters in ten seconds. So I go by the name of Wheels."

He told us about one place he had. It was in downtown Manhattan, and he said that he'd filled it with computers, blueprints, and gadgets that he was working on. "When I get a bigger place ready, I'll be able to make these weapons. That'll even the playing field a little. If you ever need a place to stay, you can contact me." He handed Callie a card with a number on it, and one to me as well.

After that, staying quiet about what I could do became even more imperative.

I didn't tell my parents about my meeting Wheels. They wouldn't have understood.

I did some checking on Wheels, though. It seemed that, as Larry Fender, he was a child prodigy, finishing high school at the age of thirteen, then entering MIT a year later. His major was quantum physics, and he was considered the brightest of the bright.

He'd graduated MIT at the age of seventeen, then worked for a think-tank for a few years, but for some reason, at the age of twenty-five, he dropped off the map. Now, he'd resurfaced, and he was offering us shelter, if we needed it.

As fate would have it, it turned out that I needed his help, after all, as one day, one-hundred-eighty days into my seventeenth year on Earth, I came home from school to an empty house. It had been tossed from top to bottom. In the kitchen, I found a note stained with blood on the floor. *The government came for you. We love you, son. Take care.*

Callie and I took Wheels up on his offer. I tossed my personal belongings into a backpack, and we went to New York a day later.

Upon our arrival, we called him. He met us at the bus station and proceeded to lead us to his subterranean lair where he'd set up shop. In an abandoned subway tunnel, he'd found a large enough space to work on his contraptions, but being underground wasn't my thing.

Eventually, I moved, though, as I needed my own space. So did Callie. We started dating, we had fun, but it was all quite innocent. I had no clue about women, and she wasn't all that experienced, either.

We went to movies, spent time in coffee shops, took walks in the park...all those things young lovers did, except we never got past the kissing stage. Callie said that she wanted to wait, and I was okay with that.

The main thing was that we had fun, we had our own places, and we were safe. That setup worked well...for a while...

I remembered the hideout, though. Things had been comfortable there, even though we couldn't go out very often. Going out meant going up to the surface, and there was always a chance of being spotted.

One thing that I had going for me was my relative anonymity. Since I'd never registered my name with the government, outside of my parents, Callie, and Wheels, I'd thought that no one knew me or what I could do. But I'd been wrong. My parents had been taken. That meant that someone in the government must have been watching us.

Rumors could kill, so I did the get-lost thing, did the New York thing with Callie, and Wheels eventually set us up with our own apartments. They were nothing special, but that was all in keeping with the concept of maintaining a low profile. Add in my bank account, and I was good to go. Callie had a similar setup.

Everything worked. I had no idea where Wheels got the cash from, but it didn't matter. It was just enough to keep me going. "Only one rule," he'd said. "Tell no one who you are. Trust no one except me, yourself, and your girl. That's it."

He also told us to stay safe, and his plan had worked...until it didn't. New York was an exciting city, one that was always on the move, and it was a huge change from my formerly sedate Tacoma lifestyle.

At the same time, there was always an element of danger, and I never deluded myself into thinking that I was safe. So I started my nighttime patrols again, just me, my mask, and my changeable body. Robbers, potential rapists, carjackers, drug dealers...they were all fair game.

I never killed anyone, but I beat the living hell out of a few. Once the rumors started to fly about a metal-man dispensing justice, I toned down my act at Wheels' request. He knew what I was doing, and like my father, he asked me to lay off.

It was good advice. Things were quiet after that, up until the AMA started their roundups. People were scared, they said, and they wanted to keep order. Society was built on rules, built on order. It was for the public good, they said. A few people had to be taken in and questioned. It would make society safe. Safety was their priority. That was all they wanted.

Of course, it turned out to be a lie, and soon after, everything went to hell.

The present.

I came back to reality with a start, wiped the sweat from my face, and got up to get a glass of water from the kitchen. My apartment was small, with only the basic necessities—a small kitchen, a tiny living room with a fold-out couch that doubled as my bed, a small television set, and a closet for my clothes. Oh, and a toilet and shower that actually worked.

Living rough hadn't been easy, and I downed two glasses of water. It tasted tinny, like it had a high iron content, but beggars couldn't be choosers.

Chapter Four

CALLIE RELATIONSHIPS were tricky things, even for people with more experience than I had. However, if a person didn't know anything about relationships, to begin with, they were doubly tricky. In my case, I fell into the latter category, and meeting Callie opened up a whole new world for me.

Wait, that was a cliché, but then again, first meetings and first-time relationships were often rife with clichés. Cliché number one—becoming cooler among my peers. I'd always been a loner, short for my age, slender, with a mop of brown hair and brown eyes, and the bigger kids at school often ignored me. With the exception of Bruce Rondo, erstwhile bully, I wasn't seen as a threat, even by the girls. As one of them put it, *"He isn't worth beating up."*

So I went my own way most of the time. I was the typical nerd, someone who preferred books over battles, and reading over rambunctiousness. My parents were both quiet by nature, and perhaps they knew what I was going through, trying to deal with school and life in general. In their wisdom, they largely left me alone. They did so even more after they found out what I could do when it came to my molecular transformations.

And after I found out what Callie could do, it was as if I'd found a kindred spirit. Like me, she enjoyed reading, watching movies, and playing video games. "Sci-fi, fantasy, mystery...it's all good to me," she said after I'd asked her what she liked to read or watch. "And give me a good action movie any day of the week."

Great minds thought alike, and we often passed the time at the public library. What with the internet, places like libraries often found themselves outdated, but they were perfect for us, quiet and comfortable, and we spent the time reading everything and anything.

It was only natural that we'd lean together and share a kiss, and unlike what other kids said about their first kisses, it wasn't strange or icky at all.

I once asked her what she saw in me. Call it a lack of self-confidence, but I had to know. "I mean, there are other guys. They're bigger, better-looking..."

My voice trailed off, and I felt like a total wuss, but before I could say anything else, she put her hand against my lips. "And they aren't you. Other guys see me as a pretty face. You see me as more. That's why."

What else could I say, save, "Thanks."

She leaned over to kiss me. "You don't have to say that," she murmured.

"Ahem!"

That came from a middle-aged librarian who'd stepped over to glare at us doing the lip-lock thing...

When Callie came to my school one day after the final bell had rung, the other kids gaped, not quite in awe, but almost. Small though she was, when she moved, others made way. Perhaps it was the quiet badass vibe she gave off, or perhaps everyone couldn't believe someone that attractive would spend time with me. "She's...she's your girlfriend," one of the guys said in a flat, I-don't-believe-it tone.

His name was Mark Cullough, he was captain of the football team, and he ruled the school. He had more girlfriends than I had fingers and toes, and yet, when he saw Callie, he wilted in her presence. "Man, when you got it, you got it," he said with respect.

On that day, yes. "I guess I do," I replied in my best you'd-better-believe-it tone. Call it payback, in a way. Most everyone thought I was a loser, and now, one of the hottest girls around had shown up to see me. They simply couldn't wrap their minds around it. So that was my too-cool-for-school moment.

I put my books away in my locker and slammed it shut, spinning the dial on the lock with what I hoped was a certain amount of flair.

Callie took my hand and led me outside. I didn't bother looking back, but I had the feeling that everyone's gaze was on me. On the way to her place—she wanted me to meet her host family—she asked, "Are you into self-defense?"

Me? Weak-ass me? Without using my abilities, I couldn't fight to save my life. "I guess I should learn."

She offered a brilliant smile. "I can teach you. I learned at the orphanage and also fighting at school before my mother adopted me. C'mon."

At her foster family's place—the Rothman's, who lived about fifteen minutes away from us—she introduced me to her foster mother, said that she was going out back with me to practice, and that I was one of her kind. "We're just going to practice, ma'am," she said.

Mrs. Rothman, short like my mother, with a curious birdlike look to her, her eyes roving over everything and forgetting nothing, greeted me cordially but added, "Be careful, Callie. You never know who's watching."

Like my parents, she was afraid of how the government, not to mention the general populace, would react. It was a natural thought, but Callie told me not to worry. "High walls," she said, pointing at eight-foot fences on either side of the yard. "That prevents nosy neighbors."

Hopefully, no drones were flying around, but a look at the sky confirmed that there was nothing there save the sun and a few fluffy clouds. "Ready?"

Callie's question jerked me back to reality. "Uh, yeah. Ready."

Here came cliché number two—learning how to fight, or, nerd becomes a semi-stud. At first, Callie showed me how to set my feet in a boxing stance. I was naturally left-handed—she was, too—so we worked on shifting our feet, jabbing, throwing hooks, uppercuts, crosses, and various combinations. At the outset of our training session, I was awkward as anything, but I soon developed a rhythm.

Sparring came next, and Callie brought out two pairs of makeshift gloves that she'd rigged up. I really didn't think she'd be so tough, but I was wrong. She was small but mighty, with a wicked left hook. Bottom line—she kicked my ass. "I can't blast people with my light ray for long, so this is my backup plan," she said while we took a five-minute break.

I rubbed my jaw where she'd repeatedly tagged me. She hadn't used her full strength, I felt, although she could have. "What if they have powers that don't conk out?"

"Then I'm screwed."

I silently hoped it wouldn't come to that.

Mrs. Rothman was incredibly nice. After Callie and I finished sparring, we went inside for something to drink. Over tea, Callie explained that she'd been protected by Mrs. Rothman from a system that didn't look out for those who were the most vulnerable. "My life with my old foster parents was rotten. I had to get out of there," Callie explained, tripping over her words at first and then gaining more confidence as she went along.

"My foster parents—my foster mom and her boyfriend—were alcoholics and scum. I'm an orphan. I first got taken in when I was twelve. I never found out who my real parents were, but the name Sanda...someone named me that when I was born. I don't know who, and my foster parents didn't know, either."

She bit her lip. "I told you before that they died, right?"

Her tone sounded defensive, but she had her reasons. "Yeah, you did."

"All right. Well, they were big into drinking, but they sometimes took drugs, and when I came home from school, I found them on the kitchen floor. Cold. Dead. I freaked, and then I called the police. Long story short, the police called Social Services, but the system isn't into taking care of older teens. They age out, they're a drain on money...so I was lucky when Mrs. Rothman took me in."

"We're the lucky ones, dear," her foster mother said while patting her shoulder fondly.

Callie smiled and returned the gesture. "Me, too. I'm here now. It doesn't matter where I came from. This is all that counts."

"I could never have children. Callie's like our daughter," Mrs. Rothman said with genuine affection. "My husband's off at work, but he'll tell you the same thing. If anyone asks, we just say that Callie's our niece. Only a few people know, and Callie stays at home most of the time. She'll be safe here."

And...cue cliché number three—me and Callie starting off as friends who became more than friends. In our case, Callie and I were almost inseparable. She came to my house, met my parents, and showed off her abilities.

Naturally, they were apprehensive at first, but they liked her. As my mother mentioned to my father—they were in the kitchen and I overheard their conversation—they sounded positive. "At least, Eli's got a girlfriend, she's nice, and they're the same. That's important."

Things went well. I learned how to box, Callie taught me some other moves, just in case, and time passed peacefully. That is, until the AMA was formed, which led to cliché number four—tragedy. The crackdown by the authorities began, and that fateful day when I was seventeen, I came home after school, only to find that my house had been trashed.

Besides the wrecked furniture, there were bloodstains on the carpet. Someone had been here, and my parents must have put up a struggle. At least, I wanted to believe that they had.

The AMA had taken them. I saw the note, and that was all there was to it. I sat on the floor and cried. They were gone, and they weren't coming back.

Five minutes later, Callie came over, tears running down her face. She carried a small backpack. I invited her in, and after she gained some control over herself, she said that the same thing had happened to her.

"My foster parents are gone, too," she sobbed. "The AMA took them. It couldn't've been anyone else."

I hugged her tightly, and then we talked about what to do. No legal organization would help us, so we were now effectively orphans. And, as such, we couldn't stay there anymore. "Tacoma's dead to me, too," she declared. "Beaverton's gone, this city is gone...AMA's everywhere...we have to leave."

"And go where?"

Callie reached into her pocket and brought out Wheels' card. "Let's find a payphone. I can't be sure that the AMA hasn't bugged your line. And I'm not sure that they aren't going to come back. They might even be watching us now."

Her statement set off my alarm bells. "We need to pack."

"Take only what you need."

Once I packed, we set off, and at a nearby convenience store, we found a phone, and Callie placed the call. I listened carefully as she held up the receiver. A voice said, "Hello?"

"It's us," Callie said. "Your old friends from the arcade."

"You ready to come in?"

My girlfriend looked at me, and I nodded. She answered, "Yes."

With that, he gave us a place, a time, and told us to look at the card. "Got it," Callie said and hung up.

As we exited the phone booth, I asked her what she meant about the card. "Look at what's written on yours."

I did, and...what? The place and time listed there were different from what Wheels had just said on the phone.

"The information he gave us over the phone was to throw off anyone who might be listening," Callie said with a somber air. "He's a little paranoid, but after what happened to our parents, it makes sense, doesn't it?"

I had to agree. We went to the bus station, bought one-way tickets to New York, and got on the earliest bus out of Tacoma. Fortunately, it was an uneventful trip. Callie and I got off the bus just long enough to use the facilities, buy food, and then take our seats once again.

We arrived in Manhattan two-and-a-half days later, at noon. From the bus terminal, we went to a small café near Central Park. Wheels picked us up there. He had a van, and he drove us to an underground garage. From there, we went through a side door. It led to a blank wall. "What now?" I asked.

He pressed an indentation on the wall, and it slid aside to reveal a set of stairs that led to a lower level. "Subterranean hotel," he said with a grin as we followed him down. "Not the Hotel Ritz, but it'll do."

His place turned out to be an abandoned subway tunnel. It was gloomy, and the air was thick and hot. Sickly yellow lights strung overhead provided the necessary illumination, and he showed us a few rooms that he'd cleaned up. "One for you. One for Callie," he said.

Wheels then took us to see his workshop, a separate room far down the tunnel. It had a lot of blueprints, half-made contraptions, and work tools on tables and on the ground. Wiring and transistors were everywhere. A miniature gate around two feet in height and a foot in width sat in the center of the room with a small console beside it. "What is that?" I asked.

"Interdimensional gateway, a prototype," he answered. "Something I started working on in high school. When I went to MIT, we started building a gateway, but we never finished it due to budget cuts."

He ran his hand over the console in a loving manner. "After I got out of MIT and the private sector, and after the AMA came around, I got what I needed from our old lab in Cambridge and came here. It took me a while, but I've got all the computer calculations figured out."

Was he serious? Apparently so, as he flipped a switch on a console, and the gate lit up. "I siphon the power from the city's electrical grid. I have a program running to cover what I do. I don't take much, just enough to power things up for about half a minute."

Wheels took a pencil from a nearby table and slipped it into the gateway. "Look here," he said.

I bent over and peeked at the gateway. The pencil had arrived in a dark place. It was difficult to make out the surroundings, but it looked like a field. "Is this real?" I asked.

"It is."

A moment later, the portal closed with a snap, and he admitted with a rueful air, "That's as far as I've gotten. I can send objects through, but I can't bring them back—yet."

He then shut off the machine and changed the subject. "Callie mentioned you're a molecular shifter. Let's see what you can do."

I showed him, and he flipped. He then asked to examine me when I was in metal mode. He had some kind of metal detector, and when it beeped, his jaw dropped. "Your body...it's like a mixture of titanium and something else I can't identify. My guess is that you're practically invulnerable."

I'd wondered about that. "Uh, what if someone shocks me?" It hadn't happened—yet—but it was possible.

"You mean with a taser?"

I nodded, and he shrugged. "It might damage you, but as for killing you...not sure."

Well, at least I knew the danger. "I'll try not to get shocked."

"Good idea." He smiled. "You'll be safe here."

And we were...for a while.

But then the AMA came around, Wheels told us to get out, he torched the place, and Callie and I barely escaped with our lives. After that, we figured that there would be no safe place for us unless it was with our own kind...

Chapter Five: Hiding Out

THE PRESENT. MY APARTMENT, New York City. Manhattan. Early morning...maybe.

I woke up in a sweat, my heart pounding. My dream about meeting Callie had ended with us breaking up, me traveling all over the country, trying to stay one step ahead of the authorities, and eventually finding my way back to New York.

But when one dream ended, another one began, and I flashed back to Eric's fight and subsequent loss to the AMA. When Callie and I had joined up with Wheels, he'd introduced me to a few of the enhanced. Eric was one of them.

A guy in his early twenties, he said that his fire powers had come around at the age of fourteen. He'd been doing the good Samaritan thing ever since. His problem was that he'd had no guidance earlier on in life. He and his parents had never gotten along, and after his powers came around, they threw him out of their house.

Eric was also a very private person. He refused to say where he'd been born, and if someone tried to dig for details, that was guaranteed to start an argument, which almost always ended in a fistfight.

However, once Wheels stepped in, Eric's personality changed. Wheels had the ability to listen and offer wise counsel without sounding condescending. Often, he and Eric would sit at a table and talk about life, with the older man simply listening. After a while, Eric would begin to smile, and he'd visibly relax.

That translated into a better relationship with me and Callie. Eric told me that I'd made a good choice in being with her, which made me feel better. We often patrolled the seedier side of New York, usually at night, so we wouldn't be spotted, but sometimes, we did so in the daytime.

During our patrols, we wore casual clothes, and whenever we saw something bad going down, we stepped in and stopped it—quietly. That meant taking the bad guys into an alley or an abandoned building where we settled it, mainly by beating the living hell out of the punks who wanted to beat the living hell out of the innocent.

Was it the right thing to do? In my mind, it was. We lived in New York, a city always on the edge of exploding into violence, and it was no stranger to racial or religious strife. However, we never killed anyone. It was against our code.

After I'd gone on the run with Callie, Eric often appeared on the news. He'd donned a bright red uniform. He didn't apologize for it. He got into trouble by laying heavy beatings on the punks he hunted, and he didn't apologize for that, either. He'd said that he was out to help, but now...he'd never be able to help anyone again.

To calm down, I looked out the window. It was night, and hot air blew inside my apartment, making it feel like an oven. The stars shone brightly, twinkling their eternal light. I used to love the night, mainly because I could go out and practice my transformations without anyone seeing them. It was me, the stars, the night air, the insects, and no one else.

But things had changed. Nowadays, the AMA often came calling in the late or very early hours. It was so much easier to nab someone when they were half-asleep. To get some cool air, I closed the window, then found the remote control for the air-conditioner and pressed the *on* button...nothing. The battery was still good, but the machine simply wasn't working.

"Damn it, this is an apartment, not a sauna."

Words I muttered while rummaging through my small closet, and voila—I found an old electric fan. Once I plugged it in and turned it on, it blasted out a welcome breeze. New York summers were always hot, and they'd gotten worse each time I came back. Many right-wing morons had long argued against climate change, but the proof had arrived in the form of hotter weather every year.

Crops wilted, famine set in, and people died. But the business leaders of the industrialized countries did nothing about it. They had the cash, and most of the regular people out there—enhanced as well as non-enhanced—didn't. This planet was slowly dying. If a world war didn't destroy it, then environmental neglect surely would.

I tried closing my eyes, but sleep wouldn't come. Ever since leaving home, I'd slept with one eye open, always aware that someone might be looking for me. Call that paranoid, but that kind of thinking had also kept me safe.

Since going back to sleep wasn't on the menu, I turned on the television. The clock in the lower-right corner said that it was twelve-thirty at night. A news report was on, so I turned down the volume and clicked on the closed-captioned titles. *Late breaking news flash...talks between the US, Russia, and China, have once again stalled. Russia threatens to annex Ukraine and the Crimean area, as well as the former satellite countries. China has reversed its formerly peaceful stance and has threatened the sovereignty of Taiwan, as well as the sovereignty of Japan. Our president has responded forcefully, saying that the US will not be intimidated. Japan and Taiwan are under our protection, and if they are attacked, we are attacked.*

According to the White House and our top military leaders, we have now moved into a yellow danger zone. President Anderson has stated that if we reach the red zone, then we must be ready for an all-out conflict. Our opponents on the world stage think that we will back down in the face of their aggression. We will not. Our nuclear capabilities are beyond anything our rivals possess, but if we use them, what will the cost be...

With a grunt of disgust, I switched to another channel, but the news report was the same, only this particular channel was extremely right-wing and xenophobic, anti-Semitic, and anti-Muslim, in addition to being extremist when it came to Christian ideology. In short, it was a cesspool of humanity's basest values.

Pass. I'd heard the anti-Semitic jokes while growing up. Being Jewish, although not deeply into my faith, I knew what it was like to be a minority. To the bigots out there, they only knew that I was the other. That was enough for them.

It wasn't for me, though. I had to take it before my powers came around, although there were times when I refused to. Once my powers developed, and once Callie had taught me how to fight, confrontations remained few and far between.

However, while being enhanced saved me from beatings, it didn't help a lot of the enhanced vis-à-vis family relations. A study a year ago about the enhanced coming out to family and friends showed that in ninety-seven percent of all the cases, non-acceptance was the rule, rather than the exception. Religion, race, creed...none of it mattered. What mattered was the mindset. Fear the different.

And that fear turned to hatred. In turn, hatred turned to action, which accounted for the AMA in the United States. And every single country around the world had their own agency or agencies that had one mission—find out who the enhanced were and then stamp them out.

No wonder no one wanted to show their true face anymore. Sticking one's head out was asking for it to be shot off. My parents had been right. I couldn't reveal myself—ever.

Simply thinking about my parents brought tears to my eyes. They'd always been there for me. They'd done their best to raise me right, teach me how to handle certain situations, and be a good person. And for that, they'd paid with their lives. I was sure of that.

The irony of it all was that the government had been after me, not them, but they were the sacrificial pawns in this venture. And they'd sacrificed themselves to spare me the indignity of jail, torture...and death...

Wait. I heard the sound of footsteps, and they got louder. Some drunk coming home? No...the footsteps were regular, heavy, and then whoever it was stopped outside my door. "Hey, in there. Open up."

Who the hell is that? A light went off on my television set. It was the motion sensor light, a gift from Wheels. It meant that someone was fiddling with the locks, and that meant they were up to all bad.

The man's voice—harsh and authoritative—repeated the command. I went to the window and quietly opened it. My apartment was on the third floor of my building, and the fire escape was the only way out.

"Marks, we know who you are. You're on the wanted list. You never registered. Now, open up!"

Holy God. My adrenaline rush spiked. The AMA had finally found me, but how? The last time I'd transformed was in Dallas a couple of months back. I'd been staying at a youth hostel, it was night, I'd gone out for a walk, and a couple of drunken morons had decided to make me their next target.

Bad choice. I'd put them in the hospital, then returned to New York, thinking that no one would come after me. Call that foolish and shortsighted. Apparently, the AMA had known about me all along, or else someone had ratted me out, but who...

"Marks!"

A loud bang sounded at the door. It quivered, and then another smash caused it to cave in. I was halfway through the window and caught a glimpse of the two AMA men as the hallway light illuminated their features. Both were tall, wide-bodied, and they sported thin, cruel-looking lips.

Put them in the category of that breed of people who never played nice. I'd faced maggots like that before—bullies who beat up the weak because they could. Moreover, they enjoyed it.

I went out the window and swung my legs over the railing. Three flights down, and I jumped, shifting into metal mode to absorb the impact. It jarred me, but I could still move...

"He's down there," someone yelled. "No guns. Get him!"

No guns. That was a relief. I moved off, only to confront two more AMA dudes who carried tasers. "Shock him," one of them said.

Tasing me in metal mode might kill me, so just before the shocks hit, I shifted into wood form. The tasers stung, but I grabbed the wires and yanked—hard. AMA Dude One and AMA Dude Two got pulled off their feet, and then I laid into them. "Ever hit a hard log, guys," I yelled while beating them from head to toe. "Ever think about how the log feels? Well, this time, the wood hits back."

Whack, whack, whack...blood spurted, all of it theirs. I left them, then, and started to move off when the first two guys who'd surprised me at my apartment appeared dead ahead. "You're not going anywhere, Marks," one of them said, breathing heavily. Running down the stairs at top speed would cause anyone to be breathless. However, he still had enough strength to pull out a small handgun. "Dead or alive, you're coming with us. We'd prefer alive."

Why did the bad guys always have to use clichés? *You're not going anywhere. This is where it ends.* And, of course, they'd just uttered the best threat of all. *Dead or alive, you're coming with us.*

Truthfully, I was tired of it, and so I charged, using my wooden limbs to maim them, break their hands, and then slice up their faces. A moment later, my powers left me. I shifted back to my default form and staggered around before some of my strength returned. While a sense of shame hit, as well as remorse for doing what I'd done, this was a case of my life versus theirs. I chose mine, and I ran. Soon, I'd left AMA's worst far behind.

But it was night, and I couldn't go back to my apartment, not now, and not ever. I had to find somewhere to stay. I also needed to eat and lie down. Such was my existence.

I kept moving, stayed in the shadows, and I found an empty alley full of discarded crates and cardboard boxes. It was better than nothing, and it was warm. I found a large box, pulled it behind a dumpster, and stink from the garbage or not, biting insects or not, I sacked out, and found that I could sleep...

Hours later. Morning.

I woke up stiff, sore, and incredibly hungry, and crawled out of the box to greet the day. The sun was already up, and it was hot, but the streets were practically empty, so I figured it was around six-thirty in the morning. There wasn't much in the way of food, and dumpster diving was a last resort.

Luck was on my side, though. I found a plastic bag, probably one that belonged to a homeless denizen, and inside was eighteen dollars in old and crumpled bills, along with some change. I could've dipped into my bank account, but paranoia took over, saying that the AMA was watching every financial institution.

That left the bag of money. At first, I felt guilty taking someone else's savings, but there was no ID, and this was a case of staying alive. I pocketed the contents and moved out, keeping close to the alleys as I walked along the streets. Every car that honked made me think it was a police cruiser or AMA vehicle. Just passenger cars, though so that was something to be grateful for.

A nearby twenty-four-seven coffee shop provided me with cover. I bought a cup of coffee, two large sandwiches, and a donut, and I carried my goodies to a booth at the rear of the shop. No one else was inside, but I chose a booth that was swathed in shadows.

The only person on duty was the middle-aged guy who'd served me, and he didn't pay attention to anything except the money I handed over. Anyway, I was hungry, and feasting ensued. Once I was done, I exited the shop, keeping my head down.

What now, I thought. What now? The police surely had my description, although the AMA didn't like cooperating with the local law. They were into handling the cases of the enhanced on their own, so what to do...

"Hey, you, over here."

My heart jumped into my mouth, but the voice belonged to a tall, strongly built man who was accompanied by another man who was just as tall, but much, much fatter. They wore jeans, tight-fitting t-shirts, and they carried pipes. "I seen your description," the more muscular man said. "Authorities are after you. They're promising a reward for your capture, and we aim to collect."

Wonderful. These two idiots were the AMA's lapdogs. It was bad enough that the AMA was out and about, arresting innocent people. It was worse when ordinary citizens forgot about being decent and turned on their fellow citizens. Spying on each other was the lowest thing around, but for those willing to sell their souls, it guaranteed advancement.

However, I couldn't think about that. All I thought about was the cliché they'd spouted over collecting a bounty. "You talking to me?" I asked, well aware that there wasn't anyone else in the vicinity. An alleyway lay two steps away, and that was it.

"Yeah, you. You're Eli Marks, ain'tcha?"

Oh, yeah, someone had been doing their homework. Well, since there was no avoiding this... "Guys, my name's Eli Marks, but I'm not the guy you want."

Mr. Wide smirked. "Boy, stop lying. We know. Now, you gonna come quietly, or do we have to teach you a lesson?"

In that split-second while cursing the AMA and also cursing my bad luck, I formulated my responses, and they went as follows. At first, I could've said, "You and what army?" That was an old line, but it fit.

Response number two was, "Guys, you have the wrong person. I'm innocent." While I *was* innocent, good luck in getting these two idiots to believe it.

Finally, response number three went as follows, "Can't we all just get along?" That was another oldie, but it also fit.

Another split-second went by, and I decided to forget about my clichéd responses. There was a time to back off and take it, and a time when I didn't have to take it anymore. This was a case of the latter. "Okay, let's go into the alley and have it out. But I have to warn you, you won't like what's coming."

Mr. Jacked grinned, exposing yellowish-green teeth. "We got pipes. You don't."

No one could be that stupid, but perhaps they didn't know what I could do, or else they felt confident enough to take me out with their weapons. I backed into the alley, shifting as I did so. When Mr. Wide took the first swing, he dropped the pipe and clutched his hand. "Man, what the hell are you?"

I couldn't resist. "You mean, what am I made of?" I stepped into the light, and when his jaw went slack with shock, I smashed that jaw into oblivion. He collapsed. One down.

Mr. Jacked didn't lay off, though. He didn't even stare at his friend's downed form. Instead, he took out a taser and shot me. Stupid, I told myself. I should have been expecting that, but no, I'd gotten overconfident.

Overconfidence could cost a person. A shock wave traveled through me, practically shorting out my senses. *So that's how it feels.* I ripped the wire off and slumped back against the wall, half-stunned.

My opponent grinned. "So, you can be hurt. Nice to know."

He went all batter up on me, but I ducked and changed into wood mode. It was better than nothing, and I hoped that he didn't have a lighter handy.

Luck was on my side for a change. His pipe whacked me upside my head, but in wood form, I barely felt the impact. In response, I morphed my fingers into sharp points, and I replied by stabbing him in his shoulders and arms, then switched to slice-and-dice mode.

However, my mission was to disable, not to kill. "S-stop, man...stop," he pleaded as the blood spilled from his body. "I'm done." Fine, I backed off. I'd never killed anyone in the time I'd gotten my abilities, although the urge was always there, and it was a constant battle to stop myself from ridding the world of another asshole.

Now, that urge came back, as he took a laser knife out of his pocket and slashed my shoulder with it. Right, I'd spared his miserable life, but he just had to go there. His laser knife took out a chunk of my shoulder, which hurt like hell and caused me to bleed.

No more Mister Nice Guy. I slashed open his legs, and he fell against the dumpster, more of his life's essence leaking from a double-dozen cuts. "Like that, you jerk? Like that?"

He didn't answer. He was too busy groaning in pain, although he managed to say, "You're...you're still a freak," before passing out.

"I'm still standing, you maggot. What's your excuse?"

Right, I was speaking to an unconscious moron, and yes, it was a lousy line, but I'd never been the pithy sort. I moved out of the alley and into the light, staggered along the street, now back in default mode. Being flesh now, blood dripped from the wound. Those damn laser knives were lethal.

By now, a few people had gathered around to see what the rumpus was, and they'd followed me. Didn't they have anything better to do? Obviously not. One man shied back after he caught sight of my forearms. There were still traces of wood on them. "You...you're one of them," he cried. "Mutant!"

God, I hate that word.

One man started toward me with his fists raised. Oh, wonderful, another tough guy. Well, if he wanted to...

But it never came to pass, as a bright light exploded out of nowhere and blinded everyone—me included. A collective scream rang out, and a small, soft, but firm hand grabbed mine. "It's me, Callie," a voice whispered in my ear. "I know you can't see. Hold onto me. I'll get us out of here."

She pulled me away from the action, and a few seconds later, my hand touched metal. I heard something being opened. "It's a car," Callie whispered. "Get in."

My vision was beginning to clear, and I made out the back seat and dove in. Callie slammed the door shut, went to the driver's side, and took the wheel. "Keep your head down," she ordered as she started the car and drove off. "We've got places to go."

"Is this your car?" I didn't know she could drive.

"Nope," she replied cheerfully. "Someone left the keys in, and I decided to borrow it. Anyway, we needed transportation. Oh, and by the way, I don't have a license, but I learned how to drive. Practice, you know?"

Fine, she knew how to drive, but stealing a car? Well, it could've been worse. I had another question, though, once my vision cleared and we'd moved well away from the crowd. "How'd you know where to find me?"

"I've been in New York for a few weeks," she replied nonchalantly. "I found out that you'd moved back to New York, and Wheels ordered me to watch out for you and the AMA. Lucky I was here on time."

"Yeah," I muttered. "Then you saw those thugs try to take me down. They had it coming." My tone was defensive, and why not? I'd been targeted and in only the foulest way.

Callie's response wasn't what I expected. "You shouldn't have done that. They deserved it, but you shouldn't've done it."

"They had it coming," I repeated, tired and drained from shifting. "In case you haven't noticed, my shoulder's bleeding."

I couldn't shake the feeling of defensiveness. It was wrong, yes, but I'd been the object of their hatred. The AMA was after me, and I'd grown tired of people seeing me as a freak. I only wanted her to understand where I was coming from.

"I see it," she responded. "I know they had it coming, but you can't show yourself in public. And before you tell me, I used my powers, too. C'mon."

She drove skillfully through the streets, avoiding any cars that were out, and within twenty minutes, we found ourselves on the highway. "Relax," she said. "You need something to eat?"

My stomach growled. "Yeah."

Callie opened the glove compartment, rooted around in it, and came away with two chocolate bars, which she handed to me. "It isn't much, but it should keep you going until we get to our destination."

Chocolate...I tore the wrappers off and crammed the candy bars into my mouth. The sugar rush hit, but I felt better, and my healing powers came to help. I'd always healed up faster than normal, and now, I was grateful for my enhanced condition. After that, I must have dozed off, but a jolt woke me up. "What? Where...what happened?"

"Sorry," she said. "Had to change lanes."

Well, so much for my nap. I felt better, though, and I checked out the sights from the highway. Manhattan was an immense city, and I kept my eyes glued to the magnificent skyline. "How much further?" I asked.

"About half an hour."

Half an hour. Whatever, as long as we were out of harm's way. Our journey continued, and after twenty minutes, she took an off-ramp. The scenery gradually changed from concrete jungle to the green countryside. A sign up ahead said, *Royce Township, three miles.* Royce Township was in upstate New York, near the Catskill Mountains.

High hedges lined the gravel road we'd turned onto, and a sense of peace filled me. It had been a long time since I'd felt that way. We kept going, but then Callie said, "We're just about there. Hang on." In a swift move, she pulled the car over to the side of the road, reversed direction, and then stopped. "Out."

I got out, she took the keys and tossed them into the brush, then took something from her pocket and put it on the dashboard. "Let's move."

We started walking, and a dull boom sounded from behind us. I turned around to see that the car was on fire, although it soon burned itself out. "You torched the car," I said, stating the obvious.

She smiled. "No traces. That fire-bomb can wipe out any trace of human DNA, including fingerprints." She turned her attention to my wound, peering at the split flesh in wonder. "It's halfway healed. You'll be fine."

Wonderful, I had a nurse. I refrained from tossing her a snarky answer, opting to remain quiet. Our trek continued, and after five minutes, Callie reached into her pocket, brought out a smartphone, punched in a few numbers, and then waited for the connection to tie in. I heard a voice say, "Yeah?"

"It's me," she replied. "We're on the road leading to Royce Township." She listened intently and then added, "Got it."

With that, she turned off the phone, dropped it, and stamped on it until it was totaled. She picked up the remains and tossed them into the brush. "That's so no one can track the signal. If you think I'm paranoid, then ask yourself how the AMA found you."

That made sense. As we made our way along the road, the sun began to rise in strength and intensity. Finally, I broke the silence. "Did you say that Wheels sent you?"

"He did, but he needs time to get ready," she replied, still on the lookout for more trouble. I'd taken care of those punks, but who knew if they'd try again. People like that were unpredictable, and now that I'd exposed myself and what I could do, it wouldn't be long before the government came around. I cursed myself for losing my temper, but it was too late to take it back.

The sound of an engine approaching interrupted my bout of mental castigation. We had company. The sound got louder, and Callie pulled me over to the side of the road. It was just us two, but we couldn't be too careful. A few seconds later, a black van pulled up alongside us, and a bearded man poked his head out the window. "Remember me?" he said.

It was Larry, AKA Wheels, but he'd changed. He used to be clean-shaven and chubby, but now, he had the full hippie-slash-homeless look going on, complete with a scraggly beard. His face, formerly round and full, was narrow and drained of vitality. He looked more than exhausted.

"Look who I brought," Callie said as she opened the sliding door. We got in, and I found a seat in the back next to a folded-up wheelchair.

Once we got underway, I snuck a look at our driver. His hands flew like lightning over the console. "I gotta concentrate," he said. "Shove the wheelchair over if it's too cramped back there. Gimme ten minutes, and we'll be home."

Callie chose to look out the window, and we drove fast and hard down the road, making a turnoff onto a gravel road. A sign that hung from a rotting wood post read *Windermere Drive*. We continued up the gravel path to a cottage. "Here," I asked. "Here?"

My seatmate giggled. "Wait."

We kept driving, and Wheels flipped a switch on the console. The ground opened up in front of us to reveal a ramp leading down. Holy geez...

"Hang on," he said, and we accelerated another twenty miles per hour down the ramp.

We entered a vast underground garage. Wheels skidded to a stop, breathing heavily and let out a loud whoop. "That entrance always gets my heart pounding. Okay, you two, out. Callie, can you pop my chair, please?"

She quickly got out, grabbed the chair, and unfolded it. Callie then wheeled it over to the driver's side. Wheels opened the door and slid into the chair. He wore jeans, but the material flapped around his thighs like sails. His legs must have been sticks. "That's better," he said with a sigh. "I like driving, but I'd rather be sitting."

A rueful look came over his face. "No, actually, I'd rather be walking around like everyone else, but that ain't going to happen anytime soon."

He led us over to a side door where a console was in place of where the handle should've been. After he pressed numbers two and four, the ramp closed up, and the lights came on. The area was empty save for his van and a large object covered in a tarp. Thick cables ran from under the tarp into the ground and along the wall.

"Secret project," Wheels said with a wink. "Something I've been working on for a while."

That was all the information he volunteered. He spun his wheelchair around and pressed eight, nine, and five on the console. After a beep, the door opened. "Welcome to the lair," he said as he propelled himself inside. "Relax. You're among friends."

Chapter Six: Dornaught

ALTHOUGH OUR NEW DIGS were in an underground bunker, the kitchen was brightly lit and well-ventilated. Our guardian opened the refrigerator long enough to show that it was fully stocked. "Can you look at Eli's shoulder?" Callie asked, her voice full of concern. "Laser attack. I figure he'll be okay, but I'm no doctor."

Wheels pulled out three cans of cola, put them on the table, and said, "Take off your shirt, Eli, and drink up. I'll have a look at your shoulder."

Right, my shirt off, Wheels probed the wound with gentle fingers while Callie fidgeted. In the end, he let things go. "You seem to be healing okay without any help. If I were you, I'd just let it heal on its own."

His medical assessment jived with what Callie had said. After I'd downed my drink, I felt better, so I decided to let nature take its course and donned my shirt. Wheels then asked us to follow him. His chair had a motor attached to it, but it must have been ultra-light as Callie had lifted it easily.

He pressed a button on the right-hand armrest to guide it along. "I don't usually use the motor. I have to get some exercise in, somehow, besides lifting weights."

I noticed that his upper arms, as well as his forearms, had a lot of muscle. His chest and shoulders were just as jacked. We followed him around, and the more I saw, the more amazed I grew. This place wasn't simply a fallout bunker. It was a complex. Five spare rooms for those who stayed with him. Besides the kitchen, there was a large lounge-slash-living-room, and also a fully equipped gym that included a combat area.

Then there was a workshop where Wheels said he was in the process of developing a variety of gadgets. I saw transistors, pistols of various sorts, and bolts of cloth. "Uniforms," Wheels said. "I figured that someday, some of us will want to look cool."

It seemed like a good idea. The tour went on, and we viewed five other rooms that served as storage areas for various pieces of equipment, plus Wheels' clothes and a huge number of canned goods and MREs. "The MREs are just in case we're stuck down here for a long time," he explained. "If the worst happens, like a nuclear war, this complex will sink a hundred feet into the earth."

"Is it safe?" I asked.

Wheels gave a confident nod. "I have air filtration systems in place, enough water for a hundred years, plus backup filtration systems, medical supplies, and mini-nuclear power generators that'll supply lots of energy."

His excuse for such a large place, as well as bankrolling me and Callie—a rather sizeable inheritance. "My parents owned a lot of real estate, including over one hundred fifty hectares in this area. It's been in the family for over a hundred years."

Well, that answered one question I had. "Don't people know who you are?"

Wheels shook his head. "There are only around a thousand people here in total. The permanent residents number around eight hundred. The rest are vacationers who rent the cottages during the summer season. The nearest cottage is about ten miles up the road. No one bothers me."

He went over to a table covered with a series of rolled-up papers. He sifted through the pile and then unrolled one. It was a map of the area. "Look here," he said. His finger traced a wide circle around the area where we were. "All this land belongs to me. My folks died a few years back, just before the AMA came around.

"In addition to this land, they owned seven buildings in Manhattan, and they also had sizeable investments in blue-chip stocks, so I sold off some of those assets to fund this place. After taxes, I still came out way ahead."

I marveled aloud at how he'd been able to construct such a well-designed and built complex. His answer? "I hired six different contractors to build one section down here. All of them used to work for my parents, and they're all loyal to them—and to me. Their blueprints showed five different survival basement-type areas, along with one storage room, so that's what they thought they were building. Bunkers to ride out a nuclear storm, you know? Survivalist stuff."

"They must've thought you were crazy," I said, only half-joking about it.

A harsh laugh emanated from Wheels' belly, worked its way up through his chest, and then out his mouth. "Eli, if you're poor, you're a nut. If you're rich—or people think you're rich—they put up with your eccentricities. No one really knew what the other sections were. After each section was completed, I blocked it off and had the construction crews start on another section. No one found out."

It was like the ultimate plan. I had another question, though. "Can't the AMA trace who owns the land?"

He chuckled. "If they do, they'll find that the owner is one Mark Russell, rich retiree. He's an old friend of my father's, and he stayed here during the construction and supervised things, while I stayed at a hotel. No one found out. Russell acts as my proxy. If the AMA ever goes to him, he's got the documents and the bank accounts to prove he's the owner. They're not going to find out."

Wheels seemed to have planned everything down to the last detail. "You knew what would happen, didn't you?"

He shrugged. "I'd like to say yes, but I'm no fortune teller. Even I didn't think the feds would go this far. But when a friend of mine in the government said something about registering those who had powers, I started planning. Call this place a just-in-case scenario. And if anyone comes snooping around, I've got motion sensors, trip wires, and mounted machine guns on the trees. I've also got surveillance cameras set up."

Perhaps he'd sensed an upcoming war? No, he'd simply thought ahead, while I'd failed to see the big picture. I hadn't even thought to look for his home defense system. Still, I felt compelled to point out that the AMA, as well as the government, had a variety of weapons.

"Yeah, they do," he replied. "Man-made and human ones. We have to watch out for both."

We'd gone back to the kitchen after the tour. Callie busied herself making sandwiches for us, and I marveled at her ability to construct something to eat far more quickly than I ever could.

Wheels took a bite of his ham-and-cheese concoction, inclined his head at Callie in appreciation, and put it down after swallowing and taking a sip from a can of cola. "Better than I can make. And, to answer your question, Eli, yes, they do have a variety of weapons. There are also the enhanced personnel to worry about. I have a gun that interrupts their neural system for perhaps ten seconds, but it's only got one shot." He gave a self-deprecating laugh. "You have to start somewhere."

In a quick motion, he pivoted around in his wheelchair, saying that he wanted to work on his inventions some more, and wheeled himself out. I watched him go with a sense of awe.

Callie and I were alone, and at first, neither of us spoke. She drummed her fingers on her knees restlessly, while I thought about how she'd unceremoniously dumped me over a year ago. Holding a grudge wasn't a cool thing to do, but at the same time, I also wasn't overly happy at how I'd suddenly gone from attached to unattached so quickly. Finally, Callie cleared her throat and asked, "How've you been?"

I could've given her a snarky answer, or an angry one, but in the end, I told her the truth with no emotion. "On the run. You?"

"Same." She bit her lip and then moved over to sit beside me. "Listen, I'm sorry about us splitting up before. It was my decision and my fault. I thought it was too dangerous for us to be together. I mean, it's not that I didn't like hanging out with you. I did...I do. But being together? That made us a target for the AMA. If one of us had gotten captured, that would've sucked. If we'd both been taken in, well, that's worse than bad."

She had a point. I'd read somewhere that in a person's life, they had three chances to forgive someone for something they'd done. I didn't know about the three-times concept, but to me, there was always a time for forgiveness, and this was one of those times. "So, why is it different now?"

Callie inclined her head at the kitchen area. "Wheels. He has this place, it's well hidden, and we're safe. In my book, that counts for a lot."

Again, her statement made sense. "What happened to him?"

She inhaled and blew out a deep breath as if arranging her thoughts. "He told me all about it when I rejoined his group a month ago. After the AMA raided his old hideout, they took him away. They tortured him, then shot him. His legs were paralyzed, but he managed to escape and then came here. Like he said, he set this place up just when the trouble between us and the government started."

I felt sorry for him. He didn't ask to be injured, and I said as much to Callie. Her reply was simple. "Wheels doesn't want pity about his condition. He just wants to help, and he also wants to stay hidden from the government. Can you blame him?"

"No." He had his reasons, and so did I. On the other hand, I wanted to get back at the powers-that-were. If anyone deserved it, it was those stooges in the AMA, as well as the government, who sanctioned what they did. If this setup worked, then I was all for it. "Can I ask you a question?"

Callie glanced at me, then looked away as if she already knew what I was going to say. "Sure."

"I didn't do anything wrong when we dated, did I?" I felt embarrassed to ask, but I had to know. "I mean, I knew about the AMA, and I get your reasons for splitting up, but I have to know if I, you know, pushed too hard or something."

She was silent for a time, while I stared at the floor and wondered if I'd made a mistake in asking her. Finally, she cleared her throat. "No, you didn't do anything wrong. You respected me. We were good together, and we had a good thing going on."

Callie shifted around to face me. "I liked you then. I still do. But...like I said, the situation we were both in...after we split up, every city I was in, I wanted to contact you...I really did. But I couldn't take the chance on the government not tapping the lines or someone seeing what I could do or what you could do. I didn't want to get you into trouble. That's why I stayed away and didn't contact you. It was for my protection—and yours."

A note of longing entered her voice, and she suddenly leaned against me. "Now, we're here."

Yes, we were. I hesitantly put my arm around her shoulders. When she didn't pull away, I hugged her gently. She returned the gesture, and we stayed in that position for quite some time until Callie got up and pulled me up with her. "C'mon, let's finish lunch, and then we can take a walk or something, if you want."

That sounded like a good idea.

Two days later.

Our rooms were simple and functional, blasted out of the rock by the construction crews Wheels had hired. My room had a cot, a bathroom-shower, a small closet for clothes, and a mirror, plus one light that illuminated everything. That was it, but it was comfortable. Good enough for me.

Air came in via overhead vents that had been carved into the rock. It hissed out a soft flow, but it didn't impair my sleep, and for the first time in a while, I felt safe, almost insulated from the trouble in the outside world.

Speaking of the outside world, Wheels had a large-screen television mounted on the wall in the lounge room. He said that an antenna on the surface relayed signals to his lair. *"The antenna's well-hidden. Not to worry."*

It was a good idea, but when I parked myself on a couch and tuned into a local news station, the news reports put a damper on things. China had decided to flex its naval muscle, and the results weren't pretty.

China attacked two Taiwanese freighters today, sinking one and damaging another. The loss of life exceeded one hundred people, with fifty-seven injured. China claimed that the ships infringed on their territorial waters.

Taiwan immediately protested the attack, and in a separate action, their naval forces shelled three tiny islands used by China as fishing areas. Sixteen fishing boats were sunk, with a loss of twenty-three people. Forty-four people were injured. Both countries accuse the other of fomenting war, and tensions are running high...

Great, more Chinese aggression, just what the world didn't need. As for the American-Russian Cold War Two front, Russia apparently launched a cyber-bot attack against the American Pentagon in an attempt to disrupt military communications. The US retaliated by expelling the Russian ambassadors from five of their protectorates and also launching their own cyber-attack, or so Russia claimed. Naturally, the Americans denied any involvement...

"This just in," a voiceover said. "Five of the mutants captured by the AMA are now being tried and sentenced. Our new laws have permitted fast-tracking their cases. What used to take months now takes far less time."

"No jury, just a judge and a lot of armed guards."

I looked around at who'd spoken and killed the sound. Callie had come in. She'd always favored wearing jeans and t-shirts, and she had the same getup on. Her hair was tousled. One thing I liked about her was that she never wore makeup. Her skin had a healthy glow to it, perhaps because of her inner light power.

In contrast, I'd suffered from an acne outbreak when I was thirteen and still sported scars on my cheeks. It made me somewhat self-conscious, but Callie, in her decency, had never mentioned it. Now, she took a seat beside me. "How's the shoulder?"

It had healed quickly. "Fine. What's new?"

She pointed at the screen. "Nothing, but the news still stinks. There aren't real trials anymore. Everything's done in secret. Trial, judgment, and execution...everything. That's the law these days."

As for the news, the anchors and co-anchors reported on the captured enhanced in almost gleeful tones. Fair and impartial reporting hadn't existed for a long time, not since the elections around forty years ago. Back then, most of the news stations were on the fence when it came to politics. Recently, though, they'd shifted to the far-right, even the reputedly centrist ones.

It was frustrating to try and find impartial news, and these newscasters were no different. "Convicted killer Eric Darven, also known as Firebird, part of the mutant cult, was found non-responsive in his cell this morning. He'd been injured in a fight with the authorities and had suffered the loss of an arm."

Naturally, the newscasters failed to mention exactly how Eric had lost his arm. They continued spewing the lies. "Although he'd been treated at a hospital, he'd been taken back to his cell, as he'd been deemed fit enough to be moved." Call that a cause for alarm number one.

At some point in the night, Darven asked the guard to call for a doctor. When the doctor came, he said that Eric had suffered a heart seizure. Call that a cause for alarm number two. The reporter added, "An autopsy will be performed tomorrow."

Right, the old heart attack excuse. Never mind that Eric had probably suffered severe shock when the AMA officers shot off his arm. Never mind that he shouldn't have been imprisoned after the injury.

Never mind all that. Eric had never smoked or drank, not that I knew, and he was foursquare against drugs. Medication for his depression aside, he'd been physically healthy, so their heart attack excuse didn't wash.

But what bothered me more was that the news outlets had labeled all enhanced people as part of a mutant cult. Say what? In Eric's case, he'd killed two police officers, and he should've been tried for that crime, but calling the rest of us cult members? That pissed me off.

The news anchor went on to say that Victory, Colossal Woman, Darkslayer, Ether, and Mist, were to be executed the next day. "All of them?" I asked after turning off the television.

Her face somber, Callie nodded. "What do you think? The government's fighting two wars. They've got a war of words going on with Russia and China, and that'll probably escalate."

Now, her manner turned more serious, and a note of anger combined with frustration laced each word. "And now, the mass media is calling us a cult. We're on the hit list. There are no life sentences for people like us. Ever. If we don't join with the AMA, we die. That's the reality."

While what she'd said wasn't unexpected, it was still shocking. I'd hoped that we'd have a little more time. Now, our time had seemingly run out. Showing our faces in public was a sure invitation to imprisonment, torture, and death. I was eighteen. I had another six or seven decades to go. This wasn't right.

It wasn't right at all.

The next day. Noon.

Wheels was busy working on one of his contraptions. He refused to divulge any details, but he recommended that Callie and I check out the news. "It's probably all bad, but let me know, anyway."

Requests were requests, so the two of us sat in the lounge, watching the news. Internationally speaking, things were status quo—bad—but no one had made any aggressive moves, so that was something to be grateful for. Newscasters discussed the international tension with a sense of detachment, as if they'd been expecting the worst all along.

Domestically, though, when it came to talk of the AMA, the news stations were in a state of excitement. On one of the national television stations, a middle-aged male reporter with an ill-fitting toupee that he constantly adjusted in front of the camera seemed ready to pee his pants with excitement.

"We're going to go live to AMA headquarters, located in the heart of Chicago. There, we're going to witness the first-ever aired execution of five prisoners, five of the mutant horde, who dared uproot our American way of life."

That guy was a certifiable idiot, but his words had a chilling effect, nonetheless. He was actually looking forward to people being killed. The camera then switched to AMA headquarters, panning around a large room where Ether, Colossal Woman, Darkslayer, and the others were encased in titanium tubes that stood in a row.

The covering was transparent, so the viewers could see every single detail, and the camera zoomed in to show those details. Multiple metal IVs had been inserted into each arm, their legs, and their torsos. Holy Christ that was torture enough...but not for the AMA.

The newscaster said that the head of the organization would soon come out to make an announcement. Sure enough, a minute later, a man the newscaster identified as Thomas Dornaught, entered via the main door. He waved his hand at the technicians and then said that the execution would commence immediately.

Dornaught was a man in his forties, with slicked-back black hair, a thin face, glasses, and a tall, rangy physique. He exuded a scholarly air combined with quiet menace. He also gave me the impression that he enjoyed his work a little too much.

"This...is going to be bad," Callie said. Her voice shook. "I...I can't watch this."

She got up and hurried out of the room, leaving me to witness this horrid display of inhumanity to man. At Dornaught's request, five technicians, each assigned to a different capsule, flipped a switch, and greenish-silver liquid flowed in a slow but inexorable manner from massive tanks at the base of their consoles through the tubes, and into the bodies of the captives. My stomach began to roil. Oh, God, this maniac was going to embalm them.

"This is considered more humane," Dornaught's voiceover said. "We can't shoot them, as they're bulletproof or they can absorb the metal. But their organs and blood are the same as a regular human's organs, and by infusing their bodies with liquid *salvem*, a material I devised, these mutations will never trouble our human populace again."

The liquid hit their veins, and they bulged with the pressure of the salvem entering their circulatory systems. Screams of agony emanated from inside the capsules and reverberated around the room. Some of the techs glanced up in alarm, then they went back to their jobs. A few of them quivered in shock over what they'd done.

Let them quiver. They'd sold out to the AMA. They were still alive. The same couldn't be said for the enhanced in their mini-prisons. All of them writhed and twisted as they were literally choked from the inside, and their cries for help went unheeded. Soon, it was over, and they lay still.

"We now return you to our regular broadcasting," the announcer with the toupee said. "Thank you for tuning in..."

I shut off the television, feeling sick at heart and even sicker to my stomach. All of this was so unnecessary. I got up and wended my way to the kitchen where Wheels had a mug of coffee in front of him. Callie nursed a can of ginger ale. "Newscast's over. That Dornaught," I mumbled as I took out a can of cola from the fridge. "He's a real Doctor Demento."

"Define that, please," Callie said as she took a sip of her beverage.

I described the execution and tried not to choke on the words. Fortunately, I managed to make it through my description and finished off with, "Demented is the best word I can think of." I popped the top on my can but didn't drink...I didn't trust my stomach, not yet.

A bitter laugh clawed its way out of Wheels' throat. "He's a sadistic scumbag. I know all about him."

"How?"

Wheels' answer was that, as head of the AMA, Dornaught had been put in charge of interrogating suspects. Interrogation meant torture, plain and simple. "Dornaught's ex-military. Before he joined the army, he majored in biological chemistry at university, which meant he liked practicing on people with the concoctions he whipped up in the laboratory. He got kicked out in his third year for doing that.

"He then enlisted, served overseas, mainly in security, and he was known for being cruel to prisoners. The army liked the information that he gathered from prisoners, but they didn't appreciate his methods, so they forced him to take an honorable discharge.

"Dornaught came back stateside, and someone recommended him for the job of heading up the AMA after that anti-mutant law was passed. He's got clearance up to the highest levels, and the president is ex-military, too. He and his boys stick together."

I wondered what could drive a person to be so sadistic. As if reading my mind, Wheels gave me the details. "Like most of the anti-enhanced brigade, he fears us, and that fear's turned into hatred. I heard a rumor that his mother was enhanced, but that's only a rumor. Dornaught calls himself a patriot, but he's turned xenophobic."

He took in a deep breath and blew it out slowly. "After they caught me, they took me to their headquarters in Chicago. It's a big building, lots of levels, but they took me to the top level, near as I can remember. That was where they did their dirty work. They wanted what was up here"—he pointed to his head—"the secret to my portal calculations, among other things. Torture doesn't begin to describe what they did to me. They strapped me to a table, used electroshock, and when that didn't work, they beat the living hell out of me."

His voice took on the inflection of someone detached from the situation, but he wasn't totally detached. It was just his way of sparing himself from reliving the psychic pain. "After torture session number ten, Dornaught shot me in the back. Blew out my spine, put me in this damn wheelchair for the rest of my life."

Now, the anger at past injustices surfaced. "He wanted me dead. He tried, oh, he tried, but I didn't die. After I came out of surgery, he figured that I'd end up as a prisoner in his complex, but a friend on the inside helped me escape. He died during our run, but before he did, he slipped me the keys to his car. I started driving, and I didn't look back. Dornaught's been after me ever since. Good luck in finding me, though."

I finally took a sip from my can, but after listening to Wheels' torture story, I couldn't drink it, so I put it aside. Wheels stopped his narration to heave in another deep breath and puff it out. "That's why I'm working so hard on weapons. I don't want a war, but if push comes to shove, I'm going to give you and the others a chance to get back at them. All of them."

His rant—which wasn't a rant but a declaration—over, he wheeled himself out of the room, saying that he wanted to be alone in his workroom and didn't want to be disturbed. Callie watched him go with a sad expression. "He's a really decent guy. He didn't deserve what happened to him."

None of us deserved what had happened to us, either. "It seems we all have scores to settle. I know that I do."

Callie turned to look at me with a stricken expression. "You can't be serious. Vengeance isn't the answer. I'm sorry about your parents. I really am. I miss my foster parents, too. They were good to me. It makes me sick to think about what might have happened to them."

Her expression changed to one that bespoke of the reality we were living in, one that said that no matter how much the law was on our side...it wasn't. "But going out to get revenge on the AMA isn't a great idea. They're well-equipped. They've also got the weapons, and we don't. Not yet."

In a moment of realization, what she'd said hit home. To attack the AMA now would be tantamount to suicide. I had to look at the bigger plan. Changing the subject, I asked Callie how she'd survived over the past year. For that, I got a tiny smile. "I had my ways."

"How?"

"Luck, mainly, keeping my head down and bothering no one. On the outside, I don't look like I have any powers, and I never thought about showing off."

Asking her about her income, she shrugged. "Wheels set me up with a bank account, and I used it from time to time. I got lucky, and I found part-time jobs in convenience stores and discount shops. I took a lower hourly wage, so the managers didn't ask for ID."

Callie offered a rueful smile. "I always wanted to find another decent foster family, but I couldn't take the chance. So I dyed my hair black, let it grow longer, and used makeup to hide my looks. I stayed in youth hostels most of the time, but there was always at least one person using drugs or trying to...bother the women."

Her face took on a haunted look. "Sometimes I slept in alleys. The police thought I was just another vagrant and left me alone. It was dangerous, but there was no other way."

As she spoke, I realized that her life had been like mine, one of constantly moving around to avoid detection, never getting close to anyone, and hoping that she wouldn't be found out. "You know, I've always liked New York," she said with a thoughtful air. "Something about this city always called me back. So I came back, found Wheels, and then we came to get you. Simple."

Simple for her, maybe, but not for me. "Are we still friends?"

Immediately after asking that question, I mentally kicked myself. We'd had something once, but I wondered if she still felt something for me. If so, the question was, how much?

Callie turned her face up to mine and kissed me. It had been a long time, and the touch of her lips made me realize how much I'd missed her. "We're more than friends," she whispered. "We always have been. And we always will be."

As she melted into my arms, my question had been answered, and even in this uncertain existence, her presence and warmth gave me a certain amount of reassurance that things just might work out.

Chapter Seven: A Precarious Existence

MUTATIONS ADVANCED life. That was the secret of the survival of the human race. Once modern man had supplanted Neanderthals and became the dominant species, those changes in DNA were small and had little variety.

Oh, in every generation, some people were bigger than the norm, or stronger, or faster, or more intelligent, but only recently did more and more odd mutations account for the enhanced showing the world what they could do. Perhaps it was the change in climate or Mother Nature's way of tapping into a genetic acceleration, or perhaps it was something else. Not even the finest scientific minds around knew why.

All they knew was that the genetic changes were dramatic. Some people could fly. With their own gravimetric fields, they could take to the skies and stay up there for short periods of time. They weren't invulnerable, they weren't super-fast, but they could waft along the airwaves, and that was cool.

Those who had wings also ruled the air. And then there were others who had super strength, or those who could manipulate the elements along with other abilities that were weird and cool at the same time.

However, the main problem with that concept was that non-enhanced people were afraid of what the special few in the genetic lottery possessed, and what people feared, they often hated.

"Who are they? What are they?"

"Are they here to help us, or help themselves?"

"What's their ultimate agenda?"

Lots of podcasters started their shows with the previous questions of, *"Who are they?"* Those podcasters and media influencers had their own agenda going, mainly ratings and money. However, they touched a chord with the general public. Long story short, they didn't trust us.

Call it ignorant, childish, or irrational, but human beings had never been known for being intelligent, mature, or rational. By and large, they were selfish, greedy, and often stupid individuals. Left to their own devices, those individuals weren't dangerous. They were the kooks on the internet who shouted idiotic conspiracies, who stood on a street corner and preached their word, or they yelled at clouds. No one ever took them seriously.

On the flip-side, two or three people who banded together to preach their views were to be avoided. In packs, they were dangerous. And that pack mentality caused every government to be wary of the enhanced.

Soon, the question of, *Who are they?* became, *What are they?* and then, *Where are they?* The public said that they had a right to know, which meant that they thought they had a right to control another person's life.

Ironically, when the enhanced first burst onto the scene, when Eric, when a woman named Paige Parker, and when her twin brother, Paul, appeared, they were seen as possible saviors. Eric used fire as his way of making a statement. Paige could control dirt, and, to a certain degree, small rocks.

She created sandstorms to blind her opponents, while her brother had the ability to connect with birds, commanding them to attack or dump guano on people, at his behest. He favored talking to crows for reasons he never divulged.

Of course, the authorities were leery of asking any of the enhanced to help enforce the law. Still, crime had to be fought, so the police had their own people watch the trio, go out with them on patrol, and things went well—at first. The crime rate in the major cities fell, and that was a plus to the incumbent politicians who backed the enhanced, as well as the human rights groups.

Then the government asked a few more of the genetically favored to serve in the armed forces. It seemed to be a natural thought. It was also asking for trouble. Some of the enhanced were all about going all Uncle Sam on the enemy, whoever they were. Others were pacifists and only used their abilities to help others in domestic situations. They didn't want to go to war overseas or kill anyone.

Unfortunately, that was when the government stepped in and gave them the old, *you're in our employ, so you're going to do what we say* edict. It did not for good relations make. It just made things worse. Paul and Paige retired from the business and subsequently dropped off the map.

Still, the various enhanced who remained did their bit for justice. When I met Eric for the first time, he asked me about my powers. I showed him, and he flipped. *"Man, you could do anything you want. This is going to set the world on fire."* Considering he could set any object he wanted on fire, that was an understatement.

But it wasn't an understatement when it came to dealing with the criminal element. Eric and I did our thing, but quietly. We never alerted the police as to what we were doing. Although the MRA had already passed, I'd never registered with the government, preferring to fly under the radar.

Additionally, the AMA had only recently been formed, but they had no power—yet. Therefore, for the first year or so, no one interfered with our nocturnal patrols. We stopped bank robbers. We stopped muggings, rapes, and possible murders. We felt proud of doing the public a service, felt proud of helping out. Rumors went around the internet like wildfire. *Metal-man mashes muggers. Wood-man whips would-be wrongdoers.*

Yes, the news headlines loved alliteration. But those headlines were what people liked to read. They were simple, dramatic, and effective. And the upshot was that John and Jane Average Citizen liked us. Not loved us...liked us.

Between love and like was an overwhelming ambivalence. When the reporters talked about the mystery men and women foiling robberies and other crimes, people spoke of us with respect, but underlying that was a guardedness and an unwillingness to fully accept us.

As Eric put it in a most blunt fashion, *"They'll let us eat in their shops and spend our money, but if I ask their daughter out, they slam the door in my face."*

I'd looked at him after he uttered that statement. *"Did you ask anyone's daughter out?"* I was seventeen at the time. Call me naïve to the nth degree. I knew nothing about dating, so I thought it wouldn't hurt to get advice from someone who was older and ostensibly wiser.

He shrugged. *"Yeah, a few times. It never worked out."*

"Why?" It was a stupid question, but I had to know.

Eric heaved in and blew out a deep breath. *"Man, the ladies just want someone who stays home at night. They want Joe Average, not Joe Above Average. And my powers scare them."*

I thought about what to say. *"You don't use them. I mean, we go on patrol, but it's always me who turns into wood or metal to deflect things. And I always do it from the shadows and wear a mask. No one's ever seen my face."*

He nodded. That happened to be true. I handled the strong-arm stuff. Eric wasn't always in control of his flame abilities. Being short-tempered worked against him. He'd never snapped at me, but at times, he got angry for no reason at other members of our group. And once, just once, he jerked around a suspect a little too harshly, and I had to intervene.

In a private moment, Callie asked me to be careful. *"He's on medication, in case you haven't noticed."*

It was springtime, and we were in a small café, having a light lunch while keeping watch for any trouble. However, that day, trouble seemed to be far away, and everyone was in a good mood. I put down my fork, surprised at the information. *"No, I didn't notice. I mean, Eric's a bit short-tempered, but he never tried anything with me, and he never, uh, beat up a suspect. The guy he pushed around threatened him. Eric's not into threats, so I figured he was right in doing what he did."*

Callie didn't see it that way and shook her head, muttering, *"Wheels told me that Eric's bipolar. When he takes his meds, he's calm and does his job, but sometimes, he doesn't stay on his meds because they make him sick. And when he goes dark, he gets really dark."*

"Wonderful, I'm patrolling with a time bomb."

Callie laughed, but from that point onward, I was very careful about what I said around Eric.

STILL, WHEN THINGS turned against us, it wasn't because of Eric but because of a mistake one person in our group made. Her name was Millicent Madison—code name Breath—and it was my first winter in New York. Eric and I were on patrol in the early morning, and Breath stopped by to say hello. Short, slender, with brown hair, a plain face, and with light gray eyes, she had the ability to project hard construct shapes if she chose when she breathed out.

"How's the patrol going?" she asked us quietly. She had a wispy voice that was, in part, responsible for her nickname.

Eric waved his hand at the buildings and populace around us as if to say he had it under control. "No trouble so far. It's too early, it's too cold, and the scum are smart. They're sleeping in."

She laughed. "You have a nice way of expressing things, Eric."

"I have my moments. If you're flying solo, you can always hang with us."

Breath shook her head. "It's the solo life for me. My boyfriend has the flu, so I'm on my own. I'll be fine."

Her boyfriend was Don Conlon. His powers were similar to Eric's, but in his case, he breathed fire. His nickname of *The Dragon* was well-deserved, and he was a decent, good-natured person. Millicent added that she could handle things herself.

I had no doubt of that. Millicent was small and inoffensive-looking, but she'd mastered several martial arts. Call her a badass to the nth degree. I'd seen her take down seven gang members my first few days there when they'd threatened us in a nearby park. She warned them against starting something.

"Baby, you're in over your head," the leader of the gang had said. He gestured at her with a crowbar. "Back off."

Millicent sighed and asked me to wait. "I'll handle this."

The fight was over in less than a minute. She didn't break a sweat, although she did break a few bones in the aforementioned gangbangers. Millicent had wicked moves, but she didn't use her fighting skills unless they were absolutely needed.

Most of the time, if she wanted to stop someone, she'd puff out a blanket of air and wrap them up tightly so that they couldn't move, or else she'd blow out a net that would trap them. Killing anyone who wasn't in her repertoire.

However, past badassery aside, that day, shortly after she'd gone her own way and when Eric and I touched base with her, a man in his mid-twenties ran over to us. "Hey, you...either of you got a smartphone? Call the cops. Someone's gotta stop her. I don't have a smartphone. C'mon, man, this is urgent."

"Stop who?" Eric asked.

"That breathing girl," the man replied, practically jumping up and down in frustration. "She's beating the living crap out of some guys. I don't know what happened, but...well, c'mon!"

He set off at a run, asking us to follow him. A minute later, we found Breath standing over the bodies of five men. Our informer went to get the police, while I stared at the scene. Blood stained the snow, and Millicent puffed out a series of breaths in the shape of daggers. They wafted along the airwaves and dissipated.

The body of a middle-aged woman also lay near the men, and while I had an idea about what had gone down, I still needed more facts. To that end, Eric asked, "What happened?" He went to the woman, put his finger to her neck, then looked up at Breath. "She's still breathing. Millicent, what happened?"

She didn't answer, only stared off at something in the distance that only she could see. I waved my hand in front of her face. No response. She'd gone catatonic.

A few seconds later, two police officers arrived. One officer bent down to examine each of the men in turn. Finally, he straightened up. "All dead."

"The woman's still alive," I said. "You should call an ambulance, and, uh, maybe a psychiatrist for this lady here."

"Thanks, kid," the officer replied and told his colleague to call an ambulance as well as the meat wagon. He then looked at the bodies and sighed. "This is a real mess."

A day later.

The police had taken the bodies of the men away. The coroner later issued a statement saying that their chests had been sliced open and their hearts cleaved in half, and it was broadcast on every news channel. "Nearest I can tell, those ethereal daggers that woman, Breath, tossed, were lethal." He shook his head. "They never had a chance."

As for the woman, she was in shock, but forty-eight hours later, she came out of it and gave a statement to the police, as well as the press. No racism was involved. The now-dead gang members were all white, and so was the victim. "Breath saved me," she said. "Those men...they were going to rob me, maybe rape me, and she saved me."

That was her official statement, but it didn't do much good. Millicent was arrested and charged with manslaughter. She was still catatonic, and no matter what the state psychiatrists did, she wouldn't respond.

In the end, the Attorney General dropped the charges, but because of her condition, she was committed to a mental institution. The public had mixed feelings, but the relatives of the gang members sued the city.

Many people immediately protested, and it was a farce. The mayor, the governor of New York, and even the police defended us for doing our jobs. But in a sudden turnaround, the public said that we were a danger. Never mind that Breath had saved the victim. It only mattered that they were afraid of what we could do.

A week later.

The police stopped asking us to patrol. Shortly after, the AMA started pushing their weight around. They'd gained power, politically as well as with the populace. Worse, the regular law deferred to them, and the AMA had meetings with every major politician around in order to consolidate their grip on society.

In the meantime, Millicent came out of her catatonia, but when she read about what she'd done, she suffered a nervous breakdown. Her boyfriend stayed with her, and they soon moved from New York to New Mexico, living off the grid and staying away from any possible trouble.

For the rest of us, we didn't have the luxury of living like everyone else. No more patrols, no more showing off what we could do. Instead of being the good guys, in the eyes of the public, we'd gone rogue. We had to go undercover much of the time, and the restrictions became ever harsher in scope and practice.

And it was all over someone simply doing their job. That was the biggest irony of all. In the space of a few months, we'd gone from being special people in the public's eyes to total pariahs, and it left all of us, including me and Callie, uncertain and fearful for our futures.

Chapter Eight: Fighting The Good Fight

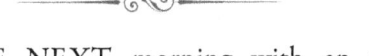

I WOKE UP THE NEXT morning with an upset stomach. Memories, unbidden thoughts and visions, had come during the night. They still swirled in my mind and in my gut, making me feel ill. Eric's death, the exile of Millicent and Don...our people being forced to hide from a government-funded death squad...it was all too much. Witnessing the death of some of our own had been even worse.

I'd been in fights, I'd spilled blood—only when necessary—but I'd never seen anything like those executions before, and all I wanted to do was to erase those images from my mind. That wouldn't happen, though. They'd been burned into my cerebral cortex, and they would never leave. Moreover, I had the feeling that sooner or later, that kind of execution scenario would happen again.

Worse, the newscast I watched at seven in the morning had an interview with some of the AMA members. They weren't regular members, but members of the enhanced squad. Wheels, along with the other people, said that he felt betrayed when he came into the lounge to watch the broadcast with me.

Listening to the enhanced brag about assaulting others and living the high life made me want to hurl. After the broadcast was over, Wheels grabbed the remote control and switched off the television. "I knew most of those jerks years back. I trusted them, broke bread with them, and now...they *would* sell us out," he said bitterly. "Good thing I never told them about this place."

He added that he'd put up a shield to block any kind of detection from the government's side. "It's an electronic shield that deflects any satellite tracking. I value my privacy, and living off the grid with no one knowing where I am is the best thing for me."

"Dornaught knows who you are," I pointed out.

"Yes, he does," Wheels replied. His tone of bitterness hadn't abated. "But he doesn't know where I am, where we are, and I'm going to keep it that way."

He left me, then, and I thought about what he'd said, mainly the enhanced joining the other side. One guy, Harvey Havoc—yes, that was his real name—had the ability to transform into a kind of werewolf.

I'd met him only once while on patrol, and after we finished our daily duties, we grabbed a couple of coffees at a local stand, and while we observed the crowd, he said that my powers were wasted by following the straight and true path. "Man, I was made for better things. So were you."

"You leaving?" I asked.

A smirk lined his face. In his default form, he was tall, slender, and hairy with pronounced lupine features. It was like he was stuck in the transition phase between man and monster. When he fully transformed, he became a terrifying were-beast, with seven-inch claws and the strength of ten men. "What do you think? Eli, wise up. Take the cash. It's the best decision you'll ever make."

He went over to the AMA shortly after. In a way, that was to be expected. Once the registration act went into effect, and once the AMA had been formed and had gained power—the life and death kind—in a quest for life as well as a livelihood, many of our kind had either gone into business for themselves. They offered their services as bodyguards, became pro athletes or assassins in some cases, or they joined the AMA as a way of avoiding prosecution and persecution.

Harvey went down that path, and so did many others. For him and the others who had obvious features that couldn't be hidden, perhaps they thought it was the best move. Perhaps they thought that they'd never be accepted, or maybe, maybe they were simply tired of being called freaks and mutants, and they decided to hang with their own kind.

In a sense, Callie and I were fortunate, as we could pass for the average citizen. Wheels had no special power save his intelligence, and a few of the other enhanced crew tried to blend in with the general populace as well...

One year ago. Green Bay, Wisconsin. Night time. Eleven PM. Summer.

After the AMA found out Wheels' underground hideout, I went on the run, moved around the country, and I never stayed in one place for too long. Currently, I'd bunked down in Green Bay. I lived on the streets, hid in the back alleys at night, while staying in libraries and department stores during the day. Sometimes, I dyed my hair blond or black. Once, I shaved my head, but it looked ridiculous, so I let the hair grow back.

A self-serve car wash near the alley where I'd staked out my territory became my go-to place to get clean. I washed my clothes there as well, so I managed to stay reasonably neat and odor-free.

However, during my second week in that fair city, I was in my cobbled-together cardboard box home, trying to get some rest. Green Bay was uncommonly hot that season, and the weather brought out not only the homeless, but it also brought out the insects, many of which crawled over me at night, feasted on my blood, and made life miserable.

However, for people like me, outside of the AMA, it was the gang bangers and some concerned citizens who wanted to make a name for themselves. All of them were after only one target—us.

So, I tried to make myself as inconspicuous as possible. My neighbor was a man nicknamed Rat. Unlike the rodent, he had no tail, but he was over six feet in height and had a lot of hair like his namesake. Additionally, he had a long, narrow face, wickedly sharp teeth, and he had paws instead of hands and feet. In short, he stood out from the crowd.

He was a nice guy, though, equally adept in hiding from the world as well as finding food. I envied him as insects left him alone. They preferred to chow down on my flesh instead. Rat also had a sense of decency that many others lacked. That night, he'd ventured out from our alley to go dumpster diving. "Brought you something," he said in a low, raspy voice when he returned from his food hunt.

In his right paw was a bag full of hamburgers. "Got these from a restaurant two blocks away. I snuck up behind a couple of the cooks when they were taking a smoking break. They cooked these up a couple of hours ago, no customers bought them, and one of the staff tossed them away. I smelled them, so, it's dinner time."

Good thing, too, as I was starving. Rat—real name, Arthur Bell—had a sharp sense of smell, ten times as acute as a normal person's. Same deal with his eyesight. He was also quite flexible, able to squeeze under doorways and into tight places that the average person couldn't. "Thanks, Arthur."

"No problem."

There were eleven burgers in the bag, along with four bags of fries. I took two of those bags and four of the burgers. Arthur had to eat three times as much as a regular person...something about his metabolic rate caused him to burn off food and calories at a frightening rate.

We ate quickly, got rid of the bag, and settled down into our cardboard homes. While I was trying to sleep, mosquitos buzzed around my face, making sleeping difficult. Additionally, sounds from outside the alley kept me from catching my much-needed zzzs.

Arthur must have heard those sounds as well. His ears, long and leathery like the rodent he was named after, were ultra-sharp, like his sense of smell. A rustling noise cut through the air, and a moment later, Arthur crept in front of my box. "We have company," he said in a low, worried tone.

"What kind of company?"

"The worst kind."

Immediately, a jolt of adrenalin hit, but I forced myself to keep calm and get ready for a fight. "How many?"

Arthur looked around, his beady red eyes checking the darkness. A lamplight just outside the alley offered some illumination, but I didn't have great night vision. Arthur did. "I see four of them...no, five. Not AMA. No uniforms, just regular clothes. Gang bangers. Get ready."

He turned around, claws out and ready for battle. Animals, when cornered, often fought. Arthur wasn't much different. He bared his teeth, and I shifted my body into wood. "Here they come," he murmured.

As he'd said, five men, all large, armed with baseball bats and crowbars, poured into the alley. For someone with no powers, facing off against angry men armed to the teeth and wanting to cause heavy bodily damage would've scared them, but our visitors didn't pay attention to their surroundings. Two, they couldn't see well at night. My friend could.

"Got us some mutants," one man grunted in triumph. A second later, he tripped over a box and fell, cursing. That was our cue.

"Get them," I cried, and Arthur led the charge, snapping and biting whoever he could. I morphed my fingers into knives and went on the offensive, slashing at the enemy. Soon, they were down, writhing in pain from their wounds. Two of the men had broken arms, and they all had numerous bite marks. Those who were still ambulatory dragged themselves out of the alley to seek medical attention.

"Tailor-made," I muttered, and then retracted my declaration. We'd fought back, but it didn't matter, as in the eyes of the authorities, we were guilty. It wouldn't be long before they arrived, so I gathered my meager belongings together and got ready to move.

Arthur slumped against the wall. "I'm tired of being a surface dweller," he panted. He stood up, checked himself for scratches, and then shook his head in dismay. "This life sucks for me. I'm leaving. Sorry, Eli."

There was nothing to be sorry for. "Where are you going to go?"

Arthur pointed to the sewer grate. "There. At least, I'll be among my own kind. If you're smart, Eli, you'll find a place to hide, too."

He nodded at me and ran out of the alley. I felt badly for him, as he'd had to resort to living with lower forms of life. Later on, after I'd left Green Bay, I heard that the authorities had gassed the sewers...

I CAME BACK TO THE here and now with a start. Arthur was one of the unfortunates who couldn't pass. He also couldn't handle being seen as a freak and not being accepted by the rest of society. I felt sorry for him and others like him, but those feelings of sympathy ended when they joined up with the AMA and enforced the law as they saw fit, with virtually no oversight.

Oversight was the key. The AMA let their superpowered people run wild with almost unlimited freedom to do whatever they wanted. Perks such as their own apartments, money, gold, and freedom to enforce their own brand of justice—which meant brutalizing others—were part of the package.

What was worse, the police often didn't do a damn thing about it. As the police chief of New York stated in a widely circulated interview about a year ago, *"I don't want to say that I approve of all the AMA's methods. Many I don't approve of. But if they help to keep society safer by stopping...undesirables, then I'm all for it."*

Of course, when he said *undesirables,* he meant the enhanced who hadn't joined the other side. Everyone knew it, and the news shows and podcasts ran with that line of thinking. In a brutal moment of self-reflection, I wondered if I'd done the right thing, staying with Wheels and Callie.

Had I joined the AMA, would I have been given the same deal? Would they have let me do what I wanted, go where I wanted, and see who I wanted, all in exchange for implementing the law their way? Would they ask me to commit acts of violence or kill someone? I'd thought about it. I was sure that others who sided with Wheels and Callie and me had thought about it as well.

But deep down, I knew it was a lie on the government's part. They wanted to own us, and then to erase us. I couldn't be sure that they wouldn't go back on their word. Years back, there'd been an absolute disaster of a president, even worse than the current one we had. This person had corrupted the entire government, placed his cronies in positions of power, sided with big business, grifted, lied, and stolen, and yet, his supporters treated him like some sort of deity.

While he was bad, people who had common sense were worse. They willingly sold themselves to the highest bidder, and it was nauseating to witness. My grandparents had never voted for him, and my parents hadn't voted for the incumbent president, who was not only a war-hawk, but who was also totally tactless, a person entirely lacking in international diplomacy.

I was in the lounge watching television when a newsflash interrupted some mindless action show. The anchorwoman, a young, attractive brunette, sounded positively giddy as she related a recent happening. "And the AMA sent a squad to the Brooklyn area to clean out a nest of mutant radicals. As you can see, the radicals didn't want to be taken in for questioning and registration, so our law enforcers felt that they had little choice in doing what they did."

Justification for crimes committed—to me, that's all it was. But I didn't have time to contemplate things, as the camera cut to footage of a woman with an oversized nose spraying acid over a couple of the enhanced. The acid came from her nostrils. It melted two of the enhanced, but it did so slowly, and their screams of pain were horrific. Thank you, Ms. Anchorwoman, for not notifying the public or giving trigger warnings...

"See that?"

Wheels' voice came from behind me. I twisted around to find him standing with a pair of heavy braces that ran from his upper thighs down to his ankles. "Experimental walking aids," he said.

He slowly turned around and lifted his shirt to show me where two slender wires with tiny nodes ran from the braces into the skin in his withered lower back. "The braces have tiny servo-motors built into them. The electrodes go right through the muscle and sit on either side of my spine. They stimulate the nerves and muscles, and they help me get around. I can't wear them too often, but I really don't like using my chair."

There was nothing I could say, except, "You really know your tech."

He shrugged as he swung around to eye the television report with disgust. "It's what I do. It keeps me sane, and it helps out." Wheels then pointed at the screen. "I knew those people, most of the AMA killers, I mean. They were colleagues once. Now, look at them. They live to kill."

I had an idea. It wasn't something I'd initially felt comfortable with, but sitting here and hiding, it would only be a matter of time before we were found out, and I didn't feel like being a target. Not now. "What if we evened the odds?"

His eyebrows arched so high that they almost met his hairline. "Are you talking about going after them?"

I'd decided. After all the discrimination, the humiliation, and the plain and simple fact that we weren't considered part of society, getting back at the AMA and the vigilante groups was worth the risk in my mind, if no one else's. "Yeah. Payback is where it's at, don't you think?"

My suggestion didn't make him any more positive. "Eli, this isn't about being a superhero. It's about doing the right thing."

To me, they were one and the same, but at the same time, I checked myself. When I was younger, the thought of being a superhero had appealed to me, and I actually saw myself as one.

Now, though, the superhero tag didn't apply. Neither did the term vigilante. This situation wasn't a cowboys-and-Indians scenario—one played out in the schoolyard. It was a matter of life and death.

But at the same time, I couldn't sit idly by and do nothing. I had the ability and felt compelled to use it, not as an ego boost kind of thing, but, as I put it, "This is about doing the right thing, Larry. I want to help."

We argued over that, but in the end, Wheels gave his blessing, although he repeated his mantra of not being seen, not getting caught, and he mentioned the risks involved.

In turn, I talked it over with Callie, and she reversed her earlier stance, saying that she wanted to help. "I think it's about time," she said.

Since she was now down with this, Wheels let us go, outfitting us with his nerve-disruptor guns, saying, "Use these as a last resort. They have only one shot, so make it count. If you find the AMA guys, don't kill them. Beat them up and place them where they make the AMA look foolish. Got it?"

We did. He drove us up to the surface and to the edge of Manhattan. After that, we were on our own. Before he left us, he gave me a small plastic box.

"What's this?" I asked.

"Protective lenses, if Callie gets all sunny. Slip them in. They'll protect you from one of her sunbursts. After that, they're useless."

I did as he asked, feeling a thin film of plastic coat my eyes. It felt odd, but I figured that I'd get used to it. As for Callie, Wheels gave her a smartphone. "Burner phone," he said. "Like before, use it to call me, then destroy it. Leave no traces."

"Understood," she said as she pocketed it. "Call you in about three hours."

He waved to us as he turned the van around and drove off. We were on our own.

Forty minutes later. Downtown Manhattan.

"First things first," I said as Callie and I skulked through the back alleys. We had to avoid the authorities at all costs, and if stealing through side streets and alleys kept us safe, then we'd do it. "We need a snitch."

"Where?"

"I know a place."

It was only a rumor, really, but Eric had mentioned that a guy named Frisby knew where all the enhanced people hung out, a special bar. Since some of the enhanced had gone over to the other side, it was a given that the non-enhanced AMA members left their enhanced brethren alone and protected them.

But they couldn't protect them all the time, and many of the enhanced I'd previously known had only hung out with their own. In that case, the rumor that they all congregated at one place was true...but only Frisby knew, if he was still alive.

We walked, hid in the shadows, and waited. Anyone and everyone was the enemy. One good thing about coming in at dusk was that it would be harder for the AMA and their lackeys to spot us. After taking our indirect route and peeking around every corner, we reached our target. Callie gazed around the area. "We're in the Bronx?"

"Fordham."

She cast a look of skepticism. "Here?"

"Yep, here. Stay ready."

Fordham had never been safe, but over the past two decades, it had gone from being termed dangerous to being termed hazardous to one's life. Statistics said that one in every twelve people would be attacked, shot, raped, or murdered in that neighborhood. If it had ever been a nice neighborhood, it wasn't now.

Garbage lined the streets, abandoned and burned-out cars sat at the curbs, and gangs walked the streets. Everyone was considered scum. Color made no difference. It was so dangerous here that even the police had written it off.

"There." I pointed at a bar with half a burned-out sign. Ordinarily, it would've read *Prime Time,* but the first letter in the first word had ceased to function, and someone had stuck a *c* in its place, so now, we were looking at *Crime Time.* It seemed appropriate.

Callie took my hand, we walked across the street, and made our way inside. It was beyond seedy, with a cracked wooden floor, half-broken tables, rickety-looking chairs, and the smell of stale beer and wine combined with desperation permeating the air. Seven people were there, and only one of them sat at the bar, nursing a glass of beer. "Him," I said, after scanning the patrons and going on the description I'd gotten. "That's Frisby."

We went over and took a seat on either side of him. Frisby was a small man, barely over five feet, with a sallow complexion, thinning black hair, and he had a face like a ferret with the beady black eyes of a crow. In short, he was a walking advertisement for stool pigeon of the year. He turned to gaze at us and slurred, "What the hell do you want?"

The man reeked of beer, drunkenness, piss, and desperation. "Information," I said, pulling a twenty-dollar bill out of my pocket. Money was precious, but information was more precious. "We need to know where some people are."

Frisby reached for the money, but Callie was faster and plucked the bill from my grasp. "Info first, money second," she said softly. "You know the drill."

His eyes narrowed as he abruptly sobered up. "Listen, I'm not telling you anything. I got no idea who you two are, and I don't care."

Fine, be that way. I reached over and morphed my hand into metal, grabbed his hand, and began to crush it—slowly. "You know what I am," I replied. "If you want to keep your fingers, tell me where I can find the others. You know who I'm talking about."

Sweat sparkled on his face, along with a look of slowly mounting agony. "Please," he said. "I don't know nothing. I swear."

"I think you do," Callie replied in a voice devoid of pity. "My boyfriend isn't patient, and neither am I, so start talking."

The bartender had been slowly reaching under the counter, but I latched onto his collar with my free hand and hauled him over the bar. He hit the floor with a thud and stared at me. "We...we get all kinds here, kid," he stammered out in a terrified voice. "Not your kind, though. I swear. Frisby's telling you the truth."

That, I doubted, and I pulled the snitch closer. "Listen, I'm not after you, but if you don't give me a location, I'll ruin your hand. Then I'll destroy your other hand, and then I'll go to town on your feet. Guess what happens after that?"

He did, and he gave me a location while gasping for air. "There's only four of them. Just four. I don't know where the others are."

"Names!"

"Crusher, Eel, Snort, and Crawler. They're at the Russell. Please...my hand..."

The Russell...that was an old hotel not far from where we were. "They're staying at the hotel?" I eased up on the pressure, just enough.

Frisby nodded his head frantically, and he stumbled over his words. "Yeah. I heard...heard the AMA is footing the bill. Four of them are...are getting ready to find someone. I don't know who, but they're staying there, partying up...they're getting ready for something. I swear, that's all I know!"

By now, he was sweating heavily, and tears were coming from his eyes. I let him go, and he fell back, clutching his ruined hand. "Thanks for the information. We're going now, and if what you told me is good, then we won't come back. But if you're lying, we'll find you."

Callie and I left after tossing the money on the counter. As we exited, we heard him call out, "My word's good, man. It's good!"

We'd soon find out.

Ten minutes later.

The Russell used to be a stately hotel, but now it was falling apart, with the front sign hanging by a thread, garbage strewn everywhere, and a couple of large people standing outside wearing soiled AMA uniforms. One man, one woman—I recognized them as Crusher and Snort, respectively.

Crusher stood around six-seven, was bald, with a heavily scarred face and muscles that would make a champion powerlifter cry. As his name implied, he was immensely strong, capable of crushing cement blocks in his hands. He could also bend steel bars with ease, but the rest of him was just as powerful. I'd seen footage of him overturning trucks with one kick.

Additionally, he had the disposition of a constipated bison. I'd heard that he'd been dishonorably discharged from the army for killing prisoners, as well as his fellow soldiers. Rumor or not, he was dangerous.

Snort was the lady in question. She was around my height, and with regular features and red hair, ordinarily, she would've been called attractive. However, she possessed a large nose, one so large that she could inhale food through her nostrils. I'd seen her do it once, and it wasn't a pretty sight.

She also used her nostrils to spray acid and kill the victims I'd seen on that newscast, and she seemed to enjoy their agony. Sadism was terrible to see, and it was even worse to be around.

When they saw us, they cracked smiles, something most unusual for them. "Look who showed up," Snort said in a pseudo-friendly voice, shaking out her arms and then balling her fists. "Where you two been? Word's out on you, and there's a reward for your capture. You ready to be taken in?"

"Are you talking about both of us?" Callie asked in the most innocent tone possible. "If you are, we're not going, but tell me, why'd you become their pets?"

Crusher laughed at that. "Well, well, aren't you the righteous one? Honey, the AMA *is* the power. They have the firepower, the strength, and they're not going to take any prisoners. I'd rather be their pet than their prey. You get me on that?"

My girlfriend wouldn't be dissuaded. "Can't you see that they're using you?"

Her plea fell on deaf ears, and I realized that it was a cliché plea, but what else was there to go on? Nothing. And right then and there, I also realized that reason wouldn't work on these people. Snort put a finger to the left side of her schnozz, and out came a green ball of snot that landed just in front of Callie's feet.

She took a quick step to avoid getting burned. "Acid," she said with disgust. "That figures."

When the pavement started smoking, it showed that Snort was not only gross but also supremely dangerous. Crusher moved forward with his arms outstretched as if to grab me. "Yeah, it does. C'mere."

In a quick move, he engulfed me in an embrace. I'd already turned metal, though, and as strong as Crusher was, he couldn't make a dent. "Give it up, man," he grunted. "Give it up."

Not yet, although I could feel the power in his grip. Moreover, he could squeeze all day. I'd already passed the two-minute mark on my internal power supply, and the clock was ticking. It was time to end this. "Callie, light 'em up!"

A second later, Crusher and Snort screamed as a brilliant burst of light temporarily blinded them. My protective contact lenses worked, as only a tiny amount of discomfort arose, and I could still see.

On the other hand, Crusher released me and fell to his knees, his hands clutching his orbital sockets. I grabbed him by the shoulders and head-butted him. Metal met bone, and guess which side won? He hit the pavement, out cold.

Snort was on her knees as well, and Callie walked over to punch her in her oversized proboscis. A loud crack filled the air, and blood spewed from her giant schnozz. Snort fell on her side, bellowing in agony, and clutching her nose. "Bitch, you broke it." She got to one knee, screaming, "You broke my nose!"

"Be glad that it's the only thing I broke," Callie replied before leveling Snort with a shot to her temple. After that, we strode inside the hotel. The lounge was empty, save for the two people who sat in the oversized chairs. Oh, and about a hundred empty bottles of alcohol.

"More opposition," my girlfriend murmured and pointed straight ahead at the two men who stood to meet us. Eel stood well over six feet. He was in his early thirties, a shapeshifter who could transform into an eel and wind himself around someone, squeezing them until they died or their ribs cracked, whichever came first. Thinking it over, they should have called him Boa, as he liked to crush his victims.

In contrast, Crawler was a squat man in late teens who resembled a platypus, with a mouth like that mammal, as well as flipper-like hands. His key weapon was his ferocious bite. He came toward us, opening his pie-hole impossibly wide, revealing rows of four-inch, razor-sharp teeth. "Can you blast them?" I asked Callie.

"I haven't recovered, yet," she murmured. "Take 'em."

Right. I was still in metal mode, so I let Crawler chomp away on my left arm. His teeth didn't make a dent, but he clamped down as hard as he could. "Why won't you scream?" he grunted through his beak.

"You haven't hurt me," I replied. All right, time to end this, so I smashed him between his eyes with my right fist. One shot was all it took, and he collapsed.

"You hurt my friend!" Eel yelled.

He shifted into his monster form, but Callie pulled out her matter gun and fired a shot at him. It stopped him in his tracks. He stood up, watching his body revert from eel to human again. His face was full of wonder. "What's going on?"

I walked over and tapped him on the bridge of his nose, just a tap, but it sent him into the wall, and he toppled over like a house of cards.

It wasn't worth offering a pithy answer, as he wasn't listening. "Nice work," Callie said. "One shot or not, these guns are pretty decent."

We grabbed our foes and dragged them outside to toss them on top of their already unconscious comrades. Now that I was back in default mode, I reached inside my pocket, pulled out a piece of paper and a pen, and scribbled a note, leaving it on top of the human pile.

AMA, this is what happens when you send the least of your worst to fight us. Do better next time.

Callie laughed when she read it, and then she pulled out her smartphone to call Wheels. Once she finished, she crushed it underfoot and took my hand. "Wheels is going to pick us up at the drop-off point. Forty-five minutes. Let's go."

We walked through the messed-up section of the city, taking note of the drunks, druggies, and gangbangers who stared at us as we walked past. One man who sported a scruffy beard and torn clothes, called out, "Are you with the freaks?"

Did he know something I didn't? I wondered if he was working for the AMA. "What if we are?"

He hawked out a glob of mucus as if to show his displeasure at our being there. "I ain't seen you around these parts. I seen them mutants acting tough and showing off their powers. They think they're going to run the world. Guess again. This turf is ours." He ended his speech on a defiant note, pointing at the ground and drawing an imaginary line. "Ours."

Callie turned around to nail him with a glare. "For what it's worth, mister, I'm not interested in running this part of the world. It's all yours."

Her response shut the man up. Grateful that he didn't recognize us, I took Callie's hand and turned in the direction of freedom. None of the punks followed us, and forty-one minutes later, we reached the spot where our guardian was waiting in the van, the motor running. "All good?" he asked as we got in.

What else could I say? I answered him while taking out my contact lenses. "As good as it's going to get."

"Can't ask for more than that," he grunted as he threw the van into gear, and we motored off to our safe haven.

Chapter Nine: Marked

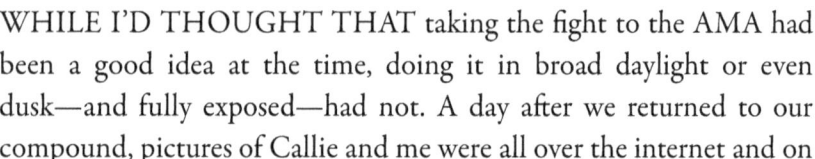

WHILE I'D THOUGHT THAT taking the fight to the AMA had been a good idea at the time, doing it in broad daylight or even dusk—and fully exposed—had not. A day after we returned to our compound, pictures of Callie and me were all over the internet and on television news reports. Where they'd gotten them was obvious, at least in my case. My pics came from my school. *Thanks, hall of semi-higher education.*

As for Callie's pic, it was an artist's digital rendering, and I was pretty sure that the man we'd met the day before had called New York's finest and given them my girlfriend's description. "It's a pretty good likeness," she remarked with good humor. "They made my nose too big, though."

So now we were marked. The newscast went on to mention the assault of some of the enhanced. Their injuries weren't life-threatening, but charges against us for assault had been filed with the local authorities.

"And while the whereabouts of Eli Marks, formerly of Tacoma, Washington, and Callie Sanda, formerly of Beaverton, Oregon, are still unknown, it is believed that they are still somewhere in New York City," the announcer intoned. "A reward of fifty thousand dollars for each suspect is in effect. Any and all information to the AMA will be kept confidential..."

Callie switched off the television. "Nice to know that we're worth that much money. I could use that cash to go to university."

She could talk. "My grades aren't high enough," I responded, trying to see the bright side of things and failing miserably. "But it could come in handy for an early retirement fund."

My girlfriend laughed, but this was serious, as the news had said that any and all information should be reported to the AMA, not the police. That meant the AMA was running the show, and the police were simply figureheads. Handle the easy stuff, it seemed to say. The AMA is here for your protection.

No, they were there to rule, but the general populace didn't seem to care about that. They were after their own safety and security, and any manufactured threat against the enhanced who weren't working for their benefit made them fearful as well as hateful.

Additionally, the news from overseas wasn't any better. Russia and China were still hellbent on ruling the waterways. Our country decided to test that theory, and the news said something about American submarines sinking a Russian oil freighter, as well as a Chinese submarine.

For their part, the Russians and Chinese laughed off those news reports, saying they'd repelled the American imperialists once more. They then had to admit the truth when both the wreckage of the freighter and the submarine were recovered, and the pictures were uploaded to the internet.

And so, it went. Our fight was at home, and Callie and I went to our leader to ask him about another foray against the AMA's lackeys. All we got was a headshake. "You two were lucky the first time. What makes you think you'll have the same luck the next time?"

"We don't," I said, realizing the possibility of failure, but knowing that we had to try. "But what else can we do? Hide? We have to do something."

His response was to mutter that we were on the high side of idiotic. "I'm working on something right now that might help, but it's not ready. Another few days, maybe."

Callie asked what it was, and Wheels, cryptic as always, said we'd have to wait and see. "For now, do you want to wear disguises?"

Disguises could work. Callie dyed her hair red, and it looked decent enough. She also wore padding to make her look bigger, and some skillfully applied makeup disguised her looks to a great degree.

As for me, I went with dyeing my hair blond. It didn't look that authentic, but what with the crowds and us keeping our heads down, perhaps no one would look too closely. Callie showed off her expertise at makeup application, teaching me how to alter my features with tape, charcoal, and rubber.

A jagged strip of rubber down the right side of my face gave me a scar. Along with makeup, it looked more than passable. She then penciled in thicker eyebrows. The tape pulled the right side of my mouth up in a snarl. A glance in the mirror showed a stranger. Hopefully, that would be enough to throw people off.

I also took along a balaclava, just in case. Armed with our power-suppressing guns, we went out the next night. Wheels drove us into Manhattan, parked at a gasoline station near Broadway, and Callie and I decided to walk the streets to see what we could see.

"Two hours," he said. "It's seven-thirty PM now, so at nine-thirty, we leave, mission accomplished or not. I'll be here."

He'd shaved off his beard, but he left a thin mustache that gave him, as he put it, the Pancho Villa look. He even wore a sombrero. The streets were busy with citizens of all shapes and colors walking around, talking, and eating, but they were jumpy. Every time a loud noise happened, they jerked their heads around. If a car's engine backfired, they ducked. If someone dropped a bottle and it shattered, someone invariably screamed. The tension was palpable, and it seemed to cut across all racial, religious, and socio-economic lines.

Noticeably, there were very few officers of the law around. No one from the AMA was there, either. Both groups said that they were all for law and order, but when it came to protecting the citizenry, they seemed to be on a permanent donut break.

At the very least, no one was looking at us. To the rest of the New York crowd, we were two kids out for an evening stroll. "So, who are we looking for?" Callie asked. "We can't go and ask that guy Frisby again."

"Maybe we don't have to," I replied and pointed straight ahead. "Look."

A couple of the enhanced walked out of a jewelry store, carrying boxes of ill-gotten loot. The owner, a tall, skinny man with a toupee that kept slipping off his sweaty dome, ran after them, begging them to stop. "And...here we go," I said as I took my balaclava out of my pocket. I hated the feeling, but since I didn't have a cloak of invisibility...

Callie walked ahead of me, ready to unleash her bright burst of power, but I held her back. "You know those guys?" I asked.

"Does it matter?"

Actually, it did. I recognized one of the men—Malon Dipp—and I warned Callie about him. Short and wide, wearing clothes that were a size too small and that made him look like a mutated sausage, Dipp waddled over to a car. His code name was Mud Bomb. As the nickname indicated, he could hurl clumps of mud at his opponents, mud that his body manufactured. The mud would soon harden and immobilize his victims. I'd met him once when I first came to New York, and he had a nasty disposition.

He was also jealous of Wheels, often saying that our leader had a big ego with no powers to back it up. When the AMA crashed our first hideout, I had the feeling that Malon was the one who'd ratted us out, although I couldn't prove it.

As for his partner, he was under five feet and built like a fire hydrant, wearing a pair of sweatpants and a t-shirt. He had a cigarette shoved in the side of his mouth, tough-guy style. "Move it," he said in a gravelly voice. He turned to the store owner, took a drag on his butt, and flicked it at the man. "You got insurance."

Man, if that didn't beat everything. Those two morons were robbing a store in full view of everyone without using disguises, and they had the stones to tell the store owner to call his insurance company.

Callie grunted with disgust. "And they call us outlaws," she stated and strode over to them, not heeding my warning of hanging back. "Hey, you, fat man and little boy. Over here."

I donned my balaclava, and as I did so, they turned around. Mud Bomb let fly with three shots of mud that spread out upon the air like mini-blankets. Callie ducked, and the projectiles sailed over her head, landing just shy of my feet. He stared at me, his lips moving. Did he know who I was? Maybe, although his eyes betrayed nothing.

His partner, though, nodded. "Mister, you better back off. I may be short, but you're messing with the wrong guy."

In a flash, his body turned a dull gray. Another metal-man...wonderful. Sighing, I did the same thing. Mr. Short-And-Metallic gave me the once-over and hmmphed as though he didn't consider me a threat.

He then charged, which didn't give me enough time to take out my weapon. No matter. I waited until he was two feet away and then slammed my fist on his head. He collapsed and reverted to his default form a few seconds later. His chest was still moving. Good. Killing him wasn't on the menu.

Mud Bomb stared at his downed partner with disdain, and then he raised his arms to let loose with another salvo. Callie never gave him the chance and used her pistol. The charge hit him square in the chest, and he abruptly stopped, the mud disappearing from his hands. "What's going on?" he wailed.

"This," Callie said as she kicked him hard between his legs. He let out a scream and sank to his knees, clutching his shattered orbs. My girlfriend then cut loose with a left hook to his jaw, knocking him cold.

Our fight had lasted a grand total of less than a minute. The boxes of loot were on the ground, so I motioned to the store owner. "They're yours, right? Take them. We're not interested."

He didn't say a word, only nodded. Once he was gone, I noticed that a group of curious spectators had surrounded us. Not good. Worse, they had their smartphones out and were clicking away. "Get us out of here," I whispered.

Callie threw up her arms, and I shut my eyes tightly, turning my head away. I'd forgotten to take the protective lenses with me. A collective scream rang out, which meant that she'd let loose a burst of light. Once I opened my eyes, I saw spots, but the spectators around us were still covering their faces.

"Time to go," Callie said. "C'mon."

I changed back to flesh. Callie grabbed my hand, and we ran for our lives. No one got in our way, and once we reached the gas station, I tore off my balaclava and tossed it in a nearby garbage can. By that time, I could see clearly. Wheels already had the engine running. Callie opened the sliding door, we piled in, and he took off down the road. "How was your walk?" he asked.

"Balls of fun," Callie replied as we motored into the night.

An hour later.

Once we got home, Callie went to the lounge and turned on the television. Sure enough, a news report said that two mutants had caused a disturbance near Broadway Avenue only a short time before.

However, no names were mentioned. There were only brief descriptions of us and what had transpired. Ordinary citizens gave the details, and the reporter on duty gave her opinion. "So, is this a case of mutant versus mutant, or is there another agenda at play? As always, this is Renata Gonzalez with..."

Callie shut off the television with a snort of disgust and tossed the remote control to the far end of the couch. "Now, it's a case of mutants against mutants. They want us to kill each other, just to make it easier for the AMA to control everyone." She gave another snort of disgust and went to shower up.

Good idea, and after I wiped off my makeup, I took a shower. While getting clean, I wondered if we were doing any good. Changing everyone's mind, or anyone's mind, was a Herculean task. But I figured that if we showed everyone what the AMA was—an organization of total goons—then maybe people would see us in a new light.

Once I got changed, I went to talk to our guardian. Wheels was poring over another design and said that he was still working on something to help us. "Patience," he responded when I asked him—again—what it was all about.

All right, he had his secrets. Since he couldn't give us something to boost our presence in the public eye, Callie and I would have to do it on our own. So, the next day, we took a stroll. Callie dyed her hair jet black, while I did the dye job again, this time changing my color to something between auburn and a full-blown redhead. It looked even more ridiculous than the previous dye job, but no one had noticed me before, so maybe I'd be all right.

Moreover, we both decided to use props. My girlfriend favored using a cane, while I borrowed a pair of crutches that Wheels used to use when he first moved to this complex. "Never liked using them," he said. "But you might fool someone. Give it a try."

That we did. A day later, we went to Times Square, with our minder holed up at an underground parking garage. "I'll be here whenever you get back," he said as we left his van. "No surveillance cameras, so I'll stretch out in the back."

It seemed all right. Callie and I surfaced and joined the busy crowd that was walking in every direction. We checked out the eateries, the vendors, a few gangs of punks who were, in turn, watching others, and we made it obvious that we were handicapped. Sooner or later, something was bound to happen.

And...it did. Five minutes later, three of the AMA foot soldiers came out of an alley. One man strode ahead, holding a pistol. His two comrades carried the limp form of someone familiar. It was Rat, my old acquaintance from Green Bay. His face was bloody and swollen. When he lifted his head, he saw through my rotten dye job and crutches right away and mouthed, "Good to see you."

I replied with the same words, and a crowd gathered to watch the AMA haul Rat over to their van. Not happening. One man in the crowd called out, "What are you gonna do with him?"

"Not him," one of the AMA ghouls answered. "It. And we're going to do to vermin what we always do to vermin."

It...vermin...we'd become sub-humans, and that made me see red. Callie and I walked in front of the van, blocking the authorities. The AMA officer who held the pistol asked, "Are you going to move, cripple? I'm not above shooting cripples."

Cripple. That word went out of style years ago. What an insensitive bastard. I said, "I think you mean disabled, mister."

"I don't care what you are, just move."

"If you say so." I morphed my hand into a wooden knife and slashed the man's hand. He let out a cry of pain, dropped his weapon, and sank to his knees, blood spilling from his wound. My legs became metal, and I crushed his gun underfoot. "Let the guy go," I commanded the two remaining goons holding Rat. "Do it now. I won't ask you twice."

The people around us stepped back in surprise. "Those handicapped people," one woman said. "They're not handicapped!"

Gee, what a novel thing to say. "No, we're not," Callie answered, her hands up and ready. She then addressed the AMA officers. "My friend told you to let your prisoner go. Do it now."

They did, and Rat slowly got to his feet. I helped him up, whispering, "Can you move?"

He nodded. "Yes."

"Then run." I mouthed the words *Royce Township*. A faint smile broke through the mask of blood. Rat fled the scene, bounding from spot to spot, and soon, he was out of sight.

As for the other two AMA goons, they stared at me with sullen expressions working overtime. One of them reached for his gun, but Callie threw a jab that knocked him off-balance and took his weapon. She then gestured to the other man. "Give me your guns...both of you."

They did, and she handed them to me. I crushed them to the oohs and aahs of the bystanders, then tossed the junk away. The AMA dudes didn't appreciate their toys being destroyed, as one of them said, "You two are dead!"

My hand was still knife-shaped, and I was so tired of being threatened, so I poked him under the chin. A bead of blood appeared. "Are you going to do it, or is your buddy going to? Tell me now. I'm waiting."

He gulped and shook his head, whispering, "No. Please...don't."

Uh-huh. When he'd had the upper hand, he was merciless, but when he was on the defensive, he was nothing more than a coward. And these were the people who wanted everyone to obey them. They were more like wind-up toys than anything else.

"Who's driving?" I asked, suddenly angry that Rat had been abused and that life was made harder by the existence of these morons.

"Uh, our driver," one man said.

Brilliant answer. "Don't move." I stalked over to the driver's side, morphed my left hand into metal, and tore the door off the hinges. "Out," I said to the frightened driver. "Give me the keys."

He exited quickly and handed over the keys. I twisted them into pretzels and tossed them away. "Join your buddies."

Once he did, they watched as I turned my body to metal and began beating on their van, smashing in the sides, kicking the tires until they burst, and then crushing the entire vehicle until it resembled a metal ball. The crowd didn't make a sound. They only waited expectantly.

Once I finished destroying the van, I gave our new best friends a warning, attempting to breathe normally and not pass out from exhaustion. "This is what happens when you mess with one of ours.

This is what will happen to you, your enhanced goons, and your leader, if he keeps hassling us. Understand?"

Mute, they nodded. Callie then told them to leave. "Take off your uniforms first. Leave everything behind."

The driver remained defiant. "Lady, I'm not wearing anything underneath, you get me? These uniforms...they're hot."

"Then it's time to air things out," she said. "Or should my friend make it clearer to you? Your choice."

In a flash, they stripped and stood naked and ashamed in front of everyone, using their hands to cover their privates. A few people in the crowd tittered. Most shook their heads and turned away. "Leave," Callie said. "Kids are here, and they don't need this trauma. Me, either."

The men left, taking small steps and still covering their privates. It was our time to go, as well. As we made our way through the crowd, one old man stopped us. "You kids...you're the, uh, new breed, aren't you?"

I'd never heard that term before, but I understood what he meant. "Yeah, I guess we're the new breed. We're not here to hurt you. We're not the bad guys. The AMA is. If you don't believe me, check out what happened to that rat person. He didn't ask to be born that way. He just wanted to live his own life, and then the authorities stepped in. Well, all we want is to live our own lives."

He nodded and wished us luck. Callie murmured, "Time to go," so we took our leave. Once we were safely ensconced in the van, Wheels tore out of the underground parking lot, and we got out of the city as fast as possible.

"Was it worth it?" he asked once we got on the highway. "Oh, if you're hungry, I brought some food." He reached over to the passenger seat, took a paper bag, and handed it to us.

It contained sandwiches...very thoughtful of him. As Callie and I chowed down, I thought about his question. We hadn't done that much, really. On the one hand, we'd saved Rat. On the other, the people there saw us humiliate the AMA lackeys. Maybe they believed us, maybe they didn't.

But if we could change one person's mind about who and what we were, then call it a success. "Yeah," I finally said. "It was worth it."

Chapter Ten: Should We Leave?

WHILE CALLIE AND I celebrated our mini-victory, in all truth, we'd been lucky. We hadn't met any of the enhanced that time out, and the sad truth was there were far more enhanced people on the AMA's side than on ours. For those who'd gone over to the AMA side, they reaped the rewards, and they didn't care what happened to anyone else as long as they got paid. In short, they were perfect droids.

Money was also a factor. The bounty on our heads had started at fifty thousand dollars each, and it soon went up to twice that much. Pretty decent cash, so that meant we'd more than likely run into some tough customers. They had nothing to lose and everything to gain. On the other hand, we had everything to lose, but we couldn't stand by and do nothing.

So, with Wheels' blessing, Callie and I went out again two days later, this time to Queens. A news report said that some ordinary citizens had been injured by a couple of the overzealous enhanced. "If you two are up to it, go," he said. "Have a party."

Callie chuckled. "Party is our middle name. Who are these poster children?"

Arm and Hammer were the two lackeys. Arm—real name, Nick Fortos—had a right arm that was capable of flattening pretty much anything with one smash.

As for Hammer—Stanley Morton—he could morph his hands into the shape of that special home improvement tool. He also had ultra-tough skin, not quite like mine, but close. That made him dangerous. Oh, and both were ex-military, also dishonorably discharged for conduct unbecoming, whatever that meant. AMA took only the best people.

J.S. FRANKEL

Wheels drove us into Queens, letting us off a ten-minute walk away from the action. "I'll be here," he said. "You're not wearing disguises, and the AMA might have set a trap. Watch your surroundings, and don't take too long."

"On our way," Callie said. We started walking and found our quarry sitting in front of city hall. The bodies of seven people lay near them, mashed to a pulp, and blood flowed down the steps and stained the sidewalk. A small group of onlookers watched us approach and made way. They seemed frightened, as well as curious, and sure enough, they took pictures of the carnage. Why people had to do that was beyond me. Maybe they got bonus points from the networks.

When Callie and I approached, our enhanced foes rose and offered polite bows. "We heard that you took out Snort and Crusher," Stanley said, flexing his muscles. He stood around five-eight. Height-wise, he wasn't a giant, but he was built like a pro bodybuilder, and he liked to show off his physique, hence his apparel of a t-shirt and shorts that did nothing to hide his musculature.

"They're friends of ours," Nick added. Unlike his counterpart, he stood around six-seven, and he wasn't particularly well-muscled, save for his incredibly huge right arm that he flexed and swung around, as if warming up for the battle ahead. "And you're not."

Callie stepped up. "I just want to ask you one question. Why are you doing this? The AMA is a goon squad. You know that they'll never accept you."

"Neither will ordinary people," Stanley retorted, shaking out his shoulders and arms. "Let's not pretend that we're part of this society. We're not. We never were...never will be. If it's all the same to you, let's get this on. Our bosses aren't here, now. It's just us, and my buddy and I want to collect the reward on you. Oh, by the way, their policy is to bring you in, dead or alive. I prefer dead."

So be it. Nick started things off by swinging his oversized arm around like a hammer thrower getting his hammer up to speed. The onlookers backed off in fear as his arm became a blur, and he slammed it down in our direction, cracking the pavement and sending us flying. Callie picked herself up and urged him forward. "You know what I can do," she said.

Nick grinned. "I know. I'm wearing special contact lenses. Do your worst, kid."

That was new, so maybe it was true, maybe not. Too late, as he came at her, but Callie stood her ground. Nick's arm whipped around in a blur, faster and faster. "Kid, you're going to get smashed. You're going to...augh!"

Good old threats. They never worked, especially when someone kicked the bad guy in the nuts. My girlfriend had aimed well, and Nick fell, holding onto his crushed balls. Her standard left hook laid him out.

"All right, you and me, Marks," Stanley said. "C'mon!"

In a rush, he barreled toward me, and as he did, I shifted into metal mode. His hands hammered a tattoo on my head and made it ring. I replied with punches to his gut and mouth, and after trading blows back and forth, he started to wilt. I was running out of time, though. My five minutes was just about up.

Desperation hit, and I grabbed him in a bear-hug and started squeezing. Stanley let out a whoof as the air left his lungs. "Just a little more, Stanley, and your ribs are going to crack," I grunted. "Give it up."

He continued to struggle, and the sound of bones slowly breaking echoed in the air, much like ice cracking off a glacier due to a sudden warm spell. "I...I...give," he gasped and fell limp.

Fine with me. I let him go, and he dropped to the ground, unconscious. "We have to leave," Callie said. "You up to it?"

I shifted back to default mode, bent over at the waist and breathing heavily. I wasn't back to full strength, yet, but we had to leave. "Yeah...yeah. Let's go."

As we made our way back through the silent crowd, an old man asked, "Are you going to protect us?"

I couldn't answer his question at that time, but Callie answered for me. "Think about which side you're supporting. I'll give you a hint. Don't back the AMA."

No one responded, and we hustled back to where Wheels was waiting. He drove us home, and once there, Callie hit the showers while I raided the refrigerator. Two cans of spaghetti and a loaf of bread and butter later, I felt normal. After a shower, I went to my room and passed out.

Seventy-two hours later.

We nursed our wounds over the next three days. A few hours after the fight, I woke up stiff, sore, and black and blue. But I was still ambulatory, and after I stretched out, the stiffness went away, and the bruises faded. Enhanced healing rocked, and Callie informed me that she felt fine.

Good enough for me. We checked out the daily news for any reports of our fight with the two sellouts. Oddly enough, there was no news of our fight with Nick and Stanley, even though there'd been witnesses. Either a news blackout on that was in effect, or else those whose butts we whipped hadn't reported it.

However, when it came to international news, in the space of a few days, relations between the superpowers had spiraled downward even further, if that was possible. Talks had broken down between the US, Russia, and China, and we'd already recalled our ambassadors from those countries. They'd done the same to us. It was a shit show, and it was about to paint and taint every single corner of every single part of this world.

China had already sent part of its fleet to venture into Taiwanese and Japanese waters. The US countered with a third of its fleet—the largest and the most powerful in the world—to shore up those countries' fleets and defend their shores if necessary.

Russia decided to invade Ukraine—again. Last time, they'd lost. This time, they were back, bigger and badder than ever. Daily bombings, missiles, and other terrible weapons of war were thrown against the people of Ukraine.

Naturally, the Ukrainians fought back with everything they had, and the US had also sent machinery, missiles, and jets to help out. So far, the war hadn't gone well for the Russians, but they'd always sent everyone they had as cannon fodder. And their leaders were only too willing to sacrifice their people.

As for the rest of the world, the smaller countries hadn't joined in—yet. They would, though, if their borders were threatened. And the US stood loud and proud, as they always had in the face of adversity. The president gave a speech, live and without notes, and with patriotic music playing in the background, he presented a heroic image, one that many, if not all, Americans, appreciated.

"Our political leaders cannot and will not allow any aggression by our counterparts in Russia and China. Perhaps there are certain elements in those countries that will try. They will not succeed. We have the mightiest army, navy, and air force in the history of mankind, and we will not shirk our duty in the face of these intolerable invasions by our Asian and European counterparts."

It sounded noble, but what it really meant was a no-holds-barred world war. Half the countries in the world possessed hydrogen bombs, the US, China, and Russia had neutron eliminators—ten times as powerful as hydrogen bombs—and the US was rumored to have a planet buster, a bomb rumored to be so powerful that it could conceivably crack the Earth in two.

Even if they detonated a bomb half that size over a country, the shock wave would be enough to wipe that country off the map...if it didn't destroy the planet first. MAD stood for Mutually Assured Destruction, and it was equally mad that the leaders had devised such an insane plan. They didn't want to be first—they wanted to be the last country standing.

Of course, the government never confirmed nor denied the existence of such weapons. Keep the enemy in the dark as to the military capabilities each country had—that was the mindset, and it proved to be most effective.

As for the populace, they were, as usual, unwilling pawns. I was part of that populace. "I'm scared," a mother said when asked about a potential world war. This interview took place in Las Vegas, and the sounds of cars honking and people yelling somehow underscored her statement. She held the hand of a girl who couldn't have been more than six. "I trust our president, but if war comes...my husband will have to leave us. He's on reserve duty now, and..."

She didn't finish her sentence, but she didn't have to. She was frightened for both her husband and her daughter. I couldn't blame her.

"It's the fault of them damn mutants," a fat man in his thirties stated as he stared at the camera. That report came from Atlanta, Georgia, and the interviewee spat out a wad of chewing tobacco and wiped his mouth with the back of his hand. "They started this damn war. All for them and their rights. You can quote me on that."

When the interviewer pointed out that the world conflict was due to aggression by Russian and Chinese elements, the man shook his head. "That's what they want you to think. No, it's all them damn mutants."

The reporter cut the sound, but the man continued to rant about two minority religious groups that were usually scapegoated for everything. The closed-captioning told the entire story. He finished with, *"You can quote me on that, too."*

Another whack job, but what else was new? Callie came into the lounge, wearing a pair of slacks and a t-shirt. "Any good news?" she asked and then yawned.

Seriously? "No, all bad."

"How are you feeling?"

Fairly decent, all things considered, but I didn't tell her that. "I'll make it. You?"

"Same."

She sat beside me, running her hand playfully over my head. It was just a light touch, but it sent a shiver through me. Was it too early to think about having fun? No, but we were in someone else's house, and it wasn't polite to get it on...

"Morning."

I turned around at the sound of the voice. Wheels sat in his wheelchair, and my thoughts of having fun went out the proverbial window. Our guardian yawned and waved his hand in our direction. His eyes were bloodshot, as if he'd pulled an all-nighter. "Come with me. I've got something to show you."

Callie took my hand as we got up, and we followed Wheels down to the garage area, where his van and that big tarpaulin-covered object were. He moved over to the object, yawned again, and quietly groused about the implants giving out and being stuck in his chair again. "I've been working on this all night, and I think I have the problem fixed."

All right, now I was curious. "What is it?"

He pulled off the tarp to reveal a large, metal, circular object that sat on supports two feet off the ground. It couldn't be...but unless I was dreaming, I was looking at a gateway that was roughly six feet in diameter. A computer console and an array of thick cables that went through the concrete into the ground made the setup look impressive. "What is it?" Callie asked.

"A portal to another Earth," Wheels replied in the most serious tone imaginable. "I started working on the schematics in university, and then once I moved here, I started building it. It wasn't as difficult as I thought it would be."

He had to be kidding, and I stared at the contraption with awe. "I saw the miniature at your old hideout. I didn't think you were serious."

He shook his head. "Eli, I never kid about things like this. When Dornaught caught me, he took the schematics for the portal, but he never got the equations that link our universe to others. Those, I have in my head, and his science guys aren't smart enough to figure things out.

"As for the concept of parallel Earths, that isn't new. It's something that scientists have kicked around for decades, but now, it's not science fiction but science fact."

Wheels *was* serious. "How?" I couldn't think of anything else to say.

Our guardian chuckled. "I'll give you the short version. Each universe operates on a set series of vibrations. They're almost identical, but there are slight variations. All I did was find the variations, and I tapped into them."

Callie then asked about the power consumption. It had to be enormous. "Yes and no," Wheels replied. "Remember how I told you I owned the land around this area?"

We nodded, and he continued, "Well, Royce Township used to have an old electrical plant that received its power from a nuclear power plant just outside of Manhattan."

"You mean, Indian Power Point, don't you?"

Wheels' eyes widened. "You know that place?"

I'd heard about it and told him so. He rubbed his hands together. "Good. Well, the Indian Power Point is one source. The other source is Six Mile Point near Lake Ontario. Now, the electrical plant here was shut down years ago, but when I inherited the land, I inherited the power plant, too. All I do is reroute some of the power from the two other places and send it through the Royce Township plant. I can turn it on and off, but only for about eight minutes."

Callie asked, "Has anyone figured out where the power's going?"

Wheels shook his head. "No. It takes five minutes for the charge to cycle up, then a gateway opens for a max of two minutes, and then I have to shut things down. That takes another minute. Short vacation, longer stay, if you know what I mean."

He wet his lips. "As for them finding out where the power's going, like I did at my old hideout, I hacked into their systems and set up a program that says all is normal when I siphon off the power. So far, no one's bothered to look. I also have a program for monitoring the power output of any nuclear or water or electrical power station on the eastern seaboard. Just type in *Graph xkkli-one-five-six,* and it'll show you."

I did so, committed the password to memory, and...voila. A series of graphs came up. Call Wheels a genius and then some. As for the idea of visiting another Earth, my curiosity intensified. "Can we take a look?"

He laughed. "You read my mind. I'll fire it up, but you can only go in, and then you have to come back when I say so. I haven't worked out all the kinks, yet. You won't be able to actually touch anything. You'll be in the bubble."

"Bubble?"

"It's to protect you," he said with a patient air. "Deal?"

Callie and I looked at each other, and we said simultaneously, "Deal."

Wheels flipped the switches, the power built, and my heart began to race. This was way over my head, something out of a sci-fi movie, but still...a fact. A few seconds later, a crackle of energy sounded, and an opaque film formed on the formerly empty space. "Go," he said. "Clock's running."

I took a deep breath and walked inside, holding onto Callie's hand. As we moved, another opaque bubble formed around us, like a cocoon. We emerged in an alleyway. Although the cocoon made the view blurry, I made out the sun's position overhead. It was around noon, and even through the protective covering, I felt the heat. Summertime on another Earth? *Call that amazing and then some!*

I felt a smile cross my face. When I looked at my girlfriend, her expression mirrored mine, and she called back, "We're here. It's all good. Can you hear us?"

"Yeah." Wheel's voice sounded like it was at the end of a long tunnel. "One minute, fifty-two seconds left."

I tried to pick up a newspaper, but I couldn't grasp it, so I knelt down and read the top line—barely. "I think it says, *Happy Valley News, Virginia.*"

Callie squatted beside me, whispering, "This is fantastic."

It was...and Wheels called out, "One minute, forty-one seconds!"

Fine. The cocoon moved with us, so I poked my head out of the alley and saw large cars pass by, men in suits, and women in long dresses. It looked like something out of the nineteen-fifties. I'd watched movies from that era, but those were movies. *This is real, and we're in it!*

"Fantastic," Callie said again as she came up to watch the scenery with me.

Our guardian's voice came again, and he sounded worried. "I'm having trouble with the power grid. It's jumping all over the place. Get back here."

Call that disappointing and then some, but with no choice in the matter, we returned, and once we were home, the bubble around us disappeared, and Wheels shut down the machine. "How was it?" he asked.

What a rush! I felt another grin begin to form, and there was no sense in stopping it. "It works."

Fifteen minutes later.

We sat in the kitchen, coffee cups in front of us, and gave our reports. "It was so real," Callie said. "I mean, we just stepped onto another Earth."

She wore a silly smile, as if she couldn't realize the magnitude of what had happened. I probably wore the same smile, although I couldn't see my expression. "Well, you did," Wheels replied, calmly sipping his coffee. "Initially, the power field was stable, but after thirty seconds, it started to fluctuate. That was why I called you back. Initially, I didn't use that protective bubble. However, I added it, just in case the power containment field failed and I had to yank my volunteer back in a hurry."

Volunteer? "Who was it?"

"Eric. He made a few trips for us, but so far, only the Earth you visited shows any promise."

That Earth? "Uh, how many have you seen?"

He took another sip of his beverage to keep us in suspense a few moments longer. "Three others, so far," he finally said. "Before you came to live with me, Eric made a couple of trips to the other Earths. That was just before he, well...you know."

We did. "Go on," Callie said.

Wheels drew in and puffed out a series of small breaths. "Eric said that the first Earth—we called it Earth Two—was too hot. Apparently, it had the temperature of Venus, and it was only because his body could adjust that he survived. He was there for a grand total of eight seconds. There's no way you or Callie could live there, and if you can't, people who aren't enhanced have no chance.

"As for Earth Three, it's one of eternal dusk, but there are no humans. The air is the same as here, but instead of people, he said that he encountered only animals. No, that's not right." He shuddered. "Not animals...things. Eric had to kill two of them in order to escape."

Wheels let out a sigh, as if only now accepting the finality of failure, although the failure certainly wasn't his. "Finally, Earth Four is mainly one of water. The amount of land is perhaps five percent. He was lucky to have landed on a small spit, but when he examined the water, he found that it had a high ammonia content. Totally unsuitable to sustain human life.

"Now, Eric did go to Earth Five, the Earth you two just visited. He did an air test, a water test, and from what he saw, he said that there's no difference between that planet and ours. It all looks good on our end..."

His voice trailed away, and what was the problem here? "You, uh, didn't finish what you were saying. What's stopping you from using this machine for, uh, the masses?"

"Time," Wheels replied after I posed the question. "The power I used, like I said, comes from the old power station. Outside of the rerouting program I mentioned, I set up another program that'll bounce any attempt to trace the signal off two thousand satellites."

He inhaled a deep breath and blew it out, almost like a sigh of regret. "But sooner or later, someone will wonder why the lights suddenly go on in an old, abandoned, energy plant, even though the nearest neighbor is two miles away. If the AMA gets their hands on this, then goodbye Earth Five. They'll be able to invade that new Earth, and that's something I don't want.

"The second problem is that I can only keep the gateway open for a short time. You guys got about a minute. Eric stayed on Earth Three and Earth Four about as long as you did. The power field is unstable, and I'm trying to fix that.

"Second, I want to try to get all the North American enhanced to come with us. I've sent out coded messages, and I'm hoping for at least fifty people to show up. It's not that I can't take them...it's the time factor. I can keep the gate open for only so long."

He heaved a sigh of regret. "We're the unwanted, here, and if I can save people like us, then this world can—and probably will—go to hell. Maybe it's better that way. I don't know."

Something he'd said about saving people hit home. "What about the rest of the people? I mean, the regular people out there."

Wheels sighed. "If I could, I'd build a million of these machines to take everyone to the other Earth. Even if some of them are bigots and losers, I'd offer them the chance. But I also can't be sure that the AMA hasn't already developed something similar to what I've created. I won't let anyone pervert my work. It's better if no one uses it...except us."

His comments, harsh though they were, made sense. There was no place for us here. Wheels took in and blew out another deep breath before finishing off his coffee. "Bottom line—only a finite number of people can get through. It also takes a minimum of five days to retune the settings from our world to Earth Five. I'm trying to fix things, but right now, this is the best we've got."

He then excused himself, saying that he had to lie down. I sat at the table, and while Callie busied herself making something for us to eat, I wondered if leaving was the right thing to do. I didn't want to believe that a war would come, but nothing seemed to be able to stop it, and if it came to that, then there was only one place where we'd be safe.

Chapter Eleven: There And Back

A WEEK LATER. OUR SANCTUARY. Three PM.

With the world spinning on its axis, the various countries sniping at each other, the authorities being authoritarian, and the citizenry complaining about everything, it seemed as though humanity was determined to destroy itself and us with it. If ever there was a time to leave, it was now, but...

"I'm still having trouble balancing the power field," Wheels said in consternation when we asked him about sending us through again. "That's the one thing I've never been able to get right. I'll tell you this—I don't want to risk anyone else's life on it, although I have a feeling that someday I'll have to."

He added that he'd work on the portal device as often as possible. "It's a fine balancing act," he said while adjusting his laser torch and tinkering with some gizmo on the gate. "Too much power on one end alters the readings just enough to send you here, too little power on another end jumbles the readings and sends you there. I'm always trying to balance things out."

Danger or not, I wanted to try it again, and I patted the side of the portal. "When you get it ready, I'd like to go, but without the bubble. I mean, I get that it's for our safety, but when we went to that other Earth, we couldn't see that well or touch anything."

Our guardian-slash-mechanic-slash-genius stopped working and put down his laser torch. He squinted at where he'd soldered things shut, and then turned to us. "You realize that if the power fails and you end up on a different Earth, you're screwed. If you end up on the superheated world or the ocean world, then you won't live very long. If you end up on that twilight version of Earth, I won't be able to get you back for a week, maybe more."

Understood, but I still wanted to give it another shot. "Wait. Be patient and relax," Wheels said as he started working again. "Spend time with your girlfriend. Don't watch too much television. It'll depress you and rot your brain."

He sounded like the proverbial controlling parent, but he meant well. Callie chose that moment to come downstairs and sauntered over to lead me away, saying that we should leave the genius alone. "We'll be in the gym," she said.

"Fine." Wheels let out a grunt as he soldered a few more wires. "I'll keep working on this."

My girlfriend pulled me along. "Workout?" I asked.

"Fight training," she replied with an innocent smile. "We have to keep sharp."

Uh-huh. I had the feeling that she wanted some practice in kicking my ass—and I was right. We put on boxing gloves and headgear, warmed up slowly by throwing a few tentative jabs...and then we went at it. Round one was a draw.

Round two, though, started out with me dominating and taking the fight to her, but then her left arm exploded out of nowhere. I felt the impact on my jaw, saw stars, and the next thing I knew, I was staring up at the ceiling.

Callie bent over me, a concerned expression working. "You all right?"

"I'll live." My jaw hurt—a lot.

She smiled. "Good. Three more rounds."

Ninety-six hours later.

Wheels said that he was ready to try things out again. We met him at the gateway where he was inputting the equations on the console, and he greeted us with a cheery smile. "I think I've managed to get the power field to hold for more than a couple of minutes. I've also removed the bubble. You'll be able to walk around freely, but I wouldn't stray too far from the gateway. You'll see it as an opaque blob hanging in the air. Just step through, and you're home."

My heart began to beat faster. This was it. Wheels fired things up, Callie grabbed my hand, and we stepped through...into a world of eternal dusk. It was warm, perhaps seventy-five degrees, the sky was clear, and the air smelled fresh, but there were no buildings, no alleyways or businesses...

Shit, this isn't the new Earth! "We're on Earth Three," I said, half in wonder and half in shock. "This is not good." And we'd forgotten to take weapons with us. "This is so not good!"

Anger hit. How in the hell could Wheels have been so careless? Half of me wanted to scream in frustration, but the other half told me to keep calm. It wasn't like he hadn't warned us about the possibility of a mistake. Callie's comment of, "Let's go back," jolted me out of my anger-surprise mode.

We turned around, but the gateway closed up abruptly with a snap. Callie let out a moan of frustration that soon segued into a series of muttered curses, and then she finished with, "What now?"

A look around the area showed that we'd landed in a field of thigh-high, tangled greenish-blue grass. As my eyes adjusted to the dimness, the nearest safe place—if this world was considered safe, and according to Wheels, it wasn't—lay about three hundred yards away. An outcropping of rock, high and jagged...it was a cliff. Get to the top...that was our only hope.

"Target, straight ahead," I said and pointed to our goal. "Go."

My heart began beating fast, and Callie's breathing became shallow. "Go," she repeated, and we ran through the grass. The only sound that came through was a growling sound that came across as a cross between a bear and a lion. Those growls got louder and more intense as we ran.

"Keep going," I said, panting. My fear level was at an all-time high, but adrenaline spurred me on, and we reached the rock outcropping. About sixty feet up lay the top, near as I could see. Cliffs sometimes had caves. Danger or not, we couldn't stay on the ground. I pointed upward. "There."

Callie replied that she didn't think she could climb it. Right. She could kick my ass in sparring, she never backed down from a fight, but she couldn't climb a rock? A look at the smoothness of the cliff's surface made me realize that there were no handholds or footholds. "Fine, I've got this," I said, morphing my hands into metal pitons. "Hang onto my neck."

She did, and I dug my hands into the rock, hauling us up to the top. There, our sanctuary waited, but we hung back, waiting at the edge. "Wheels said that there were, uh, creatures here," Callie said nervously as she disengaged her grip. "Maybe they're in the cave."

"How about you shed some light on the subject?"

Despite our dire situation, she grinned. "Close your eyes."

I did, covering them with my hands, and a second later, she told me that I could open them again. "Beast at twelve o'clock high," she said in a frightened voice. "It's coming fast."

Beast didn't half-describe it. It looked like a cross between an octopus and a bear, with four arms like the former, and the body and face—sort of—like the latter. Whatever it was, it snarled as it pawed its eyes, and when it lunged at us, foaming at the mouth and bellowing in rage, I shifted my left arm into a metal spear and drove it through that thing's neck. It collapsed in an instant. "Cave is safe," I declared.

Half an hour later.

We'd made a perfunctory search, but the cave was empty. It had an uneven surface, but there were no projectiles, and we didn't find large eggs or slimy critters waiting to jump on our faces or tear our hearts out. For the moment, we were safe, although the stress caught up to Callie, and she started to freak out. She'd already freaked when we landed here, but now, it was worse. She shook all over, crying silently, with the tears coursing down her cheeks.

"Hey, we're going to be all right," I said. "We need to make a fire. It's warm here, but the fire will keep the monsters away."

My words had little effect, as she alternately sobbed and shook her head. I grasped her shoulders, whispering, "Callie, I need you on this. Stay with me, please."

I repeated my plea again and again. Finally, she nodded, heaved in a deep breath, and let it out slowly. "Okay," she said in a small voice. "What's first?"

Fire...we needed wood. "Find something that we can burn. Sticks, sagebrush, whatever."

We went over every inch of the cave. Nothing, so I told Callie to stay put, and I climbed down to the bottom to search. Heart thudding in my chest, I kept low and downwind, listened to the growls—they were far away—and then started my search for firewood.

It took a while, but I collected enough sticks to make a bundle, used part of my shirt to tie it all together, slung the bundle over my shoulder, and then climbed back to the cave, heart thudding in my chest whenever the growls sounded—and that was often.

"How was it down there?" Callie asked.

I tried to act as nonchalantly as possible, but it was hard. "Uh, well, I made it back. That's enough." Maybe she knew I was terrified, maybe not, but she hugged me, and that made up for a lot.

After we made a base for the fire, we waited until I was ready to morph again. I turned metal, found a rock, and struck my forearm repeatedly until a spark landed on the wood, and it began to burn. "That's a start," I said with a sense of satisfaction.

"Yeah," she said in a tiny voice that held only a trace of hope in it. "But how long do we have to wait before the portal opens up again?"

"A week, maybe less," I replied, scanning the area for anything that flew, crawled, hopped, or lumbered. Nothing. "It all depends on what Wheels can do."

Since we couldn't control what might happen on our other Earth, we had to think of our survival first. "We need food, and we need water," I said to Callie while getting up and surveying the landscape before us.

"Food, water," she echoed as she rose to stand beside me. "If this planet is just like Earth—I mean, the same atmosphere—then it has to have water somewhere. But what about food? How do we know that this bear-octopus thing isn't poisonous?" She pointed at the dead creature.

Good point. "We don't. We can skin it and cook it over the fire...that should kill anything poisonous in there. We'll eat just a little. A little can't kill us."

Well, hopefully, it wouldn't.

AN HOUR LATER, DINNER was roasting over the fire, the fat popping, and the smell was...different. I'd morphed my right hand into a knife, skinned a small section of the creature, and sliced off a few chunks of meat. It smelled gamy, but hunger overcame caution, and Callie and I took turns roasting it over the fire. The fire itself was a good idea. Although the sound we'd heard earlier reverberated over the area, it didn't seem to be coming our way. "Meat's ready," she said.

Time to test things. I took a slice and saluted her with it. "Here goes."

I took a tentative bite, chewed it...it tasted like venison. I'd eaten deer meat a few times, and this tasted just like it. "Not bad," I said. "Not bad."

Callie tasted hers, pronounced it decent, and we finished our share of the meat off. Dinner over, I dragged the carcass of the creature inside the cave, leaving it near the entrance and telling my girlfriend, "It should be safe here."

Hopefully, nothing that flew would come down and snatch it. If it did, well, we'd have to find something else. Callie and I sat against the wall. She leaned against me, murmuring that this couldn't be considered an overnight camping trip. "No, I guess not," I said, and I started to laugh. "I've never been to camp. I never even joined the Boy Scouts."

Callie joined in the laughter, but then she abruptly sobered. "I never joined the Girl Scouts, either. I never sold cookies. My foster mother in Beaverton wanted me to sell drugs. She was a drunk, couldn't keep a job for more than two months, couldn't kick her habit, and had a different boyfriend every week, but she always had enough cash to buy booze."

My girlfriend turned her face away, although I caught the hint of a tear trickling down her face. I definitely heard the catch in her voice. "She thought that dealing drugs was a good way to get rich. I mean, what kind of scumbag would tell a little kid to go out and get crystal ice from the local dealer and then sell it to other adults? I had an innocent face, they said. I was a natural, they said."

My girlfriend shook her head at the bad memories that poured out of her, and all I could do was listen. "I had to leave. I waited, went to school, lived with them, worked hard, cleaned their damn house, hid when they got drunk and tried to beat on me...I put up with that...that shit for twelve years."

A hiccup of a sob escaped her throat, and she turned back to face me. In the firelight, her eyes looked haunted. "Then, when I came home from school one day, they were on the kitchen floor. I lied before when I said that they were dead. They weren't."

Call that a shock and then some. "No?"

Her voice was small. "No. They were drunks, but for some reason, that day they tried getting high. It must've been a bad batch because both of them were on the floor, waving their arms and legs in the air, like cockroaches that had eaten poison. My foster mother begged me for help. Her boyfriend—his name was Jamie—he just stared at me. Foam was coming out of his mouth. He was trying to say something...and I...I turned away."

I was watching guilt surface in a major way, and there was nothing I could do to assuage her grief. The only thing I could do was to let her talk. And she did, the words pouring out of her.

"I could've called the hospital. Maybe they would've survived. Maybe not. But I thought of all the times they yelled at me, beat me...one of my foster mother's boyfriends wanted to rape me when I was thirteen. I couldn't take it anymore."

Tears flowed down her face unchecked. "So, I waited. I waited for Jamie to stop moving, and after five minutes, he did. My foster mother...it took her fifteen minutes to die. Then I called nine-one-one. The ambulance came, they said there was nothing that they could do...then I went back to the orphanage, but Mrs. Rothman took a chance on me and helped me to turn my life around." She looked around and sighed. "Now, I'm here."

Callie wiped her eyes. "Some confession, huh? We're here, and no one except you knows."

She leaned against me, and I held her tightly. Who was I going to tell? It didn't matter. My girlfriend obviously felt bad about it, although her anger was justified. In the end, she was the one who'd have to deal with it. I could only offer my support, and that would have to be enough.

WE STAYED ON GUARD during the first few hours after dinner. Callie went first, sitting by the fire and feeding it, and I spelled her roughly four hours later. It wasn't optimum in terms of sleeping, but this world didn't allow for deep sleepers, and who knew what was out there, lurking, waiting to maim and kill and then eat us?

Nothing came our way, though, even though the growling never faded away. Our creature's carcass remained untouched. But while we had food, we also needed to look for water. Sleep came first, and after we'd gone through two cycles of guard duty, it was time to search for that magic elixir.

Since the temperature hardly varied, I tore off another part of my shirt, wrapped it around a stick, and lit the end. Now, we had a torch. Callie did the same, and we went to the back of the cave, checking for any water sources. "Nothing here," she reported.

I checked my side of the cave. "Same here. Nothing." I hoped that I didn't sound too disappointed. A person could survive without food for at least two weeks. But two days with no water would weaken us to the point where we'd be easy pickings once the monsters out there got over their fear of us.

"I guess...we'll have to go outside," Callie said, not without a little anxiousness.

Outside meant going down the face of the cliff. I gave my girlfriend my torch, did the morph thing to turn my hands into pitons, and we went down to the bottom to find water and gather wood.

At ground level, we stayed low, waving our torches in front of us. The growling sounds continued, neither growing closer nor moving further away. "You smell anything?" I asked as we slowly moved away from the cliff.

"Not yet. But...wait."

"What?"

She sounded uncertain. "I'm not sure, but I think I hear water flowing."

That sounded too good to be true. Still, I had to trust her, and we crept along, Callie in the lead. A few minutes later, I heard it as well. "Maybe two hundred yards ahead," I whispered.

"Yeah," she replied with satisfaction. "Glad I was right."

"Let's hope the water's good." That was my main concern.

We continued to follow the sound and were rewarded when we found a fast-moving stream. "I'll guard you," I said to Callie. "Drink up."

She kneeled, tentatively tasted the water, and then cupped her hands and drank. "It's good. Your turn."

I got my fill, and then we headed back to the cave, stopping occasionally to gather sticks for the fire. A nearby growl, followed by a rustling in the bushes, signaled an imminent attack. "Stay back," I said while shifting my body into metal. "Something's here."

That something turned out to be another bear-octopus. It burst out of the bushes, charged our position, and when I grabbed it, it bit my shoulder. It couldn't make a dent, though, and a moment later, I crushed its torso and it fell, dead. After that, we returned to the cave, and while Callie sacked out, I stood guard for the next few hours.

AS WE'D ENTERED A WORLD of eternal twilight, there was no way to keep time. We spent what must have been the next four days watching out for dangerous animals, cutting up the carcass of the octopus-bear, and making trips to the stream to tank up on water. We didn't have canteens, but the skin of the animal served as a makeshift water sack.

After a while, I got tired of eating alien meat. Anything would've been better, but on this world, I saw no vegetables or fruit—or what passed for vegetables or fruit—so we ate the meat and pretended that it was enough.

While time passed slowly—too slowly—I thought about the people I'd known in my life. Besides my parents and Callie, the only person I'd gotten to know was Wheels. An intensely private person, he rarely mentioned any details about himself.

WE WERE IN THE GYM one day. While I did my squats and other leg work, he chose to work his back with pulldowns and some bench rows.

After I finished, I started to walk out, but his words stopped me at the door. "Eli, you and Callie are good together."

I turned around, surprised at his statement. "You think?"

He nodded. "Yeah, you are. I...I never had time for anyone, not seriously. I was always too busy with my projects. After I...I got shot, women simply weren't interested, so I have my work to keep me going." Although he spoke without a trace of pity, from the downcast expression on his face, I knew that he was hurting.

"You might find someone," I said, striving for the right thing to say. A mirthless laugh came from him. "Yeah, one day. Anyway, you watch over Callie. She'll do the same for you."

"Thanks." I meant it.

That was it, and we never spoke of it again.

MY THOUGHTS CAME BACK to the present when Callie asked me if I thought that we'd be stuck here forever. She'd always been the stronger of the two in our relationship, and stronger mentally in any situation we were in, but this turn of reality was something neither of us had counted on. It was necessary to keep up a brave front. "Wheels has got it under control," I said. "He'll get the portal open. No one else can do it."

She offered a wan smile and said that she'd keep an eye out, just in case. I told her that I'd do the same. "I, uh, have to tell you something," she said shyly as I stoked the fire.

"What?" I fed another branch into the flames.

"I never told you that I loved you. I mean, I know it's a cliché, but if you can't tell someone you care for them under the worst circumstances around, then when can you tell them?" A nervous laugh accompanied her statement.

It was the first time she'd ever told me, and it stirred the emotions inside me. Since that was her confession, I made mine. "I love you, too, Callie. I always have."

She scooched over to kiss me. "You sure?"

"Yes, and we'll get out of here. Trust me."

And our routine of standing guard and sleeping continued for perhaps the next three days...until a flash in the distance told me that something was happening. Callie was sleeping, but my cries woke her, and she got up, asking in a groggy voice, "What?"

"Look!" I pointed ahead. An opaque oval had formed at our original entry point. "Time to go."

It would take too long to climb down, so I shifted into my metal form, gathered her in my arms, and jumped to the ground. Sixty feet straight down, and while the shock was incredible, I stayed on my feet and lumbered forward in the direction of the gateway. Callie yelled at the top of her lungs, "It's us. Hold it open, Wheels."

"Hurry," a voice said faintly from the other universe. "Hurry!"

I ran for my life, still carrying my girlfriend, and then a giant shape loomed up ahead to block our way. It was similar to the creature I'd killed on our first day here, but much larger, with more arms and fangs that flashed in the dim light. "Callie, power up!"

She flung out her arms, and before I closed my eyes, my girlfriend's sunburst revealed a horrid monster that shied back from the brilliance. The portal was close, so I pushed myself to run faster, and I tore past the creature.

My strength began to flag, though, and spots appeared in front of my eyes. Going temporarily blind wasn't on the menu. Still, I was almost out of time in terms of shifting, so I kept pushing, and the portal drew ever closer. Seventy feet...fifty feet...twenty feet...

"We're through," Callie said. "Put me down."

Breathless and spent physically, I stopped. The portal snapped shut behind us, and Wheels spun around in his wheelchair, a grin on his unshaven face. "Welcome back."

Those had to be the most beautiful words I'd ever heard.

And home had never looked so good.

Chapter Twelve: Captured

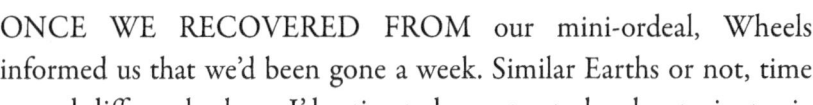

ONCE WE RECOVERED FROM our mini-ordeal, Wheels informed us that we'd been gone a week. Similar Earths or not, time moved differently there. I'd estimated our stay to be about ninety-six hours, but since every Earth wasn't the same...

"I'm sorry about what happened," Wheels said as we sat in the kitchen, downing can after can of cola and eating huge bowls of pasta with meat sauce. He'd done the cooking honors, and I was glad of it. Having eaten alien bear-octopus meat for a week turned me off those two species forever, and my stomach appreciated the influx of proper Earth food.

"Well, we got back okay," I said as I shoveled more of my meal into my mouth. Once I downed my portion, I added, "And the portal gizmo works, so...whatever. You made a mistake."

Although I'd initially been angry, I realized that sometimes, science made mistakes. Good thing that science hadn't killed us. Wheels muttered, "It wasn't what I intended. There was a power surge at the last second, and it shifted the coordinates."

He seemed most contrite. It was enough for me, and he filled us in on what had transpired during the past seven days. Our fight against the two enhanced AMA goons had gone viral. Someone had taken a short video of me and Callie kicking ass, and they'd sent it to a news station.

Naturally, news being news, and people being people, everyone had plastered the images all over the internet. New York was New York, which meant that in the space of a few seconds, the entire population had seen what had transpired.

While the news of the battle was bad enough, worse, the authorities—the police, as well as the AMA—had seen our faces. It's not as if they hadn't seen me and Callie before, but now, the vitriol against us intensified tenfold.

"They tried to murder our people," Dornaught said in an interview. If an award for self-righteousness existed, he'd have won it many years in a row. "They deliberately targeted them, used their superior abilities to maim our people, and we will not rest until justice is served."

His concept of justice and mine differed radically, but he was in a position of authority, and people listened to him. Soon, the obligatory APB went out. In the case of the police, they'd probably arrest us.

In the case of the anti-mutant gang, though, that was our death warrant. We'd just come back from a deadly situation, but for some reason, this pronouncement was much more visceral, like a series of punches to the gut with a sledgehammer.

"That...is not good," Wheels said with a philosophical air after we'd finished our meal and relaxed in the lounge. The newscast had painted Callie and me as wanted fugitives. "I suppose it was inevitable. You fight crime, you look out for the little guy, eventually, you pay the price."

His voice then turned harsh. "For the moment, you two are laying low. No more joy fights against the other enhanced. I know that you want to get out and have fun, but these are your lives we're talking about. We have enough supplies to last for a year and maybe more, if necessary. I'm working on something, but you two, you sit tight."

Sit tight, he said.

Apparently, Wheels wasn't familiar with the term cabin fever. It was most definitely real. Living a life of relative luxury in a golden cage was one thing, but not being able to go out and enjoy it was another matter entirely. My routine was to get up at six in the morning, work out in the gym—sometimes, Callie joined me, but usually she slept in—then eat breakfast, watch the news, which was all bad, and then talk to Wheels, or my girlfriend, or both, until it was time for lunch.

The rest of the day wasn't any more exciting, and after a few days, Callie and I carped about our situation to our guardian. "I'm working on something to help you out," he answered in his usual cryptic manner. "Give me a few more days."

A few more days turned into a period of eight days in which crime was its usual rotten self, and politically, it was the US and its allies against everyone else. Just as I thought I was going to have a mental breakdown from being cooped up, on the eighth day, Wheels announced at dinner that he had a gift for us. "It's experimental, but it might help you for a time."

Call me interested, and Callie perked up right away, asking, "What is it? It's not about the portal, is it?"

"No, I'm still working on that. This is different." Wheels pulled two small watches from his pocket and proffered them. "Put these on, and don't ever take them off. They're waterproof and shockproof, and I want to see how they work."

"Do you have to wind them, or are they battery-operated?" I asked after putting mine on.

For that, I got a thin smile. "Trust me. They tell the time, but you'll see two tiny buttons on the right side of the face."

I did. "Yeah?"

"Press the top button."

I obeyed, and Callie gasped. "Eli, you're...you're..."

"What?"

"A woman."

A woman? I went into the bathroom, and sure enough, the mirror showed a tall black woman in her thirties with a close-cropped Afro, narrow, regular features, and brown eyes. Whoa...from every angle, I looked like a woman. The clothes this projection had on—a purple skirt and matching blouse—even moved with me. Amazing. "Wow."

That exclamation came out of me unbidden. Not only did I look like a woman, I sounded like one, too. When I came back, Wheels was sitting with a short Asian woman in her mid-twenties who wore a black skirt and a white blouse. "Callie," I said. "You're—"

"Japanese," Wheels cut in. "You, Eli, are Carol Brown, age thirty-one. Callie is Julie Fukuhara, age twenty-four. You make a nice couple. Oh, and if you want to turn off the device, press the bottom button."

We switched off our devices, and I took my seat, astonished at how real it all was. "Those holograph projectors took me a long time to build. I used voices from the internet, and an AI app did the rest. You'll look and sound like women."

"I like mine," Callie said. "Do you have any others?"

Wheels shook his head. "Not yet. I'm still working on male versions with different ethnicities and races to throw the AMA and the police off. Thing is, I don't know how long your devices will last, though. The prototypes shut down after half an hour in order to regenerate. That takes about two hours. Eli, I recently tested yours. It's an upgrade. It tested out at forty-five minutes, but you'll have to be careful. Same deal for you, Callie."

"Did you do a field test?" I asked.

A grin came from him. "Nope, just motored around this complex until the time was up. You get the honor of testing them for real." He dug into his pocket, pulled out some laminated cards, and handed them over. "Now, I made up some IDs for you. Birth certificates, social security cards, and driver's licenses. They'll pass muster in a store—probably—but I'm not sure the police don't have a better fraud detection system. Bottom line—don't get caught."

He then wheeled himself out. At the door, he stopped and added, "Field test is tomorrow afternoon. I'll drive you into the city, give you a burner phone, and once you're ready to come back, call me and come to the pickup-drop-off point. I'll give you two hours, tops. If you don't call after two hours, then I'll assume that you got nicked."

That was it, and Callie leaned over to kiss me. When she pulled back, I asked her how it felt to kiss another woman. She whispered with a sly smile, "Perfectly normal. Now you know how the other half lives. Just remember to cross your legs when you sit."

The next day. Noon.

Wheels drove us to the edge of the city. "Drop-off point is here," he said. We were in an empty lot at a convenience store. Cars passed by on the busy road, but no one stopped or even slowed down to glance in our direction. And, best of all, no police cars or AMA cars came our way, either. So far, this was shaping up to be a successful outing. "Don't forget where I parked."

He then handed me a smartphone, which was already on. "Remember, when you're ready, just press the call button. The phone will do the rest. After that, destroy it. Enjoy your day. I'll be around."

"Will do," I answered. We clicked on our holograph watches, our disguises were set, so I took Callie's hand as we walked off.

It was a beautiful summer's day, hot and full, and we strolled hand in hand for a while until Callie said that we shouldn't hold hands. "Not that I'm homophobic, but someone might be, and if we get into a fight, our devices might get damaged."

Her comment made sense, so I dropped her hand, and we continued on our trek. I didn't have any cash on hand, so I took a chance and paid a visit to an ATM machine. Good ol' Johnny Dollar alias—it was still working. I withdrew three hundred dollars, and Callie and I ended up at a small upscale café near Central Park. We sat outside, just two ladies enjoying the day.

No one gave us a second look. Second looks were for those they found suspicious. For all the rest of the customers knew, they were looking at two women who were sipping ice café lattes and nibbling on chocolate scones. What could be more innocent than that?

It was a great change from the food we usually ate, and couldn't all days be like this? Rhetorical, as the reality was that they couldn't.

The world had moved in a different direction than most people wanted. New York had always been a city on the edge, one filled with excitement and danger, but now, the atmosphere was charged with tension.

A television behind the counter was set on a news channel. The sound was on, but over the chatter, it was impossible to hear. At least the closed-caption switch was working, and the subtitles told us the whole story.

An incident in China today has underscored the need for diplomacy. Four American tourists were beaten near a university in Beijing. Police arrested the Americans for allegedly inciting violence, although witnesses said that the attack on the Americans was unprovoked. Their injuries are not life-threatening, but they were arrested.

In a separate incident in Los Angeles, police arrested five Chinese nationals for allegedly exporting semi-conductors to China through a dummy corporation. The Chinese embassy has protested, but our police have the evidence, and the trial is sure to be swift...

I turned my gaze away. Diplomats were the best choice to handle international relations, but they were definitely falling down on the job. The couple at the next table seemed to think so. A fat man in his forties with pasty skin, beady black eyes, and a suit that was a size too small, was busy shoveling a bowl of meat and pasta into his maw.

His equally heavy partner wore slacks and a blouse that couldn't hide her excess. She was scarfing down a bowl of chicken and rice. When they came up for air, the fat man opined that the world would be safer with a few less foreigners in it. He didn't look at anyone in particular, simply shared his views with the other patrons.

"And what's with the Chinese thinkin' they're so much better'n we are? If y'ask me, they should expel all them Asian persuasions, not only from here, but from our allied buddies. Let 'em go back where they came from."

Well, that marked him as a prime bigot, but what else was new? He sniffed the air and wrinkled his nose as if he smelled something bad. He then gazed at Callie, who was in her guise as Julie Fukuhara.

Callie didn't take the bait. She simply returned the gaze, which by now had deepened into a stare that held hate. "Something I can do for you?" she asked in a deceptively calm voice. My girlfriend didn't have the most even temper around.

Mr. Fat nodded. "Yeah, you. You got eyes I don't like. You got skin I don't like. You and all the other China people think you own the world." He raised his voice. "This is America for Americans."

A few people glanced in our direction. Mr. Fat's companion hissed at him to stop, but he waved her off. His expression was smug to the nth degree, and he gave passive-aggressive—as well as the word asshole—a whole new meaning. "Hey, Lily, just makin' conversation."

All right, if he wanted it, he could listen to a few words from me. "So, by saying America is for all Americans, you mean only white people, is that right?"

His beady-eyed gaze switched to meet mine. Although he said nothing, his twisted lips, flecked with meat sauce, spoke volumes about a deep-seated hatred, something instilled in him from birth onwards.

He kept silent, so I decided to up the ante. "Here, let me help you. You want America to be like it was three hundred years ago, mostly white, with slaves and plantations, all the slaves saying, *Yassuh*, or *Nossuh*, right?"

"In your case, yeah," he replied. "So, what are you? A couple of gay ho's?"

What an idiot. Callie muttered, "Prime slime," under her breath, and I couldn't disagree. She leaned over to kiss me and then smiled at him. "I suppose so. What's your answer to that?"

Ms. Fat uttered a strangled sound of disgust. "Do you have to do that here?"

"No better place," I replied and kissed Callie back. It was a long, lingering kiss, and while some people looked away, most of the patrons didn't seem overly bothered by our display of affection.

Mr. Fat's response was to clear his throat noisily. "You and your black lady buddy, you're as bad as the mutants. First, we get rid of the foreigners, and then we get rid of the freaks."

His partner abruptly reached over to try to grab Callie's shoulder for some unknown reason. My girlfriend responded by smacking her soundly across her chops. "Touch me again, you get twice that," she warned.

Ms. Fat recoiled in shock and horror. A few of the patrons cheered, and most of them laughed. A man in his fifties walked over, wearing a blue uniform. Large and definitely in charge, he announced his intentions in a cheerful but forced manner. "Ladies and gentlemen, my name is Frank. I'm the manager of this establishment. If there's a problem, all of you can settle it outside. Not here."

"Hey, they started it," Mr. Fat said, pointing his stubby finger at me. "Them two lezzies, they started it by showin' off their orientaltation, and you're accusing me?" He snorted and stared in defiance at the manager.

In return, Frank the manager gave him the same stare, and when he spoke, all trace of friendliness vanished. "Hear me good, mister. I was watching you and listening. That's part of my job. So I'm giving you and your companion a warning. Keep your mouth shut except while you're stuffing food in your piehole. One more racist crack, and I'll make you pay for everyone's lunch here. Then I'll toss your fat ass outside and maybe kick it a few times. Got it?"

Mr. Fat stared at him sullenly, then nodded. Frank left, and while the amused onlookers gave him a round of applause, Callie and I finished our coffee and treats. "Time to leave," I murmured.

We got up, and Mr. Fat couldn't resist saying good riddance. He also added a racist epithet. Fine...but his savage grin of triumph turned red when I belted him in the mouth. Frank stalked over to our position, and he was fuming. To us, he said, "Ladies, I'm going to pretend I didn't see that." He then raised his voice and addressed the rest of the patrons. "Did anyone else here see that?"

A collective, "No," answered him.

With that, he turned his wrath on Mr. Fat. "You really don't listen, do you? Just for that, you're paying for everyone here, and if you don't, guess what happens next? My brother's a police officer."

Mr. Fat, bleeding like a stuck pig, got the message, and after he'd wiped his mouth and hurled daggers at me and Callie with his peepers, he reached for his wallet. That was our cue to leave, and I tossed a few bills on the table. I didn't want anyone paying for me, especially him. Outside, my girlfriend remarked, "That was fun. What do we do for an encore?"

"It was fun, but we shouldn't bring attention to ourselves," I reminded her.

Callie's reply was that we already had. "Let's go to the park. It's just over there." She pointed straight ahead.

Why not? Bigots or not, I wasn't going to let anyone ruin this day. We strolled among the green grass, neatly trimmed flower beds, and the bad experience of before slowly began to leave. Perhaps nature was the answer to a person feeling depressed.

I stopped to smell the air. Unlike the rest of the city, this place, right now, smelled fresh and new, an area rife with possibilities. Time passed slowly, and we chatted about things we'd do if the situation was different. Callie's reply surprised me. "Finish school."

"Seriously?"

She bobbed her head. "Yeah, I liked school. I mean, when the trouble started, when my foster parents found out what I was—I mean, the Rothmans—and what I could do, school was always a safe place for me."

I wished that I could've said the same. "For me, school is...school. I was just average. Going to college wasn't going to happen, and when I changed, well...that *really* wasn't going to happen."

Callie then asked me if I regretted having powers. I had to think about that. "No," I finally said. "I learned to accept them. And I liked them. I liked being thought of as a superhero, at least, in the beginning. It made me feel good."

"But they set you apart from everyone else," my girlfriend pointed out.

"Even if I didn't have powers, I'd never have fit in with anyone at school. It just wasn't there."

My girlfriend nodded. "I liked studying, but, yeah, friendship wasn't there, either. Maybe it was my fault or theirs—or on both sides. But I can tell you, I wouldn't change anything."

And there it was...the acceptance thing. I'd never fought against being what I was. I'd learned to accept it and liked it, but I'd also never thought of myself as being better than anyone else. Or any worse. I was me and no one else, and the world would just have to accept that.

Or not.

Callie leaned against me, just us two in the middle of Central Park, no one else in the vicinity, and all was quiet. It was a rare and special moment, especially in the crowded metropolis that was Manhattan. "I wish..." she began.

"You wish...what?"

"I wish there was a time machine we could use so that we could go back to how things were before..." Her voice caught. "Before these laws came, before the groups came...before all the hate came. Why can't it be like it was?"

Her question, asked so simply, nearly broke my heart, and I realized then and there that things could never be as they were because certain evil elements in society wouldn't let it happen. "There's no going back, Callie," I said, feeling the same way as she did. "Things weren't perfect fifty or even a hundred years ago, either. They were simpler, I guess, but there was still bigotry and racism. It's just, uh..." I searched for the word. "It's more overt, now."

My girlfriend nodded, as if accepting the inevitability of what I'd said. In that split-second, I also realized that our holograph disguises were no longer working. "Callie," I murmured. "We have to go."

"Why?"

"Look at yourself."

She did, uttering a soft, "Oh."

With another burst of surprise, I understood why the place was so quiet. "Listen," I muttered, looking around. Metal glinted in the bushes and trees. "When I say run, you run."

"Why?"

"Trust me."

I took her hand, and we started to run, but a nanosecond later, a bright, metallic object landed at our feet. What the hell? Before I could shift, it went off, hurling us in opposite directions, and I landed hard in a clump of bushes. It was some kind of stun grenade...it jangled my senses and totally disoriented them. I felt something wet on my upper lip...blood from my nose.

I wiped it away, and when I looked up, my vision was still blurry, but I made out three AMA agents hauling my girlfriend away. She was struggling, and she managed to kick one man in the stomach, then jerked her left arm free and knocked down one of the agents.

In response, another guard gave her a love tap on the back of her head with the butt end of his pistol, and she collapsed. He yelled, "We got her. Let's move!"

With an effort, I got to my feet, but the world spun, and I found myself flat on my back. My ears rang from the impact of the sound-shockwave that the grenade gave off, and the only thought I had was that dying sucked.

A mini-eternity later, my senses returned to near-normal, the sound of a car's engine came through. When my vision finally cleared and I turned over to view the scene, I was alone.

Chapter Thirteen: The Offer

AS I GOT UP SLOWLY, feeling myself all over in case something was broken, I experienced the greatest sense of loss in my life. While losing my parents had been bad, I hadn't been there.

It didn't hurt any less, of course, but seeing Callie dragged off to a fate unknown, it was so palpable, so visceral and so overwhelming on an emotional level that for a moment I experienced a brain fart and couldn't move, couldn't think, only watch dumbly as the woman I loved was taken away.

Slowly, my body began to function again. On a physical level, my nose stopped bleeding, my ears stopped ringing, but mentally...no, I was far from okay. Still, I'd deal. I'd have to.

I brushed myself off and started to retrace my steps to the convenience store's parking lot. Curious onlookers peered at the park and ignored me as I moved past them and made my way along the street.

No one seemed to be following me, but when I passed an alley, a voice spoke from out of the darkness. "Eli. Eli Marks."

Curious, I stopped. "Who's there?"

A whisper came from the dimness. "Eli, listen carefully. I have something you'll want to hear."

The voice...it sounded familiar. "Dornaught?"

Although I shouldn't have entered, I figured that I'd be able to shift into metal or wood if things went south. Bad idea, as a second later, I felt a stab of something in my right rear deltoid area. He was faster than I thought, and I was a fool.

Immediately, my body began to freeze up, every nerve seemed to stop firing, but my heart, while beating fast, continued to work. "What the..."

"Stop talking and listen. Yes, it's me. You can't move on your own, can you?"

He sounded rational, almost friendly, and at that moment, all I wanted was to wring his neck, but my body betrayed me. I couldn't do a thing. "No."

"Good." A hand came out of the shadows and gently guided me to a spot filled with empty crates. I walked as stiffly as someone would if they'd just emerged from an ice bath, and then I found that my lower body was seizing up. "Sit here."

I sat, and then I couldn't move at all. "Listen carefully," Dornaught said in the same calm, pseudo-friendly tone from behind me. "I just gave you a shot that's paralyzed you. I know that you can transform into metal or wood, but even if I hadn't given you the shot, you wouldn't have been able to do it fast enough."

Fine, he had the drop on me, I couldn't shift, and what did he want? As if reading my mind, he gave me the information willingly, almost gleefully. "You're probably thinking why I haven't killed you or asked my men to take you in. Yes?"

What could I say? "Yes."

His soft laugh sounded disarmingly friendly, and then he came out of the shadows to face me, wearing the grin of someone who held all the cards. "The answer is easy. Number one, the drug will wear off soon. Number two, all my men are on their way to Chicago. It's just me. I haven't notified the police, and I don't intend to. This is between us, and I don't want the local law interfering."

He cleared his throat. "Number three, I want you to be on my team. I want your lady friend, Callie, to be on my team. It's very easy. We have a problem, and if you join us, I promise you that the problem will go away."

"How, by killing us?"

Another laugh greeted my question. "No, that's not it. I had to do away with some of the people you know. Eric Darven, for one. He had abilities, but he was unbalanced, and therefore, that made him unreliable. The ones we...embalmed, they never would've sided with us, and in my world, if you're not with us—"

"Then we're against you," I finished, realizing that I'd uttered the stalest cliché in existence.

He nodded. "Exactly. This isn't just a battle for the soul of America. It's a battle for the whole world."

It sounded so noble, but I also knew that Dornaught was a vainglorious asshole with delusions of godhood. He proceeded to tell me of how he'd been recruited by the president to head up the AMA. Why he felt compelled to give his BS side of the story was beyond me, but considering that I couldn't go anywhere, I had to listen.

After telling me about his wartime record and playing up all the activities he'd been involved in, he told me that he and the president were close friends. "He and I, we're both ex-military men. We know what kind of war this is. It's a war that only one side can win—our side, the human side."

"In case you hadn't noticed, I'm human, too." I threw all the sarcasm possible into my answer, but it didn't sway him one bit.

"Most of you is," he answered as a cruel smile crept across his face. "But your powers—and they are formidable—set you apart from the rest of humanity. You weren't accepted by the rest of society, and you never will be."

The cruel smile faded, and his voice took on a persuasive air. "However, if you join up with my organization, you'll have an easy life. If you want to continue with school, we'll make that happen. If you want to do field work, we can make that happen, too. For you, and for Callie, the possibilities are endless."

He proceeded to list the goodies we'd get. An apartment in Manhattan, if we wanted, but if we desired to go to LA or another major city, then we'd get our wish. "And then there's the money," he added. "Lots of it. You'll have more than enough to do whatever you want. You're young, and you both have abilities far beyond what most people have. We want to help you develop those abilities to the utmost."

"For what?" I really had no idea what he was getting at. "I mean, what's the endgame here? You want to get rid of us. That's been your goal from day one. You have your own regular human goon squad, and you have your own little league of the enhanced working for you. What more do you want?" I tried wiggling my fingers and toes. They began to move, but the rest of my body still felt totally inert.

Dornaught's answer sounded most reasonable, and he leaned over to stare me in the eye. On the surface, to anyone else, he might have appeared normal, but below that normality lay madness. "Eli, it's not only about control. It's about conquering first, and *then* controlling. Do you know what Project Juggernaut is?"

I'd never heard of it. "I suppose you're anxious to tell me."

He wagged his head from side to side as if considering it. "No, I don't think that I will. Not yet. But since you're here, I'll tell you what I want."

Ah, here it came, the offer. Turn to the dark side, make that leap from decency into indecency, sell my soul...the clichés were endless. "Let me guess. You want me to tell you where my friends are. You want me to join up with your hit squad, help to kill my friends, and then Callie and I can enjoy the good life together. Am I getting warm?"

Dornaught grunted out an answer that I took as an affirmative one. "Pretty close. What I want is for you to join up with us, yes. Because as we speak, as I mentioned previously, your friend is being taken to our headquarters. We're going to experiment on her. If you come to Chicago within forty-eight hours and willingly give yourself over to us, then we'll let her go. Come alone. If we find that you have help, you know what will happen to her. It's that simple."

Was it? In that moment, I thought about his offer. He was right about one thing—society had never accepted me or Callie. It never would. It didn't matter what we looked like. It was what we *were* that mattered.

And, to be honest, in that moment, the money angle was tempting. I'd never had enough since being on my own. More money, more chances...that was how I looked at it.

However, just as suddenly as the positives presented themselves, the negatives also surfaced. Assuming the AMA let me live, I'd still be a pariah to the human community. I'd still be hunted, only by a different group of people. And, worst of all, I'd be their possession, their toy...their slave.

While I was thinking things over, my body began to feel different. Lighter, more normal, and with a shock that wasn't one, I realized that the drug was wearing off.

Dornaught obviously saw what was happening, and a look of alarm flashed in his eyes. He began to back up. "Think it over, Eli. Your lady friend's fate is in your hands. I know you'll make the right choice."

A moment later, he was gone. Although I'd made my decision, the awful fact was that I was alone again, Callie was a prisoner, and I had to get her back.

Chapter Fourteen: Breakout

———— ⟲ ————

THE DRUG FINALLY WORE off, and all feeling returned to my body. It was like I'd woken up from a deep sleep, but I hadn't slept. I'd only been an unwilling participant in my own interrogation. I stretched out, checked myself all over for any injuries—none—and then decided to leave.

After I emerged from the alley, I began walking, but when I got to the pick-up point, the lot was empty. Wheels had already gone. Head down, I started my trek and hoped that the police wouldn't notice me. Luck was on my side. No one did.

For the next hour-plus by my estimation, my feet ate up the pavement. The thought came that maybe they weren't after me, although Dornaught had said that he wanted me along for the ride. It made me wonder why. Physically speaking, I was stronger than Callie, but after thinking it over, her powers were off the scale in many ways. A lot of the enhanced were strong, and a lot of them were shifters, but as far as I knew, there was only one Sunburst.

And, as Dornaught had said, they'd experiment on her, the thought of which made me alternately rage and grow fearful. What if he didn't like the results? Would he embalm her, like the others?

He'd threatened to do so, and he wasn't the type to lie about something like that. People like him were filled with purpose. It was twisted, it was vile, but it was something that made him do what he'd done, and I knew that he'd carry through on his threat.

I kept going, one foot in front of the other, beating a steady path toward my goal of getting back to the lair. It would take me well over three hours, at this rate.

Absentmindedly, I pressed the button on my watch. Nothing happened, so I figured it was recharging or broken, whichever came first. However, a couple of minutes later, a car pulled up alongside me, and a middle-aged man's voice said, "Need a ride, Ms., er..."

I looked at my legs...a purple skirt covered them. Nice that my holo disguise had decided to work again. Hopefully, this time it wouldn't burn out and shock the living hell out of my driver. "Yes, please, I'd like one. I'm going to Royce Township."

"I can take you most of the way."

Very kind of him. I'd always been leery of hitchhiking during my roaming days, never knowing what kind of psychos had gotten a license to drive. However, this guy didn't give off any bad vibes. His name was Corey Lefton, forty-seven, short and slight, with plain features, mild blue eyes, and a mustache. He had an air of eternal optimism about him, a rarity in this day and age. As a salesman for a pharmaceutical company, he was constantly on the go. "Can't get many sales these days, but I try my best," he said as we motored along.

"Have to keep trying," I said, trying to be polite.

"Yes, we do."

Lefton mentioned that he was married, on his way home after a business meeting, and he expressed hope that things would turn around, domestically as well as internationally. "I work like a dog for my wife and daughters. It's not for me. It's for them."

"You seem to be doing well for yourself."

Doubt clouded his features for a brief moment. "I don't know. What with the world going on the way it is, I'm not so sure. But...I have confidence that our government will turn things around."

I wished that I had the same confidence. At any rate, he fell silent, and I didn't offer anything in the way of topics, either, for the forty minutes. He stepped on the gas, and time seemed to pass more quickly.

"This is as far as I can go," he said as he pulled over to the side of the road. We'd arrived at the main intersection that led to Royce.

"Thanks for the lift," I replied. He waved at me as he veered left. I turned right and made my way back to the lair, looking over my shoulder every couple of minutes. Luck was on my side. I was alone. No drones, no sounds of cars...nothing. It was a good thing, as my watch gave out, and I returned to my default state once more.

Fortunately, once I got near the cottage, the ramp opened. Wheels was home. I ran into the compound with the last of my strength, and once I was in the kitchen, he made me a few sandwiches, gave me water, and listened to my side of the story.

"She's in Chicago," I said once I'd eaten and calmed down enough to speak without tripping over my words. "We have to get her back. And we have to do it soon."

"That's all?" Wheels arched his eyebrows. "And?"

And...and? "What more do you want?" I asked, filled with anger and worry. "They got her. We have to get her back. And what's Project Juggernaut?"

He shook his head. "I have no idea. I can take a guess, but without more information, it's just a guess."

Since he didn't know about the project, I repeated my earlier plea of rescuing Callie. Impassioned though they sounded, my words didn't make much of a dent in my guardian, as he replied blandly, "You and what army? That's what Dornaught and his goons want you to do. They want you to make an assault. They know you will, so save your ass."

Saving my ass wasn't on the menu, not if Callie wasn't on it with me. "Can't do it, Larry. I have to go. If you won't help me, I'll get there, somehow."

I got up to leave. His hand shot out to grab my elbow. "Sit down."

Wheels had a hell of a grip. Although I could've pulled free, reason overruled passion, so I sat. He sighed. "I figured you'd probably go off on your own and try something half-cocked. All right, I sent coded messages to a few of the old gang to come in, but they're still thinking it over. They're scattered throughout the country, so getting them to come here isn't the easiest thing."

I started to say something, but he raised his hand. "Hear me out. If you're still hellbent on going, I've got a little something to help you out. The holograph watches still aren't reliable enough."

Now, I was curious. "What?"

He motioned for me to follow him, and we went to his workshop. There, he went to a worktable and picked up a syringe filled with a yellowish liquid. "This is called P-Up, short for Power Up. Stupid name, but I couldn't think of anything else. It's an enhancer to what you've already got. Call it the ultimate marriage between a steroid and an amphetamine. The way I figure it, it'll give you a huge boost to what you already have when you transform, but it won't last long."

"My own powers don't last long, either. I get around five minutes at most."

He nodded. "I know, but this is an add-on of another five minutes. Ten minutes max."

"Is it dangerous?"

At first, Wheels seemed reluctant to answer, and then he spread his hands wide in the classic I-don't-know gesture. "It's going to increase your strength around five hundred percent. But it'll also tax your heart, your lungs, your muscular system, and especially your nervous system to the max. The way I figure it, only the young can take it. That's you."

"And...if you're wrong?"

"You'll blow apart."

Well, that was some comfort—not. But I still had to go, and I told Wheels so. He shrugged. "Risks are everywhere. Once you inject yourself, go in, do what you have to do, and get Callie out of there. I'll contact Ravenna. She lives in Rochester with her husband, and she'll be our eye in the sky."

Ravenna...I'd heard about her, but I'd never met her. "She can fly, right? That's all I know."

A smirk crossed his face. "Flying isn't the half of it. Think of a really large vulture that's built like a woman. Her talons have the crushing ability of a hippo's bite. And if you ever see her in a power dive, trust me, she's beyond awesome. Oh, and in her bird form, she's got extra tough skin. Regular bullets just bounce off her. Bottom line, she's very dangerous. The perfect partner for this mission."

He grabbed a few rolled-up blueprints and leafed through them before he found the one he wanted. He unrolled it and said with a sense of satisfaction, "Yeah, this is it."

What it was, was a blueprint of the AMA headquarters in Chicago. Wheels leaned back in his chair, rubbing his chin. "When Dornaught and his crew captured me, they took me to that building. I memorized every detail that I could, and assuming they haven't changed things much, you should be able to get in."

The bottom level, he said, was a lounge. Floors two through fourteen were reserved for training, weapons manufacturing and testing, administration, and accounting. "Accounting," I echoed, not believing he was actually serious. "You're kidding."

"Nope. They're funded by the government, but even the government wants to save money," Wheels reminded me with a cynical air. "Just how it is."

I wondered aloud why the AMA was so open about what they did. Wheels coughed out a bitter laugh. "Everyone knows, Eli. It's just a matter of who's willing and dumb enough to cross them."

Right, I was facing off against a group of killers that made organized crime members look like schoolchildren. "Meet the willing and dumb one," I said, tapping my chest.

Wheels nodded. "Well, if you play your cards right, you'll be able to go in and get out with Callie. I don't know who else is being held prisoner, but you can't stop. Go in," he repeated with greater force. "Find your girlfriend, and then get your asses to the top of the building. Ravenna will do the rest."

"Thanks."

We went to the garage and I helped him into his van. After I folded up the wheelchair and put it away, I got into the passenger seat. "Get some rest, Eli," he said. "It'll take about twelve hours to get there. I'll wake you when it's your turn to bring the heat."

Off we went, and I prayed that we'd be in time.

Twelve hours, ten minutes later. Five-twenty AM.

"We're here."

Wheels' voice woke me, and I sat up, inhaling what I thought would be fresh air. It wasn't. Chicago stank. There was no other way to describe it. It had never been the cleanest city around, but in the past, it had the rep of being a bustling, thriving metropolis where the citizenry worked hard and played harder.

Not now. Although it was before sunup, homeless people filled the streets, everyone who wasn't tailing off a drunk or a chemically-induced high glanced at each other with suspicion, and police cars patrolled the downtown core.

In addition to the suspicion, the smell of rotting garbage filled the air. Apparently, the garbage collectors had gone on strike and the mountains of trash that were piled up by the side of the roads emitted a stench that would've made a demon weep.

A strong breeze blew, but it didn't cool things off. Instead, it carried the smell of everything rotten to every corner of the city. Those pedestrians who weren't part of the homeless-slash-drugged-out crowd who were on their way to work and who were brave enough to walk around in this stink, covered their noses. Many of them wore masks, which probably didn't help much.

Wheels let me off at a corner two blocks away from the AMA building. "Be careful, Eli. If you make it through, Ravenna can help you get home. I have to get to work on the gateway and do my thing with the other little goodies in my to-be-fixed-or-created pile."

"See you in a while. Take it easy." I tried to sound confident, but inside, my stomach was roiling. It wasn't every single day of the week that an innocent would walk into the lion's den, and where I was going, it was almost guaranteed to be a one-way trip.

Get in, get out, and make the twelve-hour trip back to New York. Sure thing, piece of cake, and that plan was totally lacking in details. Mainly, if I succeeded in getting Callie out, how would I get back? I hadn't thought of that.

I'd worry about that later. For now, breaking Callie out was the thing to do. Wheels had described the place to me. I'd pored over a map of the city, memorized the alleys and places to hide, and I'd seen the blueprint of my target.

However, in person, the AMA building was far more imposing. It was impossible to miss—a gleaming chrome-and-steel, sixteen-story prison for those who'd transgressed, and a death chamber for those the AMA had deemed as transgressors.

At the main entrance, two guards stood, armed with rifles. There were probably other guards at the sides and the rear of the building. If they were hoping to get some action, they wouldn't be disappointed—but they also wouldn't like the result.

And I'd seen the results of what the AMA could do. I'd witnessed the executions, and the image of the enhanced struggling as they fought against the embalming process was seared into my cerebral cortex and would never leave. I was determined not to end up that way.

It was time. My plan was to go in, smash anything that moved, and make my way to the top floor. It was simple, but it was also stupid and practically suicidal as it had to be done in five minutes. Taking the drug would buy me another five minutes—maybe—but if I couldn't find her in time, I was screwed.

However, this was Callie I was after, and that gave me the confidence to get the job done. I moved along the sidewalk, keeping an eye out for anyone who might recognize me. As I passed an alleyway, a husky woman's voice said, "Eli?"

I turned around, and a powerful hand latched onto my shoulder, pulled me into the alley, and then pushed me against the wall, her other hand against my mouth. "Shh," the figure said in a low, conspiratorial tone while glancing at the entrance and then at me. "I'm Ravenna, your contact. Are you calm now?"

I nodded, and she took her hand away. "Calm enough. Thanks for meeting me."

We peeked out of the alley, and Ravenna pointed at the building. "Did Wheels tell you where to go?"

"I guess Callie's on the top floor."

She shrugged. "I'm not sure. I could fly you to the top, but there might be guards behind the door, and there's no telling which floor your lady friend is on."

Ravenna was in her late twenties and in the realm of six-one, with a slender figure, a head of long black hair that fell to her waist, a plain-pretty face with piercing blue eyes, and she wore a black bodysuit that extended to her ankles. No shoes, no socks. "I came in earlier and did some recon," she continued. "If you manage to free your girlfriend, meet me on the roof. It's open, no cameras that I could see. I'll do the rest."

She didn't say anything about weaponry, and doubt hit. "Uh, Wheels described you to me. Not to say you're wrong, but you don't look like, uh, the person I'm supposed to meet."

Ravenna took a step back, closed her eyes as if concentrating, and a moment later, wings, black and heavy, sprouted from her back. "I'm a shifter," she said, her voice getting deeper and hoarser, and her features elongated into an approximation of a raven. Her hands became claws, and her feet, large, lethal-looking talons.

"When I say I can do recon, I can," she said with the utmost confidence. "And when I tell you that I'm up to the job, believe it. See you on the roof. Get going."

With a mighty leap, she took to the sky, the rest of her body transforming into that of a flying predator. That was my cue. I ran across the street, turning my body into metal and holding the syringe in my left hand, just in case. Two guards held rifles, and they started firing, their bullets pinging off my torso. "Try again," I yelled as I smashed them into the ground and then went through the glass doors as if they were made of tissue paper.

The lounge was empty, and I took the stairs up to the first floor. The second floor was empty. Many doors, many offices, but no personnel. Floors number two through eleven were also empty, but once I got to the twelfth floor, a surprise was waiting. Eleven men held tasers, and they immediately let fly.

Damn it!

The shock hit me right away, almost shorting out my senses and sending me to the floor. My body began to shift back to flesh, and the pain intensified. "Not so tough, are ya," one of them said with a mean smile. "Let's see how long you last when you turn human, you freak."

Through a haze of sheer agony, I saw the others grinning as well, and they ratcheted up the voltage. In a last-ditch effort before passing out, I jabbed the needle into my thigh. Like lightning coursing through my veins, the strength, the power, the feeling of invincibility hit right away. *Crank it up!*

"Holy shit," one of the guards muttered in a sudden panic. "He's...growing."

Oh, yes, I most certainly was. The power surge was incredible, and with no effort at all, I threw off the AMA officers, sending them into the walls. I'd once seen a slow-motion movie of a car crash. The bodies snapped back and then forward. Heads hit the dashboards. Bones were shattered and-or driven into the body. If not the bones, then the metal from the car went right through the passengers, and the wounds were almost always fatal.

It was like that now, only no vehicles were involved, only me pushing full-grown men and women against the walls with enough force to literally pancake them. Blood sprayed from their bodies, and they collapsed in horribly twisted positions. Seven of them looked like pretzels, with their now-broken necks at a horrible angle to their bodies.

Two others dropped to the floor and writhed around in pain before falling still. Maybe they'd live. Only one man was conscious, Mr. Grin, the one who'd taunted me. He was the person I wanted.

I got up and grabbed him by his ugly uniform, lifting him off the floor with no difficulty. "Mister, I'm only going to ask you once. Where's Callie? Lie to me, and I'll tear your head off."

He glanced fearfully at the remains of his friends, and then gulped audibly. "She's on the fifteenth floor, room four."

"What's room four?"

Terror shone in his eyes. "It's where...where we keep and interrogate the prisoners. After that, they go to the sixteenth floor."

"What's there? Tell me!"

"The...the execution chambers."

He made me sick. I pulled the maggot closer so that he could smell the rage on my breath. "Why is she a prisoner? What's she done wrong?"

He could've said, "In our opinion, she broke the law." He might've said, "She didn't register." Both of those excuses were total bullshit, but they would've saved his life.

Instead, the grin he'd sported before returned. His answer came out softly and yet covered in venom. "Freaks deserve to be put down, just like rabid dogs."

At that, my vision turned red. Although I knew it was wrong, although I knew that killing him wasn't the answer, something inside made me lose self-control. I let go of him, clamped both hands to the side of his head, and crushed it. Blood and brain matter sprayed over my face and the rest of the room. He never had time to scream.

A moment later, a wave of nausea and self-loathing hit. The drug and my own anger had almost tipped me over into the realm of insanity. Breathing deeply, I resolved to stay in control. Scummy though he was, executing him had been wrong. Destroying the other guards had been wrong, as well. From that point on, unless it was absolutely necessary, I vowed not to kill anyone. I didn't want to become like the people I despised.

Let's get this done. With the concept of room four in mind, I charged up the stairs to the fifteenth floor, found no opposition along the way, and then located the room. Knock, knock...hell no.

Kicking down the door seemed the thing to do. To my right, seven capsules, like I'd seen in the execution video, held the captured enhanced people. Their eyes were closed, so either they were sleeping or dead. I couldn't tell which.

When I shifted my gaze to the left, one man stood next to a table with Callie lying on it. She still had her clothes on, but a small bandage was on the inner part of her right elbow. At my arrival, the man began to quiver in fear. Callie's eyes were closed, and I growled, "What did you do to her?"

"Nnn...nothing," he stammered out. "Someone gave her a sedative. She's just...just sleeping." His eyes pleaded for mercy.

"What about those people?" I pointed at the cylinders.

"They're sleeping, too."

I wondered. "Did you experiment on them? Or did your fearless leader already do that?"

His face went white. "My boss, er, Mr. Dornaught, he, uh, conducted the tests. He just asked me to watch over this person."

My anger rose at the sight of helpless people being readied for execution. With an effort, I controlled my rage. "Tell me about Project Juggernaut."

The man's eyes radiated confusion. "I...I don't know what that is. Please...I'm just a tech. I've only been with the AMA for a month. I don't know anything."

From the look on his face, as well as the readout from his eyes, he was telling the truth. "Leave now," I said, totally disgusted with these people and my own growing desire to maim someone. "If you leave now, I won't end you."

He ran out the door, and I gently patted Callie's face. Her eyes opened a fraction, then all the way in surprise. "Eli, is that you?"

"Hi." I couldn't think of anything else to say.

"How'd you find me?"

I told her about my encounter with Dornaught, his two-day waiting period, and his threat to kill her. At the end, she reached up with her hand to caress my face. "You're all bloody."

Oh, yeah. "I, uh, had a little accident."

There was a sink in the corner, so I went over and quickly washed the blood and gore off my face. My mirror image showed that I'd grown a good six inches, and my body had taken on the proportions of a super-heavyweight bodybuilder combined with an Olympic weightlifter, with ridiculously exaggerated size in my legs, shoulders, and arms.

Due to my increased size, my clothes were shredded and hung from my frame. Never mind how I looked, though. I was simply grateful that Callie was alive, and I went back to the table to help her off. "If you're ready, let's go."

Callie shook her head to clear it. "They did something to me. Dornaught said he'd altered my DNA."

Altered... "How?"

She got off the gurney and told me to stand back. Her body began to glow, and I felt heat coming from her. High heat...blistering heat. Abruptly, the heat shut off, and she breathed in and out deeply. "That. Gene therapy. He said it would activate a dormant gene inside me.

Now, I can radiate heat in excess of two hundred degrees Fahrenheit. Dornaught told me that I'd be able to do it right after he injected me with the DNA mixture he'd prepared. But I can't keep it up for long."

That's why that madman wanted her. He wanted her to give heat to her light. Someone like that unleashed on a populace would be almost unstoppable. "It's a useful power."

"If I see Dornaught again, I'll fry him," she said grimly. "What about them?" She pointed at the capsules.

Although I wanted to save the others, I couldn't. "I'm sorry, but we don't have time."

Reluctantly, we left, carefully checking out the sixteenth floor for any opposition—there was none—and then we went up to the roof. Once there, the effects of the super serum began to wear off. Callie confirmed it with the comment of, "You're, uh, shrinking. How do you feel?"

Truthfully, I felt exhausted, and my heart flip-flopped in my chest like a frog jumping from lily pad to lily pad. "Tired and hungry," I replied, longing for a sandwich or chocolate or anything edible. "I'll make it."

Callie then asked the obvious question. "How are we getting out of here?"

"We got a ride," I answered while scanning the skies. A black shadow passed overhead, and I called out, "Ravenna!"

At first, no answer came from the heavens, but then a hoarse voice from directly overhead said, "Coming."

The shadow rapidly descended, and I looked up just in time to see two huge talons come in our direction. They picked me and Callie up gently, as though we were newborn babies. "Hang on," Ravenna said. "I'll get you to the rendezvous point."

Exhausted, I relaxed in her grip. Her wings beat the air, and the ground passed beneath us in a mosaic of houses, buildings, and people pointing at the air and shouting.

After a quick five-minute flight, we landed in a wooded area just outside the city limits. There, a car waited. A man sat at the wheel, and he poked his head out the window. "Time to go," he said. "Hop in."

We didn't move. Why was the car there, and who was that person? Ravenna reverted to her human form. "Get in the car. You'll be safe with him."

I'd never seen this person before. "Uh, how can we know for sure?"

In answer, she gave me a tiny smile. "He's my husband. That's how. Get going, you two." To her husband, she said, "Later, babe. I need to stretch my wings. I'll see you at home." She then shifted and took to the skies.

Callie and I clambered into the back seat. As we drove off, the man turned around. He had a nondescript face, like pudding, but it shifted into a copy of mine, then Callie's, and then back to his almost-blank form again. Okay, that was useful. "Once we get to New York, if any AMA guys are there, I'll draw them off," he said. "I can look like anyone. You kids'll be fine."

"Thank you," Callie said. "It's dangerous for you, isn't it?"

A laugh came from the front seat. "I've done this before more times than you can count." He then spoke to us in a perfect copy of my voice and then my girlfriend's voice. "And my wife can fly fast, almost two hundred miles an hour, if she has to. Trust me, she'll be back in New York in a little over four hours. We'll be fine, and so will you."

While Callie and I sacked out in the back, he drove fast and sure.

THE CAR ROCKED GENTLY back and forth, and I must have passed out because a voice said, "Hey, you two, wake up. We're here."

I opened my eyes to find that the sun was just setting behind the horizon. We were at the edge of Royce Township. He'd been driving all this time. "Are we here?" Callie asked, yawning.

"Seems so," I said.

Our driver pulled out a smartphone from his pocket. After pressing a few buttons, he said, "Yeah, it's me. I got two packages." He then crushed the phone, saying that he'd get rid of it later on.

A few minutes later, we got to the road that led to the cabin, and he pulled over to the side and cut the motor. "This is as far as I go. You kids, be safe."

We got out and waved goodbye as he started the engine, reversed direction, and drove off, waving as he did so. Callie then took my hand and led me in the direction of the cabin—and safety. On the way there, she murmured, "Thank you for coming to get me."

"All in a day's work."

Chapter Fifteen: War On The Horizon

—— ⟡ ——

WAR WAS SOMETHING THAT no rational person should've looked forward to, but in the case of the US, China, and Russia, they were far from rational, and in their case, war seemed inevitable. Over the next week, news flashes dominated the airwaves, and whichever channel we turned to, it was a guarantee that the regular programming would be interrupted by an emergency broadcast.

Things were happening too fast. Before, it had been the occasional sniping here and there, acts of sabotage, but when the Russians started their invasion of Ukraine, the situation changed.

Apparently, it didn't scare the major power players in this scenario. Over the next ten days, Russia bombed the living daylights out of Kyiv and other major cities. They blew up key bridges and convoys of supplies...it seemed to go on forever. Moreover, the Russian soldiers didn't spare the citizens. In fact, they went out of their way to kill the innocent.

The reporters read out the death toll every morning, showing names and lists of the deceased on both sides, in addition to showing graphic video footage of the injured and the dead, many of the latter group blown apart. The toll on human life was horrific.

However, the outnumbered and bloody but unbowed Ukrainians emerged from the rubble and started their own offensive against the Russian armed forces, using drone tech to find their weakest positions and counterattack.

With help from the US, Great Britain, and the other allied powers, Ukrainian forces beat the Russians back. They also retaliated against their foe, bombing Moscow and Stalingrad. News footage showed the Russian citizenry crying, walking around like zombies, and complaining to the officials. "It's a stalemate," the newscasters said. "Perhaps it's all the Ukrainians can hope for."

Their assessment was shortsighted, at best. Attrition was the name of the game. Although the Ukrainians were formidable fighters, their numbers were limited, and Russia's leader seemed more than willing to sacrifice his people as long as he could claim victory. Victory for the Russians, though, seemed a faraway goal.

As for China, it had moved into the Taiwan Strait, threatening the island's shores. Four naval heavy cruisers stood ready, and China ignored the international community's warnings to leave or face the consequences. Consequences, though, happened, and in that case, six powerful bombs planted by divers blew up the ships, leading to a loss of over seven thousand sailors.

Naturally, both sides tried to play down the events, but the tensions ratcheted up, and China said that if the US didn't back off, they'd not only blow Taiwan up first, but then they'd also occupy what was left.

"Try it," President Anderson said. "Just try it."

Those were the words he used in the UN Security Council's emergency session. Ambassadors got recalled, epithets and threats were hurled, and tensions increased to the point where the president told every American to stockpile water and non-perishable items, medicine, and blankets, seek out the nearest fallout shelter, and pray for peace.

"Is this the onset of World War Three?"

My thoughts to the newscasters' ears. They voiced what I'd been thinking. They then said that peace was the only way. "We have to find a way to tone things down."

Right...toning things down didn't seem to be on the horizon. Even the US had suffered losses. Guam, a US protectorate, had been attacked by a Middle Eastern terrorist group. A message on the internet from the group said it was in retaliation for American aggressiveness in the Middle Eastern region.

A dawn raid by them killed over two hundred foreign tourists, seventy American citizens, and eighty-four service members. In turn, the terrorists, who numbered roughly a thousand, had been annihilated—every single one.

The US blamed Iran for the attack, and then Iran, in turn, blamed Israel. The Arab countries had always made it a rule to scapegoat the Israelis for their own failures, so why act any differently now? While the US had problems, those paled in comparison to the potential powder keg of the Middle East.

President Anderson gave a press conference after the terrorist group had been eliminated. "This is an outrage," he thundered. "Expect a response from us."

The US's response was to blow up three oil refineries in Iran, as well as bomb two military bases, which resulted in a loss of over two thousand people. Iranian officials screamed, and the US effectively thumbed its nose at them. That was asking for trouble, but the US had never been overly cautious about international affairs. For the government, it was a matter of drawing a line in the sand and daring the opposition to step over it.

Officially speaking, the major news networks pushed the pro-government line, but they had no clue as to what would happen. They talked about showing strength and mentioned the attacks on Iran, but they had no idea of what the response would be or how America would be affected.

"What's going on?"

That was the question asked by ordinary citizens when the government passed a law—in secret, naturally—allowing police and the AMA to examine the identification of every citizen in cities across our nation. While the authorities couldn't get everyone, they got what they wanted—a climate of fear. People stayed home or worked from home, department stores saw a forty-six percent drop in sales, and everyone simply stopped talking to each other.

J.S. FRANKEL

On the other hand, recruitment centers for the armed forces doubled across the nation. We hadn't had the draft in many decades, but Congress considered passing a law that made the draft mandatory. Patriotism, according to the newscaster bunch, was at an all-time high. That bill had been held up by the opposition.

Still, the young, the poor, and a lot of people who were on the edge, emotionally speaking, that is, signed up. Considering that the armed forces offered them a job, high pay, and an opportunity to blow something or someone up, they jumped at the chance.

But it wasn't that popular of a law. Citizens past the recruitment age resented it. "Who's going to protect us?" one middle-aged man asked when a reporter wanted his opinion. "That's what we're paying our taxes for, and they seem to be going into the pockets of the military and not for us. We need help."

News stations showed at least twenty quickie interviews a day from the east coast to the west. Very few of those interviews were positive. Another man, young, black, and with a t-shirt that read *Militant And Proud Of It* gave his views, and he didn't hold back. "Man, I went for a job interview, and they told me to join the army. Can you believe it? I'm a university graduate, but to them, I'm just another pair of boots on the ground. Is it too much to ask for a normal life?"

It was, at least, where the government was concerned. Other citizens' groups protested against the invasion of privacy. They railed against the ID checks, and they hired lawyers.

It didn't work, as the police showed up in force when the protests began, and they put the demonstrations down with extreme prejudice. In the AMA's hometown of Chicago, in Los Angeles, in Las Vegas, Dallas, Green Bay, Boston, and other major cities, riots broke out. They were small at first, then with greater force.

Callie and I watched the news with a sense of helplessness. "This is terrible," she said as we watched the police in Salt Lake City beat a crowd back with water cannons, clubs, rubber bullets...and then with real bullets.

In response, the citizens' groups fought back with homemade weapons and then with guns. Many of the enhanced came out of hiding and fought alongside the citizenry. It didn't work, as in the space of less than two days, over ten thousand people across the country died at the hands of the police. The police had their own enhanced personnel on duty. They were considered, as the AMA termed it, *Essential for crowd control*.

Pictures of grieving mothers, fathers, husbands, wives, and children flooded the news shows, and still the newscasters blamed the conflict on the enhanced who wouldn't join up with the AMA and their gang of ghouls. Callie watched the news with me, and she was just as appalled as I was. "Can't we help out, somehow?" she asked.

"Nothing we can do," I replied with a sense of resignation. "We have to hope that things calm down."

Call that wishful thinking at its most ridiculous. As for hope, that was for the eternally positive, those who only saw life through rose-colored glasses. I didn't want to lose hope, but as of that moment, it was hard for me to be positive in any way.

To take our minds off the domestic and international conflict, Callie and I trained in the gym, and we relaxed whenever possible. It wasn't easy, not with the threat of war looming over our heads. Wheels continued to work on his various projects, and the other enhanced came in to stay, those that survived, that is.

"Aren't you worried that someone will find out where we are?" I asked Wheels one day when he took a rare break and joined me in the gym. He was wearing his leg braces and implants, so he was able to walk around and do some light leg work in addition to working his upper body.

"I told you that this place was shielded, didn't I?" His response came out confidently, perhaps too much so.

Yes, he'd told me, but all the same, the AMA held formidable weaponry, as well as possessing outlandish tech, and what with surveillance drones and metal detectors and so on, they could easily find out where we were. After that…I didn't want to think about it.

"All right, question number two. Have you figured out what Project Juggernaut is?"

Wheels had been doing some slow leg extensions on a plate-loaded machine that doubled as a leg curl machine. An expression of muscular agony painted his face, twisting his features into a tortured grimace. He got to twelve reps, and then without a break, he flipped himself over onto his stomach and did some leg curls.

Once done, he leveraged himself to his feet and grabbed a couple of fifty-pound dumbbells to do some overhead presses. Those done, he dropped the dumbbells and took a seat on a nearby bench. Rivers of sweat ran down his face, and he panted as if he'd run up ten flights of stairs. "You okay?" I asked.

"Damn, I forgot how much that hurt." He heaved in a series of deep breaths and let them out slowly. "All right, Project Juggernaut. You know what the name means, don't you?"

A juggernaut was basically an unstoppable weapon, and…oh…the lightbulb went off. "He's going to combine the DNA of all of us to create a special weapon against…everyone. Isn't he?"

Wheels nodded. "That's what I figure they want to do. I can't hack into the AMA mainframe, no matter how much I try. But it stands to reason that the AMA—and the government—wants to create an unstoppable weapon to take on any enemy and destroy them."

"How? They didn't try to take my DNA. Dornaught could've taken it when he paralyzed me, but he didn't."

Our guardian swiped sweat from his face and then rubbed his chin in thought. "He took a DNA sample from Callie, as well as from the other enhanced. That's where they started. He also might not have been after you.

"But think about it. It's all about activating dormant powers. Eric could hurl fire. Callie told me about her power upgrades. She can harness the brilliance of the sun, as well as intense heat. The others had super speed and strength, even greater than yours. They just didn't have your near invulnerability. But maybe by activating dormant genes and then combining all those powers, they can achieve the same effect."

It didn't take a genius to see what they'd do next. With a sigh of pain, as well as regret, Wheels rose, shaking out his arms and shoulders. "They're going to build an army. Creatures with that kind of power can get into any installation, get past any kind of security, can defeat anyone, and can take anything they want. I have a feeling that the president has sanctioned this. He wants a war, and these creations of his—and Dornaught's—are their secret weapon."

Marvelous, we were up against an organization that was after world domination, and the irony was that it was our own government doing it. Wheels went to the door but paused at the entrance. "They may already have the formula, but we have to make sure that no one else gets it."

Chapter Sixteen: Taking It To The Man

OUR HIDEOUT. TEN-THIRTY PM.

A day after Callie and I came home, the news reports showed an angry, vindictive Dornaught as he gave a press conference in the ruined lobby of the AMA building. "Yes, we had a break-in," he said through gritted teeth to the reporters who thrust their mics at him.

"I thought your security was supposed to be the best around," one of the reporters said.

Dornaught glared at him. "There was...an oversight on our part. The prisoner, Callie Sanda, eighteen, and her accomplice, Eli Marks, also eighteen, are still at large. They slaughtered fifteen of my best soldiers, soldiers whom I tasked with defending this great city and country of ours. I shall not rest until both of them are in my grasp."

Notably, he said soldiers, not officers. Soldiers made it seem as though a war was about to be fought. He was wrong. The war had already started. It remained a matter of contention as to who would win it, though.

And what was with the slaughter remark? We'd beaten the living daylights out of his men, and, yes, I'd killed more than five people. I still regretted it, even though I'd been there to rescue my girlfriend. On the other hand, Callie hadn't killed anyone. It seemed that lying was another skill he'd mastered.

Worse, no one questioned the death toll. Whatever happened to investigative reporting? Obviously, when it came to the AMA, the truth went out the window—and the press held that window open.

One reporter asked Dornaught if there were any other enhanced personages at the building. "There were seven other prisoners," he confirmed. "They were liquidated two hours ago."

Liquidated. Such a nice term for killing people. Such a nice term for executing innocents. Dornaught continued, his manner calmer now. "I will admit that this was a setback, but our mission to make the US safe from these mutants will continue. I expect them to try again, and I hope they will. I invite them to try engaging us. Should they accept my invitation, they will *not* like our reception."

There it was—the dare. And in that moment of anger and frustration, I knew that there was only one option. We had to attack. And we had to do it now.

An hour later.

"First off, thanks for attending," Wheels said to the fifteen enhanced who'd assembled in our workout room. "Any trouble with your rooms?"

He'd offered sanctuary to our visitors. More had come in from various points around the eastern seaboard. Three couples took the remaining empty guest rooms, while the others used the workout area or the storage rooms to sack out in. "We're fine," one slender man said. "It's nice to have a place to stay."

Some wore uniforms, tight-fitting bodysuits that had seen better days in terms of wear and tear, while others wore civilian garb. But the one thing that stood out was the look of resignation on the faces of all those who'd come.

"Putting you up here is no problem," Wheels said. "But we have more important things to think about. We have to stand together, or else we get picked off one by one."

His words didn't make much of a dent in the group. If we went in, for many of us, it might turn out to be a one-way ticket, and we knew it. At the same time, this was a clear case of liberty or death, and we had to choose liberty. Wheels then asked me to speak. "Eli, they need to hear from you."

Public speaking was so not my thing, but if ever there was a time to step up, that time was now. Although my heart beat painfully against my chest, now wasn't the time to wimp out, so I took center stage to address the throng. "Guys, thanks for coming. My name's Eli Marks. Some of you know me, maybe, but I'm guessing most of you don't. I know this won't be easy, but like Wheels said, we have to take it to the AMA. Not the other way around. If we wait, then it'll be too late."

"It's already too late," one man said while playing with the vines that sprouted from his wrists and neck. "I came in from Baltimore. Had to sneak out at night, left everything behind." His voice rose in anguish. "Man, we're getting nailed one by one back home. AMA executed my two best friends four days ago. I don't want to be next."

Other people joined in, and I didn't blame them. Fear was the operative term here, and it was difficult to fight against. But somehow, we had to make a breakthrough. One man, short and slight, shook his head. "You're asking us to put our heads on the chopping block."

"All of our heads are on the chopping block," Callie said as she took her place beside me. "I was captured, Dornaught took some of my blood and skin, and he altered my DNA."

"Which means what?" someone asked.

"Which means I'm a lot stronger, now. But forget about that. When I was captured, only Eli came to help. No one else."

A look of shame appeared on the face of the man who'd spoken. "He can do that. I heard that he's a metal and wood shifter. I can only spray mist, and that's nothing special."

"What's your name?" I asked.

"Brian Sinden. Call me Smokescreen."

It seemed an apt nickname. "If you can hide us for a few seconds, that's enough."

The others nodded, so I asked what everyone else could do. One woman, roughly four feet in height and just about as round, with bulging purple eyes, said she could fly. As if by magic, wings, long and feathery, sprouted from her back, then disappeared inside her. "I'm a shifter. They call me Pigeon," she said. I had an idea of what she could unload, but it made me feel a little dirty.

Still, we were getting somewhere. Looks of determination replaced those of resignation. Callie squeezed my hand, and that gave me the impetus to go on. We had the people, and more importantly, we had a reason to do what we were going to do.

On the other hand, taking on Dornaught and his minions was a formidable task. He had his own army, and that counted for a lot. Moreover, he had his own array of weaponry that was equal to the power our group put out and probably more.

Plus—and this was the biggest thing of all—he wasn't afraid to kill. According to Wheels, Ravenna, and a few other enhanced, Dornaught was the kind of person who'd sacrifice thousands in order to kill just one person.

And he was most definitely after us. Still, some people asked us why we should bother going after Dornaught's hideaway. "He's already gotten his butt kicked once," one man said. "He'll be on guard now. And he's probably beefed up his security. How can you get past them?"

Silence fell after that, but Ravenna spoke up, addressing Wheels directly. "Larry, Eli's been inside, and so has Callie. I doubt that Dornaught's changed the layout of his place or beefed up his security that much in a few days. He's too damn arrogant, and that's what's going to screw him in the end."

Nods and mutters of agreement broke out. Wheels looked around as if gauging the pros and cons of it all, but finally, he bobbed his head in agreement. "All right, any ideas?"

After much discussion, we settled on a three-pronged attack. In the first wave, some in our group would draw off the guards, or at the very least, keep them occupied. That would give the second wave time to cause another distraction. "There's an empty apartment building next to their HQ," I said. "If someone started a fire or planted a bomb, it might distract the AMA soldiers."

Nods of agreement there, too. Our third wave would then enter AMA's headquarters, steal all the hard data possible, and then download any other computer data we could find. And we'd have to do it fast.

After that, we'd escape. The thing was, some of our people probably wouldn't make it home. "Be prepared for that," Wheels said with a somber expression. "I don't like saying it, but there is that possibility."

He then called the less enhanced people into his workshop, giving them the tools they needed. I went to my room and sat on my bed, thinking about how it would go down tomorrow and what our odds were. Without trying to be overly negative about it, I figured we had a fifty-fifty chance—fifty percent getting killed, and the other fifty percent being captured, which was just as bad.

But then came another mind shift. We had to do it. We had no other choice. While I was thinking things over, someone knocked on my door. I opened up to find Callie waiting. "I'm going with you," she said without preamble.

From the tone in her voice, I knew better than to argue with her. She walked in, shut and locked the door, and sat on my bed. What was happening here? "Are you sure?"

Callie gave me a sad smile. "Eli, do you know why I started dating you?"

In all the time I'd known her, she'd never told me. Not really, just something about me not being like everyone else...or maybe she had and I hadn't been listening, which made me the idiot of the century. "No."

With a note of earnestness, she leaned forward so that her forehead touched mine. "It's because of a lot of things. We're the same. I don't mean enhanced, but...I mean, like I said when we first met, you see me as a person. Other guys see me as an object.

"And we also like the same things. I feel comfortable around you. And, to me, it's very simple. I decided that I can't live without you. I know that's sort of cliché, but that's how I feel."

"But—"

"Look, if we go out tomorrow and take down Dornaught and his gang, if we die, then I think it should be together. I don't want to be without you—ever. That's what I came to tell you."

"Is that all?"

"No."

Her fingers started to undo the buttons on my shirt. *Oh.* "Uh, are you sure?"

"Shh. Don't talk," she murmured as her lips met mine.

I could do that.

The next day. Six AM.

We'd driven all night from the lair to Chicago, arriving early in the morning. From a spot just outside the city limits, our transportation waited, and we moved out to take our positions near the AMA building. Team one was in place.

Ravenna patrolled noiselessly overhead, and her husband was on the ground. Dressed in rags, impersonating a homeless person, he staggered past the entrance to the AMA building, waving his arm in a careless, drunken fashion, and yelling at the clouds. The guards, six strong and all armed, laughed.

Sure, they could laugh. They had the power, or thought that they did. But then one guard said in astonishment, "What the hell...that man...he looks like me."

Guard number two yelled, "No, he looks like me. We got a shapeshifter. He's a mutant. Get him!"

Ravenna's husband took off, sprinting away at high speed. Half the security detail chased after him, while the other three moved away from the building, glancing nervously in every direction. A moment later, a bomb went off to their left at a nearby abandoned restaurant, and the guards swung their heads in that direction.

Distraction number three came when Smokescreen stepped out from an alley and spread his arms wide. A fine grayish-blue mist shot out from his body, covered the area in front of the guards, and temporarily blinded them. "I can't see through this, damn it," one of the guards yelled.

His friends started coughing from the mist. *Bonus!* That was our cue, so I yelled, "All right, let's take it to them."

Callie and I led the charge. We held our breaths as we passed through the mist, and I shifted to wood to crash through the doors. Five other enhanced followed me in. Eight guards waited there, and we beat them down to the floor. Our crew carried satchels that contained bombs, which they planted at all four points around the room. "Twenty minutes," one of them said as he armed his device. "Then everything goes boom."

"We got a schedule to keep, guys," I said. "Get ready."

I checked the downed guards. One man was still conscious. "Numbers," I said, as I slapped his face over and over. "How many guards. Tell me now!"

"Screw you."

Well, I'd expected that. One of our crew, a woman barely five feet in height and wearing a long, loose robe, sauntered over. She hauled him up as easily as a child would lift a toy and pulled him close so that their faces were only a couple of inches from each other. "You look like you could use a hug."

The guard tried to wriggle out of her grasp. "Don't touch me, freak."

She smiled, but there was no humor in it, only vengeance. "They call me Porcupine, and if you don't want to find out what I can do, you'll tell us."

ESCAPE TO YESTERYEAR

He slapped her face. Her response was to pull off her robe. Underneath, she wore a bikini. She hugged him tightly, and a moment later, quills shot out from every point in her body except for her beach wear. Those incredibly sharp points pierced every square inch of his body. He collapsed and died in a bloody heap.

"Guess he doesn't like affection," she said with a certain degree of disappointment as she retrieved her robe and donned it.

I guessed not. Grossed out though I was, I steeled myself for the possibility of more death. "Up the stairs," I said. "Floor by floor."

We mounted the stairs, running up them steadily from floor to floor. Our team planted more bombs on every level. As before, we faced no one until we got to the top floor. Dornaught and six of his goons were waiting, though, weapons in hand, but I had the feeling that his men were packing a little extra power. "You can give up now, Eli," he said with a thin smile. "Give up now, and I promise we'll go easy on you. You as well, Callie."

"Tell me what you'll do with the rest, mister," I said, seething at his callousness. "How kind and gentle are you going to be?"

"Not very," he replied, stepping back so that his goon squad could have a clear field to shoot at us. "My offer extends only to you and your lady friend."

He then snapped his fingers. One of his men handed his gun to a colleague and stepped forward, morphing into a cross between a werewolf and something else that was even more fearsome. "Give up now," the creature growled.

Crap, it was Harvey Havoc. I didn't think we'd ever have to battle each other. At that moment, I wished that things could be different, but I knew they never could be. "Harvey, I don't want to fight you."

A savage grin crossed his face. "You don't have a choice, Eli. This is it."

Yes, this was it. I decided to meet the challenge and once more willed my body to wood. Metal would've been better, but if the

183

opposition had tasers, then I'd be less than useful. Harvey came at me, and I let my fingers grow into knives. He slashed at me with sharp claws, scoring gashes in my shoulders and chest.

Pain or not, I replied in kind, and when he grabbed me in a fearful embrace, my sharp digits sank into his torso—and out the other side. Harvey let out a mournful howl and sank to the floor, dead.

I so regretted doing what I'd done, but it was necessary. My next target was Dornaught, and I looked straight at him, ignoring the agony of my wounds. "Want to try your luck?"

A look of alarm spread over his face, and he snapped his fingers again. He and his men started to withdraw, but Callie yelled, "Close your eyes," and let off a blast of light.

Spots appeared in my field of vision when I opened my eyes again, but Dornaught and his buddies were down, writhing around and screaming about being blinded. My colleagues quickly knocked the guards out, and I grabbed the fearless leader and shook him—hard.

"Information time, Dornaught. Show us the files."

He let out an expletive, so I shoved a wooden middle finger through his left shoulder, and he screamed. "All right, all right, I'll show you!"

"Good answer."

With my finger still in his shoulder, he led us to where the death chambers were—now empty, thank goodness—along with the computer records. One of our crew grabbed the data discs, but there had to be more info on his computers.

With a bit of prodding—and another knife thrust through his other shoulder—he gave us the password. One of our crew, a man nicknamed Digital, input the password, then put his thumb on the keyboard. "I need to make contact with the computer," he said. "It won't take long."

A shiver ran through him, and he shuddered for a few more seconds after pulling his thumb away. "I got it. I'll get this to the people who need it."

He and the rest of the crew made their escape. Only Callie and I stayed. I let Dornaught go, and he cried with rage, saying that our lives were now forfeit. "You're dead, all of you," he screamed while crossing his arms to cover his injured shoulders. "Dead! And I will watch you die. Bet on it."

Callie smacked his face so hard that it put him on the floor. "Considering that you were going to kill me, I'll take that bet."

We left him, then, and at the door, I turned to face Fearless Leader. "We planted bombs. If you don't want to go down with your building, you'd better leave in the next ten minutes. We're taking the stairs. I guess you've got another way out."

Out we went, and no one opposed us. I wanted to check if any of the enhanced were kept prisoner, but we didn't have the time. "About seven minutes left," Callie said nervously as we reached the third floor. "We'd better hurry."

We hurried. The lounge was empty, but as we walked outside, six guards stood ten feet away with their guns up and in firing position. I couldn't shift, and Callie said that she wasn't ready to blast them with another sun spot or her heat beams. "Oh, the mutants are here," one man said as he smiled, probably dreaming of a raise or a night out drinking. "Guess what's coming?"

A rainfall of gray pigeon poop covered them in a thick blanket answered his question. Pigeon flew past us, yelling, "Leave now!"

She didn't have to tell us twice. We ran and managed to get five blocks away before a series of dull booms signaled the end of the AMA building, and with it, the end of Dornaught's reign of terror...or so I hoped.

Chapter Seventeen: The Last Hunt

———— ⟨∽⟩ ————

SOMETIMES, HOPE WAS all a person had. After our caper, we returned to our lair and celebrated. Those who drank, imbibed freely. Those who smoked lit up and enjoyed the taste of tobacco, but since Callie and I did neither of those things, we went to the kitchen, which had been declared a smoke-free zone, and chowed down on some fried chicken and spaghetti that one of the members had cooked.

My wounds from Harvey healed quickly, and the next morning, Callie and I woke early to check the news, only to find that we faced a greater threat. Dornaught had not only survived, but he'd also contacted the president and gotten his approval to use any and all force needed to take us down.

We viewed the press conference in silence. Dornaught stood outside the ruined building. His already thin face was haggard, and he sported two thick bandages wrapped around his shoulders. "It's no secret that our headquarters was attacked yesterday," he began in a deceptively quiet voice. "The invaders took confidential data, destroyed the complex, and killed more than twenty of my men. The others are recovering from inhaling...bird guano."

Everyone looked at Pigeon, who shrugged. "I guess I gave them an extra heavy dose."

It was funny, but at the same time, it wasn't. The interview with Dornaught continued with the interviewer asking him if the president was going to continue his crusade against the enhanced. The AMA leader's eyes bugged out. "What kind of idiotic question is that? Of course, we're going to continue hunting down and executing those traitors."

His left eye began to twitch, and flecks of foam appeared at the sides of his mouth. I expected him to jump up and down like a spoiled, sadistic child. Sure enough, he did. There was losing it, and then there was already-lost-it. Dornaught fell into the latter category, and he screamed into the camera, "They're dead. Dead, do you hear me? We're going to go into every house, every apartment, every nook and cranny to hunt these freaks down. We have branches all over the country, we have the personnel, and we're..."

Wheels switched off the television. "So that's the good news, kids. We're going to have to lay low."

As we mulled his answer over, one visitor asked, "Can they do that? I mean, go door to door and search?"

Our leader shrugged. "If they have the manpower, maybe. They already started checking IDs. The government isn't going to fight them, and the police will probably help them, so...maybe."

Callie waved her hand for attention. Everyone's gaze turned to her. "I doubt they have the manpower to check every resident in New York. The real problem is that they're creating a composite super soldier."

"Online comic book crap," someone muttered.

A few people laughed, but Wheels raised his hands for silence. "No, Callie's right. She had her DNA taken. My guess is that every other enhanced person captured by the AMA had their DNA sampled as well. Mix and match...that's the name of the game, and they can do it."

His mini-speech cast a somber note into our conversation. "What do we do?" someone asked.

Good question, and Wheels gave the most logical answer. "We wait. If Dornaught and his gang of ghouls manage to create a composite killer, then my guess is that he'll test it on the civilian populace. He'll do that to draw us out and get us to commit to a fight."

Someone asked if we could win against a monster like that. Our members were strong, we all had powers at various levels, but against someone who had all our powers...that was another story. We'd have to wait and see.

The next day. Noon.

We didn't have to wait very long. One of the crew yelled from the lounge, "Hey, news flash, guys. Something's going down in Central Park."

We gathered around the television to watch a livestream. Six news crews had gathered around Central Park to update everyone on an ongoing story. Moira Mathers, a short and perky redhead in her early thirties, breathlessly supplied the narrative. "We're here in Central Park where a monster appeared only minutes ago. It immediately savaged over twenty people, tearing them to pieces. We warn viewers that the footage you're about to see is disturbing."

Well, at least they'd warned us. A switch to another camera revealed body parts strewn all over the immediate area, and blood streaked the grass. Police officers were firing at a white, naked figure that stood over seven feet in height and was powerfully built. It had no genitals.

Perhaps it didn't need them. Bullets had no effect on the creature, and it moved quickly to take out officer after officer, smashing them into the ground or rending them limb from limb. It was horrifying, and the carnage wasn't over yet.

"What *is* that thing?" someone asked.

"Dornaught's creation," Wheels said in a toneless voice while staring at the screen. "He's further ahead than I thought."

Ravenna asked why Dornaught hadn't let the monster loose in Chicago. Wheels shrugged. "He's after Callie and Eli. He knows they're in New York. That's why."

"Nice to be wanted," Callie cracked, and a few people laughed, even though this was no laughing matter.

Moira the reporter went on to ask why the National Guard or the armed forces hadn't come to help out. "And where is the AMA? If they're here to defend us against these mutants, then why are they hanging back? We need help!"

No, they needed to leave, and the monster rushed Moira's position, smashing her news van flatter than a pancake, and then flattening Moira in a frightening burst of blood and mangled flesh. She never had a chance to scream. Her cameraman caught all the action until he, too, fell under the creature's assault. The other news people quickly moved out of range.

"Well, what do we do?"

That came from Wheels. Everyone looked at each other. On the one hand, we'd made an unspoken vow to defend the ordinary citizenry, even though they didn't trust us or even hated us. Not all of them, though, but at least half, by my count.

On the other hand, this was what Dornaught wanted. He wanted us to come out and help, either to capture us or watch us get killed, whichever came first. No one said anything, but Ravenna tapped me on the shoulder. "You need a lift? I can get you and Callie there in a few minutes." She smiled, as if looking forward to the battle.

"I'll go," I said and turned to my girlfriend. "You up for this?"

"Not really," she answered, and her eyes held uncertainty. However, the determination came out in her voice. "But we have to stop this thing."

We headed toward the door, and the group called out collectively, "Wait!"

I turned around. Ravenna's husband—his real name was Harold Frankel—Smokescreen, and a few others who had strength or speed said that they'd come with us. Pigeon said she'd fly ahead and scout out the area. Wheels went to his workshop and grabbed one of his power disruptor guns. "Only one shot," he said as he handed it to me. "Make it count."

I wasn't sure if it would work on that monstrosity, but I'd try. We all headed out to face the worst of the worst, and I prayed that we'd all get back safely.

Fifteen minutes later. Central Park.

Ravenna dropped us from a height of ten feet at the edge of the park, and we hit the ground running. The monster was in the process of eating one of the reporters—who was still alive and screaming for someone to save him. Too late, as the monster crunched down on his head, and...gone. It then tossed the remains of the reporter away and turned on us.

On television, it looked horrible. Up close, it looked even worse. Its right eye was normal, while its left eye was halfway down its cheek and triangular in shape. It was also red and weeping blood.

As for its body, yes, the composites were there. The right arm was a mallet, and its left hand morphed from hammer to flipper every few seconds. Its body shifted from flesh to rubber every few seconds...rubber? I didn't know anyone who could do that.

But what got me was its ferocity. It had gone after anything that moved with a savagery that I didn't think was possible. It was also mindless, as it alternately grunted and screamed incoherently, swinging its arms around.

Callie backed off. I handed her the power inhibitor, went steel mode, and rammed into the monster at full speed. It didn't help much, as it seemed to absorb the blow and sent it back at me in a shockwave that threw me more than twenty feet from the action. *Rubber...I should've figured that out.*

When I got up, my body tingled all over, but I shook it off and got ready. The creature had turned its attention to our crew. At first, they hung back, not sure of what to do. Then they went to an all-out charge, managed to get the creature on its back...and a second later, they got tossed hither and yon, landing in messy piles far from the scene.

The police moved in again, shooting the monster, but the bullets simply bounced off. The monster then jumped high in the air, landing on two unlucky officers who couldn't move in time, and squashed them. The impact of its feet on their bodies made a loud splat sound, and the rest of the officers moved off, still shooting.

"You okay?" Callie asked when she came over.

"Getting there," I said, thinking fast. "We don't have much time. It seems to absorb anything we toss at it."

Callie stepped forward. "Let me take a shot at it." She called for everyone to step back, and when the creature came at her, her body began to glow, and a sheet of flame emanated from her and enveloped the creature. It immediately caught fire and screamed in pain, but it still kept coming. While doing so, it dropped and rolled, putting out the flames.

"I gotta...gotta sit down," Callie said as she shifted back to normal. "A quick break, that's all. What can stop rubber?"

I wasn't sure, but...wait. I had an idea. "Ravenna," I called out.

She flapped her way over and landed near us. "Bad day," she said, grimacing at the monster that was still trying to kill the world. "What's on your mind?"

I couldn't disagree. "How high can you fly?"

"My limit's thirty-thousand feet."

I wasn't sure if it would work, but... "I have an idea. Get ready."

Ravenna took to the sky, circling overhead. For its part, the monster jumped around forty feet in the air, trying to get at her. It didn't succeed, and it bellowed its rage at her and the world. One of the police officers, his face covered in fear-sweat, asked me, "Kid, are you part of this mutant crew?"

Mutant...that figures. "We're enhanced, mister. What do you want?"

An annoyed look flashed across his face, and then he heaved a sigh. "Listen, we need help."

Fine, we'd help. "Then back off and let us do our thing."

The officer immediately yelled for his men to evacuate the area, and I called out, "Smokescreen, over here."

He came on the run, gasping out, "What?"

"When I give you the word, bring the mist."

"Got it."

Next, I turned to Callie. "When Smokescreen covers that thing, do you think you can light it up again?"

A grin appeared on her face. "I'll try."

I called up to Ravenna, "Get ready!"

"On it," she replied.

"Smokescreen, you're up," I said, shouting at the monster, "Hey, ugly, over here!"

Immediately, the creature turned, grunted, and charged us, its skin smoking. Smokescreen stepped forward, and a cloud of mist emanated from him. He then ran for his life, while the monster began coughing. It soon adapted, and when the smoke cleared, I aimed the inhibitor gun and shot the creature, hoping that the energy charge would short out its powers for a while.

It worked, or seemed to, as the blast caused the creature to stumble and fall. "Now, Ravenna, now," I yelled. "Grab that thing feet first and take it for a ride!"

She swooped down, gripped his feet with her talons, and shot into the air, climbing higher and higher until she and her cargo were lost to sight. Silence fell. We waited...and then a horrid scream came from the heavens.

"Was that Ravenna or the monster?" Smokescreen asked.

I wasn't sure, but as I looked up, a white object appeared in the sky. It was the creature, and it smashed into the ground, exploding into a mess of mangled flesh and bone. Shortly thereafter, Ravenna spiraled down from the heavens and landed near us, panting heavily. "Damn thing...fought me all the way...got him, though."

Her legs were heavily scratched and bloody, but she was otherwise undamaged and seemed to be in good spirits. She shifted back to human form and nodded at us before limping over to a car where her husband waited. A few of the bystanders applauded, and I hadn't heard that kind of goodwill sound for a long time.

Still, we had to leave, so Callie and I disappeared into the bushes and clicked on our holograph devices. We emerged as our female personas, and soon, we bypassed the crowd that had gathered and found ourselves alone.

"So, what now?" Callie asked. "Hitch a ride home?"

A honk of a car's horn made us turn around. It was Ravenna's husband. "Eli, Callie, you girls need a lift anywhere?" His wife was asleep in the front seat.

I wondered how he knew it was us. Asking him, he replied, "Wheels told me all about the holograph projectors. Get in and let's motor."

Our journey back was uneventful, and once inside the safety of the lair, Callie and I collapsed on the couch in the lounge and passed out. Just before the blackness came up to catch me, I hoped that the news about us, if there was any, would be positive.

Chapter Eighteen: The Final Countdown, Part One

THE NEWS REPORTS THE next day were all positive.

Mutants Take Down Monster.

Are These The New Breed?

Call Them Heroes...

Yes, all those headlines in the papers and online were positive, even though they still referred to us as mutants. But that positivity was undercut by the reality that Dornaught and his science crew would undoubtedly try again, next time with something upgraded and similarly enhanced. We'd barely won the first time. I wasn't looking forward to the rematch.

Wheels agreed with me when I voiced my concerns. "I'm worried, too. Dornaught isn't stupid. Now that he and his scientists know what the weaknesses are, they'll try to fix their mistakes. They're into building the perfect soldier, not only for taking over here, but also for taking over the rest of the world. Be ready, just in case."

I had a question about that. "By you telling us to be ready, does that mean you still want us to go out and help?"

He raised his hands in a gesture of helplessness. "I can't tell you what to do, but if you leave, there's no guarantee that you'll make it through. I've rigged up some more holograph projectors, but they aren't a sure thing, either. That goes for anyone else who stays here. If they live in Manhattan or elsewhere, there's nothing I can do if things get out of hand."

HIS WORDS PROVED PROPHETIC, as over the next couple of days, reports on television showed more and more monsters showing up in Chicago, Los Angeles, and the other major cities. "We need to know where the AMA is and what their response is to this creature," the newscasters said, this time with the worry evident in their voices. "Are they responsible for this?"

Darn right they were. But the AMA was running the show with the government's blessing, and there didn't seem to be much anyone could do about it. Citizens' groups begged for help, local politicians begged for help, and so did the police in every city. Their pleas fell on deaf ears. The federal government wasn't listening.

Eventually, though, the president called in the National Guard, and they did their best to stem the tide. But they couldn't do much. Monsters roamed the land, killing and savaging anyone who got in their way. The morgues were filled to overflowing with the dead. The hospitals couldn't keep up with the number of injured. Our members who lived in different cities went out and fought, even though Wheels messaged them and begged them not to get involved.

But get involved they did, and they paid for it. The newscasts showed the death toll, specifically, our kind. Those enhanced who'd stayed with us went out to fight. Smokescreen and Porcupine went out to Green Bay, Wisconsin, and they died at the hands of one of the monsters. So did the vine guy, whose name I never got.

Pigeon also lost her life in a battle over Detroit, as one of the creatures jumped her when she swooped in too low, and it crushed her. Only a well-aimed RPG from a National Guardsman brought the monster down.

Sixteen more enhanced in Los Angeles, Boston, St. Paul, Minnesota, and in Portland. They all gave their lives so that others could live. In the end, there were only a handful of us left. Fear was in the air. The ordinary citizenry voiced it. The police voiced it as well, and weren't they the hypocrites?

After all, they'd supported the AMA from day one, but when their butts were on the line, they were like little children running to their mother. Callie was brave beyond reproach, but she asked me one day, "Are we next?"

I held her tightly. She'd moved in with me, and we sought solace in each other's arms at night. It was a difficult time for us, and Wheels felt the pressure grow, as well. Ravenna and her husband stayed away for their own safety, while Wheels busied himself with his inventions and rarely spoke. Work was his way of coping with the horror of reality, and I envied his single-minded obsession.

After ten days of carnage had passed, a broadcast brought more bad tidings. The killings had stopped here, but in Russia and China, reports surfaced of monsters savaging the local populace, as well as their country's armed forces.

"They've gone and done it," Wheels said with a sense of resignation. "AMA's perfected their killing machines. Now, nothing can stop them."

It seemed to be that way. In the space of a mere forty-eight hours, the creations destroyed six weapons depots in Russia, killed four thousand soldiers plus two thousand civilians, and wreaked havoc before mysteriously vanishing. "How did those monsters suddenly disappear?" I asked Wheels shortly after the death toll for Russia had been announced.

We sat in the kitchen, him drinking coffee, and me with a can of cola. He put his cup down and rubbed his chin, then slowly shook his head. "I don't know. Perhaps...perhaps Dornaught designed them to break down at the cellular level. Or perhaps he enhanced their ability to disappear. Darkslayer could vanish for up to an hour. Maybe those creatures can do it longer. I don't know. Anyway, there are other issues out there that the Russians and the Chinese have to deal with."

He was right. While the Russians lost many people, China fared even worse. Its leader often boasted about his country's army, its power, and its numbers. AMA's monsters tore through their ranks at light-speed, and in that same forty-eight-hour period, a combined fifteen thousand soldiers and citizens lost their lives.

The leaders of Russia and China initially blamed each other, and then they turned on the US. Our president's response was that he knew nothing of what was going on, and instead, he blamed insurgents. "America grieves with you," Anderson said from the White House. "But we will not accept any of the blame for the loss of life in your countries. I would suggest that you talk to your own people first. Many of them are dissatisfied with the system of government. Perhaps it would be best to look inward."

Said in a taunting tone, the Russian and Chinese delegates to the UN, long an impotent body, withdrew their countries' memberships. Good riddance, the American online newspapers, talk shows, and pundits said. Now that the immediate danger to the populace was over, they'd decided that a little swagger was in order.

"Are we headed toward a world war?"

That question resurfaced. Tensions were at an all-time high. President Anderson told the public to prepare for the worst, but he also said that he had the matter well in hand. Oh, yes, he most certainly knew what was going on with Project Juggernaut, but good luck in getting anyone to believe it. We had the files on AMA, but there was no information on the project. Everything had been kept off the books.

Moreover, the government would never admit to anything. Plausible deniability was the catchphrase, and President Anderson had to be laughing over these developments.

FOUR DAYS PASSED. WARSHIPS from every country sailed the seas, guns pointed at their supposed enemy. American bombers flew near Chinese and Russian air space. Insults flew thick and fast over the internet. The world seemed to be on the verge of imploding and then exploding.

Our compound was the sole island of peace and tranquility, but as Callie prophetically put it, "It can't last forever."

And...it didn't. A day after her pronouncement, a shrill alarm went off early in the morning, jangling my senses. Callie and I got out of bed, pulled on our clothes, and ran to the workshop where Wheels was cursing the images on his monitor. "We got drones," he said. "Somehow, they found out where we are."

Drones were one thing. The chatter of the machine guns outside sounded as they picked off the drones one by one, but white, horrid, and massive shapes appeared out of nowhere. "It's them," Wheels said in alarm as he armed himself. "The AMA's found us."

Outside, the budda-budda sound of bullets rapidly firing started up again, and two of the creatures fell. However, there were six others, and they seemed unfazed by the bullets and bombs.

And speaking of bombs, charges went off around our compound. They weren't from enemy bombers, but from the AMA soldiers who'd planted them. The explosions took out the defenses Wheels had set up, and the shock waves traveled through the ground, rattling things around. I didn't know whether to be terrified or angry. Both worked for me.

What I wasn't ready for were the screams of the manufactured monsters. High and shrill, they jangled our nerves. The sounds of bombs going off was bad enough, and the heavy pounding noise of drills made things worse.

"Whoever's out there, they're using some kind of machine to smash into the earth," Wheels said. "Let's get to the portal."

As we made our way downstairs, something large and powerful went off outside, and another shockwave, stronger than the previous ones, threw us off our feet. A moment later, another explosion and subsequent shockwave hit, tossing me and Callie over a nearby table.

We got to our knees slowly, and Wheels walked in, wearing his leg braces. Once he checked on the console, he let out a curse. "I can't reroute the power from the power station to this complex. We're screwed."

"Yes, you are," a voice said from behind us.

As one, we turned around, only to find that Dornaught had entered the complex. How the hell had he known where we were? He held what looked to be a large taser gun in his right hand, and it never wavered. It was like he'd been expecting this to happen.

"Don't worry. I'm not going to kill you—yet." In a quick move, he shot Wheels, then Callie, and then me, before I could shift. As my senses shorted out, I saw the grinning faces of Dornaught, fifteen of his men, and the blank visages of three of the monsters. Then the blackness took over.

Chapter Nineteen: The Final Countdown, Part Two

WHEN I WOKE UP, CALLIE lay beside me. Was she...no, her chest was still moving. I patted the side of her face, and she soon came around and asked groggily, "What...what happened?"

"We got invaded," I told her as we slowly sat up. I checked my holograph watch. It was ten PM, and a glance around the room showed that the lights were still on. "We've been out for around fifteen hours."

I looked at the portal machine—wrecked. And Wheels was gone. Aw, hell, that was it. Game over. "They took Wheels and wrecked the gateway gizmo."

Callie's face fell, and I tried not to cry from the sheer frustration of it all. "What now?" my girlfriend asked as she threw her arm around my shoulder.

I had no idea outside of going to Chicago, but how would we get there, and with whom? Our forces were scattered, and...

"Hello?" That voice sounded familiar. I got up and went to the ramp, picking my way through the rubble. Ravenna, her husband, and Rat were there, glancing around. "We, uh, wanted to come in and help," she said. "What happened?"

I gave her the details, and after I was done, she turned to her husband and Rat as if telepathically asking them for their cooperation. They nodded, and she pivoted around to face me as Callie came over to stand by my side. "All right, we're in," Ravenna said. "What's the plan?"

Plan? Why was she asking me? "We don't have a plan. Wheels is gone, and Dornaught's got him. We have to find him, but he could be anywhere."

"Does the computer still work?"

We searched through the rubble to find a working laptop, and fortunately, we located one. "What am I looking for?" I asked.

"The information download from Digital, remember?" Ravenna answered. "Dornaught's headquarters was destroyed, but he probably had other places in reserve."

After I connected the computer to the modem, I fired things up and searched the files. There were a double-dozen places listed. Some of them might have been homes for the gestation chambers, while others were probably storage facilities. I couldn't tell which one.

"Any luck?" Rat asked.

Not really, but then I remembered that the gateway device needed a lot of power. If Dornaught had built one, as Wheels had said he might do... "Are there any power stations between here and Chicago?"

Harold waved his hand for attention. "Yeah, there's one. The government built a nuclear power station just outside of Youngstown, Ohio. It already had electrical power stations, but the nuclear one is new."

All right, we were onto something. Another memory surfaced, and I started typing. Ravenna glanced at the computer and then at me. "What are you doing?"

"Wheels said that he could monitor the output of any station on the eastern seaboard," I replied, my eyes fixed on the screen. "He had a password..."

I typed in the command, and a series of graphs leaped up. Everyone grouped around the laptop. Every graph in every major city on the eastern seaboard showed the output as of that moment. "Youngstown, Ohio," Ravenna said while pointing at the screen. "That's showing the most power output. It's really high." She turned to her husband. "Harold, you're a genius."

He bobbed his head. "I try."

All right, we had a location. "How far is it from here?" I asked.

"About a six-hour drive," Harold replied, tapping the side of his head. "If Ravenna flies it, maybe less than two hours."

"What about the plan?" Callie asked. "Getting there is one thing, but, I mean, we can't make a frontal assault, not like last time. They'll be ready."

Rat stepped forward, his eyes bright. "Not from below, they won't."

Below? Oh...

Ravenna clapped him on the shoulder. "Good thinking. Rat and I will fly ahead, and he can scout out the place. Harold, drive the kids over, will you?"

Her husband gave a deep bow. "At your command."

For that, he got a kiss, and after she shifted into bird mode, she grasped Rat gently in her talons and flapped her way out. Callie asked Harold to wait. "I have to get changed."

My clothes were torn and dirty as well. Callie led me over to a side room. "What's here?" I asked.

"Something Wheels made up."

The room was smashed, but some furniture was still intact. Callie searched through the dressers, finally giving an excited, "Yes!"

She turned around holding two bodysuits, one red and one blue. They looked like Olympic bobsled costumes. Oh, yeah, I'd seen the cloth earlier on. Wheels was truly multi-talented.

"These are fireproof," Callie said as she took the red one for herself. "And they'll stretch when you shift."

Right. We got dressed and met Harold at the entrance, where he led us to his car and told us to get in the backseat. "You two rest," he said as he fired up the engine. "I'll wake you when it's time. I never sleep."

Callie and I relaxed, and soon, stress or not, the darkness came up to get me.

Some hours later.

"We're here."

The voice was Callie's, and a hand shook my shoulder. I started awake. "Where's here?"

Harold had turned around in the front seat to face us. "On the outskirts of Youngstown. We made good time. Let's go."

We got out. Time...I checked my watch. It was five-fifteen in the morning, cool, and all was quiet. We'd stopped at the edge of the highway. "What now?" I wondered.

Flapping wings overhead answered me. Ravenna circled down and landed in front of us. "We've been waiting. Rat found a way in. Let's move it."

Fortunately, the streets were empty as she led us to a manhole. "That's our ticket in."

"I'll do the honors," I said as I morphed my fingers into metal claws and yanked off the cover.

A horrid smell of sewage hit my nostrils right away, and I recoiled. Callie did the same. Ravenna chuckled. "Yeah, it stinks. C'mon. We're not that far away."

We descended one by one into the sewer. Rat met us on the ledge, and he gestured to his left. "They have guards up top, but no one down here. Follow me. We're about two hundred yards from the place. There's a warehouse not too far from the power station. This sewer goes directly to the place."

Well, well, we'd struck the motherload, and he led the way along the narrow ledge to a ladder. "We're behind the warehouse," he whispered. "I took a look before. It's clear."

Up the ladder we went, and when we emerged, it was in an alley. But that wasn't the worst part. The roar of jet engines overhead signaled that the enemy had found us. A whistling sound forced us to duck for cover. It got louder...and the bomb exploded somewhere fairly close to us, as the impact tossed us off our feet. "Is the war here?" Harold asked.

"Seems to be," Callie said with alarm after glancing fearfully at the sky. "We'd better hurry."

Speed was the operative word. I morphed my arms into metal hammers, but before I could do anything, a voice from behind us said, "Hold it."

En-masse, we turned around and found ten guards with their guns up. "I've got this," Callie said and let loose a wall of flame that seared them to a crisp in a nanosecond.

Once her powers cut out, she bent over and vomited. "I really...really didn't want to do that," she said between retches.

"You did what you had to do," Ravenna said while patting her back. "Eli, you do what you have to do, too."

Cue me, and I smashed through the wall, only to find ourselves in a vast room where another portal device similar to the original had been set up. It was a little smaller, the console was different in its external layout, but I had no doubt that this version worked.

Callie had recovered, and we took the lead, with our friends standing near the improvised exit. I whispered over my shoulder, "Hang back. Don't get hurt."

As we advanced, I saw Wheels lying next to the console, his face a mask of blood. Dornaught stood near him with a gun pointed at us. Six of his men stood in a line, machine guns at the ready. Good ol' Dornaught, he just had to bring backup. "Did you miss us?" I asked.

"Hello, Eli, Callie," he said in a most genial manner. "I knew you were smart enough to figure out where I'd be. So good of you to join us. Tell me, are my men outside still alive?"

"No," Callie answered with supreme distaste. "Barbecue meat."

Dornaught shrugged as if to say that's how it was. "I expected that. However, I have a backup plan, and this it." He gestured at his droids. "My men are going to kill all of you shortly, but there are some things that you should know first."

For a few seconds, time stopped, and then the whistling of another bomb and the subsequent explosion told us that we were far from safe. Dornaught's manner was still pleasant despite the danger, although his subordinates glanced up in fear. "I suppose you have some questions. As you've no doubt heard, the bombers are already here. Things are going to get very bad. Still, we have a little time."

I asked him the obvious question. "How'd you find us in New York?"

Dornaught wore a smile of triumph, the smile of someone who held all the cards and couldn't wait to show us his winning hand. "Do you remember when I paralyzed you in that alley?"

"Yes." It was then that I realized how clever he'd been and how stupid I was. Guilt hit, although I knew that it hadn't been my fault. "You put a tracking device inside me, didn't you?"

Dornaught bowed his head as if in recognition of my deduction. "Infinitesimal in size, it lodged in your liver, sent out a signal that we picked up on, and it led us to you. As for letting you take the data from our former headquarters, getting in and out was quite easy, wasn't it?"

Yes, after thinking it over, it had been easy...too easy. "You let us, didn't you?"

He nodded. "I even let you work me over, just to make things look good. My men could've put up more of a fight, but I wanted to see how much backup you'd bring, and you did. Same deal with letting my monsters loose. I had to gauge your team's strength, so a little pain was worth it."

Dornaught had played me all along. And now, since he had the firepower to support him, there wasn't much we could do. I could shift, but Callie couldn't. And even though her heat powers worked, he'd shoot her before she could do anything. I pointed at the machine. "Is this your version of the portal device?"

A smile wreathed his face. "It is. We'd already taken the basic design from Larry when we previously caught him, but our scientists thought that they could improve on the original. I have to say that it's a most marvelous invention. We've been working on something like this for years, but we never could nail the interdimensional equations down. Tell me, have you been to other Earths?"

"Yes."

Dornaught lost his smile, and his eyebrows arched so high they almost met his hairline. "Is that so? I'd love to visit one of them. In fact, that's where I'm going to go, along with my men. We have the plans, and we can make things work wherever we go. We'll recruit others to our cause. Oh, it'll take time, but it can be done."

Dornaught's expression changed from semi-thoughtful to one of determination. "However, we can only do that if we have the code. I asked Larry if he'd give it to us. The only thing he did was tell us that the machine would work, but as for the necessary equations, no...so I shot him."

Glib bastard. He'd shot Wheels like someone would step on an ant. Dornaught added, "Don't worry, he isn't dead—yet. He will be, though, if he doesn't give me what I want. The power's on, but without the necessary input, I can't make things happen."

The bombing started again. An ear-splitting whine, another shockwave, and another upending of our footing. The enemy was finding their range, and after a few seconds, one more bomb hit. The walls quivered, but they didn't fall.

"Dornaught, we have to leave," Callie pleaded and pointed at the portal.

"Yes, we do. And you're going to help me."

What a coward. All this time, he'd pretended to be this fearless leader for the AMA, but when danger called, he was the first to run. "I thought you were stronger than that," I said. "You're running."

Madness shone in his eyes. "I'm not stupid. The war has already begun. Those bombs outside? They're just regular bombs. Still quite destructive, but when both sides figure out that the war isn't going their way, then it's time to get nuclear. Diplomacy is over. It's got no meaning, not anymore. This is the final conflict."

Yes, he was quite mad...insane, in fact. No one could be that nihilistic, but he'd managed to achieve that dubious honor. "You wanted this to happen. You, the president...the cabinet...you wanted war."

Dornaught laughed again, a totally incongruous sound, considering how dire our situation was. "Let's just say that our president isn't against the concept. Reports differ on who started it. The other side says we precipitated things, and we say it's them. In the end, it doesn't matter. The Chinese bombed Taiwan, and they're going to invade Mongolia and Japan. Fine, they can have those countries.

"As for the Russians, they're bombing us and Canada, and that means our air force is probably bombing them as we speak. I'm also quite sure that our missiles are blowing up the Kremlin. It'll be a hot time in Moscow tonight! Oh, and we've dispatched a few nukes to mainland China, just in case. Sayonara!"

I decided not to tell him that sayonara was a Japanese word. It didn't matter anymore. This was what it had come to. MAD had finally come to pass, and Dornaught was crazy enough to want it to happen.

He leveled the gun at us. "And you're not going anywhere. Only my soldiers and I are going. We just need the code to open the portal, and then we're gone. This world can go to hell, and it probably will."

His finger twitched, but a weak cough caused him to stop. It was Wheels, and he leveraged himself to a sitting position. "All right, I'll help."

"You can't..." Callie began.

"No choice. Input these numbers."

Dornaught waved her over to the console. "Do as he says."

Wheels gave her the code, and she pressed the buttons. A portal opened, and our captor grinned at us. "This is where we part." He turned to his men. "Double time, team. We're leaving."

En-masse Dornaught and his men stepped through. A second later, I heard a splash and a number of blood-curdling screams. Then the portal snapped shut. "Water world?" I asked.

Wheels coughed and spat out blood. "I hope they can swim. We have to wait until...until the power recycles itself."

That would take at least eight minutes, if not longer. I prayed for a little peace and quiet, and my prayers were answered, as the sound of the planes drifted away, and we all waited nervously for the time to pass.

After perhaps seven minutes, Wheels relayed a new set of numbers to my girlfriend. As he did so, a loud drone of engines followed by a terrifying whistling sound filled the air. The enemy bombers had returned, and the whistling sounds were the bombs falling. A shriek, a second of silence, and then...the explosion.

Callie yelled, "Eli," but her cries were drowned out by the sound of the death dealers as they landed much closer to our position. Boom, boom, boom. The warehouse shook, and the gateway quivered. I shifted into my metal form and went over to hold the portal upright.

"Callie, hurry," Wheels whispered. "Hurry."

She keyed in the sequence. The machine sputtered, died briefly, and then it roared back to life as the power kicked in. The opaque wall sprang up again. Wheels' voice was fainter this time, and his eyes were starting to glaze over. He didn't have much time, and we had even less. "Hurry," he whispered, his voice weak. "Get going." He then fell over, face down.

A whistling sound overhead meant the big one was coming. I reverted to my default form, grabbed Callie's hand, and we charged toward the portal. A black blur passed overhead as we made our way through. I wondered what it was, but in that millisecond, the world behind us exploded into a great wall of noise...

Epilogue

CALLIE AND I LANDED on our stomachs in an alleyway strewn with empty crates, boxes, and empty liquor bottles. A stink of cat's pee and wine hit my nose. It wasn't an illusion. I touched my girlfriend's shoulder. "You okay?"

"Fine," she said. "You?"

"I'll make it."

I looked behind us. The portal was still open, but it abruptly closed with a snap for the final time. No one else had come through. We'd arrived...but where? Was this the Earth I'd seen once, albeit briefly?

Hot air flowed around me. It was summertime, just like on my old Earth. A brilliant yellow sun hung in the sky, and from its position, I judged it to be roughly ten AM. Wait, my watch was still working...ten-thirty-seven. I cautiously poked my head out of the alley. The streets had a few people on them, going for a stroll. Some of them had babies or young children with them.

Yes, this was our new Earth, and although it came as a distinct relief to have escaped a hellish ending, regret hit hard. All those people on my old Earth, all the good ones...they were gone. My parents, as well as Callie's foster parents...our people—Wheels, Pigeon, Eric, Smokescreen, and so many more—they were gone, too.

As for the citizens, even if they survived, what kind of world would they have? Would they rebuild, or would the US use its planet buster and destroy that which gave everyone and everything life? I didn't know, but there was nothing I could do. Our lives on our old Earth were over. We were here, now.

I brushed sweat from my forehead. A car with enormous tailfins roared by, and it belched smoke from its exhaust. Tailfins...they came from an era long ago, the late nineteen-forties or the nineteen-fifties. I wasn't quite sure, but this place, yes, it looked like the Earth that we'd seen on our first visit. We'd stepped back in time...

"Hey, look at this."

Callie's voice came from behind me. I whirled around. "What is it?"

She held a newspaper in her hands. "Happy Valley News," she read aloud. "Established eighteen-fifty-eight, Happy Valley, Virginia. A sub-division of Richmond Valley News."

More relief flowed through me. Just like before, same place, same time period. Curious now, I asked her what the date was. "Nineteen-fifty-three," she replied promptly. "June seventeenth, Thursday, assuming that it's today's paper."

An Earth of a century ago. Unbelievable, but in a way, it made sense. Not all Earths had the same timelines. Not all Earths were at the same level technologically. Not all Earths were peaceful. We'd already been to one Earth that only well-armed soldiers could've survived—maybe—and we'd sent Dornaught and his men to a watery grave on another Earth. I could only hope that our new home was a peaceful one. We didn't have any choice.

Since I didn't know much about the era we'd entered, I peeked out of the alleyway again. No one bothered looking in our direction. Not much garbage on the street. In fact, there was none at all.

A couple strolled by on the opposite side of the street. The man wore a suit with wide lapels and a fat tie, while the woman wore an off-the-shoulder dress that spoke of an English rose garden. I'd seen those styles in old movies...not much different here.

"I wonder what I can wear," Callie said, looking at her bodysuit and then at mine. "We can't go out dressed like this."

True enough, as our suits were dirty as well as quite out of place. What was our next step? We had to learn more, but that meant going out in public. "We can't hide here forever," I replied, taking her hand. "C'mon. Let's just be nice and keep a low profile."

It was our turn to take a stroll, and we walked along as calmly as possible. A man in his late thirties, short, fat, and prematurely balding, wearing an ill-fitting black suit that was a size too small, stared at us while smoking a cigar. "What are you, actors?" he asked between puffs.

Callie answered for me. "What makes you say that?"

He pointed a stubby finger at us. "Your hairstyle, young lady, as well as them clothes of yours. They're all tight and uncomfortable looking. If I didn't know any better, I'd say that you were about to audition for a spot on that show, Rocky's Interstellar Space Force."

Rocky's Interstellar...I had no idea what that was, but when he said show, I figured that it was something on television, and that gave me an idea. "Actually, sir, we are," I replied, trying to sound as confident as possible. "Our families recently moved here from Canada. I heard there are tryouts for, uh, that show in..." I had to think of an excuse fast, and then it came to me. "Richmond."

His eyebrows arched. "You just moved here from Canada?"

"Yes, sir, from Toronto." It was the best answer I could come up with on the spur of the moment. "Our, uh, parents are working for the government, and we have a house nearby, but this area's still new to us. We were just doing some sightseeing, trying to get our bearings and all that."

That had to be the worst lie around, and a glance at Callie's skeptical expression showed me that she didn't believe me, either. On the other hand, our potential ally pursed his lips. "All right, well, welcome to Happy Valley. Richmond's a good thirty minutes from here by car. You got one?"

"No. I figured we'd take the bus." Right, we had no money, no ID, and neither of us could fly.

He scoffed at that suggestion, waving it off like someone shooing away a fly. "Listen, I got business in Richmond, anyway. I'll give you a lift there. How's that for being good neighbors?"

How could we say no? I didn't get any bad vibrations from him. He led us to his car, another fin-backed monstrosity, tossing away his stogie as we went. "Hop in," he said.

Callie and I got in the back while he eased himself in behind the wheel and started his car. His car growled and shook as we went. Even though there was no air-conditioning, a pleasant breeze blew in and cooled us off.

As we motored along, our driver introduced himself as George Broadhead, a salesperson for a local brewery. "Yes, sir," he said with a great deal of satisfaction. "Being a salesman is the life for me. I love my work, I love my customers, I love what I do, and you can't get any better than that."

Callie agreed wholeheartedly, flashing him a brighter-than-bright smile from our position. He caught that look in the rearview mirror of his car and replied with a smile of his own. "I gotta say, I knew you two youngsters were actors. You have that look about you. I only watched that show a couple of times. Low-budget junk, but my kids love it. It's got them superheroes flying around and taking on those aliens and such. That ain't for me, but it sure is popular with the youngsters."

Flying? Superheroes? Point me to the station. "Is that the number one show around here?"

He grunted. "Seems to be. It's like them networks got a new show out every week. *My Father The Bicycle, War Star, Space Lost*...lots of them shows. They come and go real fast." He swiveled his head around briefly. "You sure you two don't watch television?"

"Er, we do," Callie answered. "But, uh, we always have a lot of homework, and that comes first."

Broadhead swiveled his head around briefly, grunting as he did so. "Glad you two got your priorities straight. School comes first. It comes first with my kids, but they still like their shows, so..."

Silence fell, so I turned my attention to viewing the countryside. Outside, the highway was practically empty, with only a few cars passing us by. The countryside was simple, untouched, almost pristine. The air, while hot, was also untouched by pollution, and there was no threat of war...it seemed almost perfect. However, I had to be sure. "Uh, sir, how are relations with the European countries?"

Another grunt came from Broadhead. "What, they don't teach you modern politics in school?"

Callie spoke up, covering for me. "Yes, sir, they do, but we were wondering what the adults think. I mean, you have experience, and we don't."

That sounded like a perfectly logical answer, as well as being a totally kiss-ass one, but Broadhead seemed pleased. I caught his smile in the rearview mirror. "Glad you asked. Well, Russia's still trying to make a big noise overseas, so is China, but they're goin' nowhere, not against us. We beat 'em both in the big war, and so far, what they say don't amount to more than a few peeps. We'll make darn sure they don't bother us again. Germany, Canada, and Iceland are our secondary big guns. We can trust them."

Iceland, a big gun? At first, it seemed that we'd stepped into a weird world, but then again, who wanted identical situations? It would've been boring. We thanked him for his views, and soon, we entered Richmond, where he let us off at a curb downtown. Immediately, the stares started, and saying that we were wannabe television stars probably wouldn't work...

"Television station's over there," Broadhead said, cutting into my thoughts and pointing to our right at a large antenna on top of a five-story building. The name—RLTV Productions—stood out in bold black letters on the structure. "Biggest station in Richmond, one of the biggest stations in this great state. Have a nice day."

He nodded at us, and then he drove off. We'd arrived downtown where there were plenty of shops and movie theaters. Restaurants, too. Food was a priority, but we needed money for that. Even more important was finding out the necessary information...

"Hey, turn around," Callie said and tapped me on the shoulder.

I swung around and found myself staring at a public library. It seemed like the place to go, so in we went, found the bathrooms where we cleaned up, and once we were ready, we found a quiet corner and then got ourselves a few history books. Computers were in their early stages of development, atomic power was in its infancy, and only recently had jet aircraft begun to replace prop-driven airplanes...

A shrill, jangling sound from outside interrupted our reading time. "What is that?" Callie whispered in a low voice.

"It sounds like an alarm."

Outside, a crowd had gathered to see what was happening. Across the street, three men wearing suits, fedoras, and holding guns, ran out of a bank carrying large sacks of money. They fired into the air, and those shots were enough to scare the citizens back and prevent the police from moving in.

Since no one else was going to help, I started walking toward them. Apparently, my girlfriend had the same thought, as she fell in step alongside me. "Are you going to do what I think you're going to do?" I asked.

Callie moved ahead and tossed her answer over her shoulder. "What do you think?"

"This isn't my idea of keeping a low profile," I called out.

"This isn't the time for it."

Callie strode toward the three men who'd reached a car, and the trio pointed their pistols at her. "Hold it, honey," one of them said. "We don't want to shoot you, but we will."

In response, she favored them with her usual brilliant smile, and a nanosecond later, a burst of light came from her, blinding them. They screamed, dropped their guns, and I raced over to scoop them up and toss them away.

The driver, though, hadn't been affected as much, as he got out of the car and pulled out a knife from his pocket. "Gonna cut you up," he growled. "That was a perfect snatch'n'grab operation."

A shift in my structure, I felt the molecules align as they always had...and a coating of impenetrable metal covered my body. "Not so perfect," I answered in a pleasant tone. "You got caught. Go ahead. Stab me. See how far you get."

His jaw dropped, and then he stabbed me—or tried to. Apparently, my suit was knife-proof, as it didn't tear and the blade snapped in two. Mr. Bank Robber stared at the remains of his weapon. After that, a tap on his nose from my finger sent him into la-la land.

"Tailor-made," I murmured and then laughed. I hadn't used that line in a while, but maybe it was time to haul it out of cold storage. While thinking over another possible catchphrase, the Richmond police chose that moment to step in and arrest the robbers.

Job over, I shifted back to my default condition and strolled over to Callie. "That was fun," I said. I was hungry, but that would have to wait. A glance around the area told me that the crowd, formerly only fifteen people or so, had swelled to over two hundred in a short period of time, and every single person gaped at us. "I guess our secret's out."

"Well, that didn't last long," my girlfriend replied with a grin.

Sure enough, a couple of the police officers asked us about where we were from. "Canada," I replied. "And we're here to help."

"Canada," one officer echoed. "That was some trick you did. I, uh, don't suppose you'd be willing to help us out. We could use some help."

They could use some help. "We could use a job."

A slow smile spread across the officer's face. "I think my captain will want to know about you two. Hell, even the president is going to want to know about you two."

He excused himself to radio in the happening to his police station, and while he was otherwise engaged, a few of the citizenry came over to ask for our autographs. Then a couple of reporters with notepads decided to get in on the act. Their staff photographers took pictures, while the rest of the citizenry waited patiently. We answered their questions, but neither of us mentioned where we'd really come from. I figured that only the president should know, and we'd have to get a few guarantees first.

Still, the atmosphere was positive, and Callie and I drank it all in. As we stood and listened to the people express their admiration, a familiar figure clothed in black stood at the back, wings folding into her body.

"Ravenna," I whispered.

She'd made it. Her bland-faced husband stood beside her, and he shifted into a taller, thinner version of himself. She mouthed, "Nice to see you. We'll be around, and we brought a friend." She pointed to a corner.

I followed her gesture. A pair of beady red eyes stared back at me. Rat—he'd made it, after all. Good. If anyone deserved a little happiness, it was him. Ravenna nodded at us, and then she took her husband's hand. A moment later, they disappeared into their new lives, while Rat waved and then scampered off down an alley. I wished them well. They'd done a lot for us, served our old world with honor, and I knew they'd not only survive here, but they'd also thrive.

Callie also must've noticed them because she tugged on my sleeve and murmured, "Eli, do we have company from our old world?"

"We do," I answered sotto voce. "But it's their choice to help out and all that. If they want to contact us, they will."

We continued to smile for the cameras, but soon, the crowd dissipated, although the police remained and asked us to wait, assuring us that they were on our side. I'd hold them to that. We now had a future, and I was determined to make this life on our new Earth a good one.

As for my girlfriend, she obviously had the same idea, as she turned to me and said with the utmost sincerity, "You know, I think that we're going to like it here."

The End

About the Author

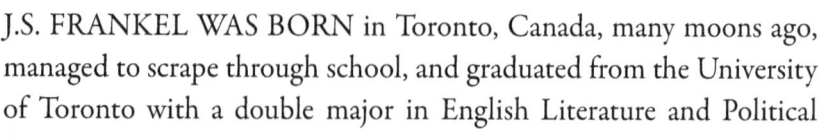

J.S. FRANKEL WAS BORN in Toronto, Canada, many moons ago, managed to scrape through school, and graduated from the University of Toronto with a double major in English Literature and Political Science.

After working for three years in Toronto, he moved to Japan and has been there ever since, teaching ESL to anyone brave enough to sit through his lessons. In 1997, he married the charming Akiko Koike. They have two sons, Kai and Ray, and they make their home in Osaka, where Frankel teaches ESL during the day and writes at night.

All his novels are in the YA Fantasy genre, the most well-known being the Catnip series, Twisted, Here, Now, and Forever, Of Dusk and Shadows, The Tower, and many more, all featuring action, adventure, and romance that readers of any age can enjoy.

www.ingramcontent.com/pod-product-compliance
Lightning Source LLC
Chambersburg PA
CBHW072051170626
46813CB00004B/1302